# Sarah Champion

A music journalist since the age of fourteen, Sarah Champion
is a global party correspondent and compiler of techno
and drum'n'bass CDs 'Trance Europe Express' and
'Breakbeat Science'.

SCEPTRE

# Disco Biscuits

### edited by
## SARAH CHAMPION

**SCEPTRE**

Introduction and compilation © 1997 Sarah Champion

For the copyright on individual stories see pages 299–300

First published in 1997 by Hodder and Stoughton
A division of Hodder Headline PLC
A Sceptre Paperback

British Library Cataloguing in Publication Data

Champion, Sarah
  Disco biscuits
  1. Short stories, English
  1. Title
  823.9'14 [FS]

  ISBN 0 340 68265 5

Typeset by Palimpsest Book Production Limited,
Polmont, Stirlingshire
Printed and bound in Great Britain by
Clays Ltd, St Ives plc

Hodder and Stoughton
A division of Hodder Headline PLC
338 Euston Road
London NW1 3BH

Doves, Playboys, Dollars, Apples, Swans, White
Burgers, Brown Burgers . . .
Dennis The Menaces, Rhubarb & Custards, White
Callies, Pink Flamingoes, Snowballs,
Kinder Eggs, Energizers, Hammer & Sickles,
Disco Biscuits . . .

Thank you to all the contributors for their enthusiasm and to Ernesto Leal (Gnash), Martin James, Susan Corrigan, Elaine Palmer (Pulp Faction) and Kevin Williamson (Rebel Inc) for helping find them.

Special thanks to Simon Prosser, Matt Bumble and everyone at Volume.

# Contents

Introduction     xiii

1   NICHOLAS BLINCOE 'Ardwick Green'     I
2   MIKE BENSON 'Room Full Of Angels'     21
3   IRVINE WELSH 'The State Of The Party'     29
4   GAVIN HILLS 'White Burger Danny'     63
5   MARTIN MILLAR 'How Sunshine Star-Traveller
    Lost His Girlfriend'     79
6   MICHAEL RIVER 'Electrovoodoo'     97
7   KEVIN WILLIAMSON 'Heart of The Bass'     109
8   JONATHAN BROOK 'Sangria'     121
9   CHARLIE HALL 'The Box'     147
10   BEN GRAHAM 'Weekday Service'     161
11   JEFF NOON 'DJNA'     171
12   DOUGLAS RUSHKOFF 'The Snow That Killed
    Manuel Jarrow'     189
13   DEAN CAVANAGH 'Mile High Meltdown'     205
14   TWO FINGERS 'Puff'     215
15   ALEX GARLAND 'Blink And You Miss It'     227
16   MATTHEW DE ABAITUA 'Inbetween'     237
17   Q 'The Sparrow'     255
18   ALAN WARNER 'Bitter Salvage'     267
19   STEVE AYLETT 'Repeater'     281

Contributors     291
Acknowledgements     299

*'Hey, Mister Pharmacist*
*Can You Help Me Out Today*
*In Your Usual Lovely Way?*
*Oh Mister Pharmacist I insist*
*Can You Give Me Somethin' That Will Assist?*
*Hey, Mister Pharmacist,*
*Won't You Please Give Me Some Energy?'*

Disco Biscuits is an anthology of nineteen stories that capture the spirit of the last decade's party culture — from illegal raves and anarchic warehouse parties to corporate clubbing. It is a world of drugs, sex, dancefloors, dealers, police and DJs. And 1997 is the tenth anniversary of acid house, where all this began.

In 1987, several British DJs visited nightclubs on the Spanish island of Ibiza where they discovered that the clubs Amnesia and Pasha were mixing black American house music from Chicago and New York with eclectic 'Balearic' holiday records, while the club's clientele were discovering a drug which would become known as ecstasy.

Inspired, DJs and clubbers brought the music (and the drug) home to London and by the autumn of 1987 Paul Oakenfold's The Project and Danny Rampling's Shoom Club had opened. By the following summer, they were joined by Future, Spectrum, Clink Street and The Trip: the Balearic scene was becoming a phenomenon — known as acid house.

Acid house became a household name that autumn, when the tabloid newspapers ran headlines like 'Evil of Ecstasy'; 'The Acid House Horror'; 'Hell Of Acid House Kids'. That year Chicago's house music and the drug ecstasy became a double-act like fish and chips. Naturally, it was predicted that this dance culture would be short-lived: that it would burn itself out in months. Little did anyone know what was to come.

From huge outdoor parties in fields in the home counties to

warehouse parties in the industrial estates of Blackburn and sweaty clubs up and down the land, the new culture grew and grew. By the early nineties the parties had become known as raves, having spread to every corner of Britain, from Coventry to Glasgow, Liverpool to Aberdeen.

Who would have thought that the guitar would be replaced by ever-diversifying electronic music? That techno, trance, garage, ambient, jungle, drum'n'bass would all be pushing the boundaries of sound further and further? That it would become the dominant pop culture? That it would entirely fill the Top 40? That the pop star would be replaced by the DJ? That it would be the soundtrack to every other TV commercial? And that *millions* of doses of ecstasy would be taken every weekend? One nation under a groove.

It was perhaps inevitable that this culture would finally influence literature too. In the fifties and sixties, jazz and psychedelia inspired writing from Jack Kerouac's *On The Road* to Allen Ginsburg's *Howl* and Tom Wolfe's *Electric Kool Aid Acid Test*. In the nineties, we have Irvine Welsh's *Trainspotting*, the book, the film and the attitude.

After all, dance culture has all the elements of a bestselling story, from drugs and sex to gangsters, police and thieves. For example, Nicholas Blincoe's crime thriller *Acid Casuals* is based on true stories of Manchester club culture (with the added spice of a hitman employed by Columbian drugs barons). It features a cast of DJs, video jockeys, speek freaks, E heads, Moss Side gangsters, dodgy bouncers and coke dealers, in an anarchic crescendo of lawlessness.

Also from Manchester, there's Jeff Noon's *Vurt*. A fresh twist on sci-fi, it features a new drug (the 'Vurt' feather) and a bunch of kids called the Stash Riders charging around in search of 'English Voodoo', the most potent and illegal Vurt.

Meanwhile, the phenomenal success of Irvine Welsh's writing, characterizing Scotland's new generation of drop-outs and drug addicts, has helped expose a new wave of Scottish writers. These include Kevin Williamson, who recently edited his own anthology and Alan Warner, whose *Morvern Callar*, told of a supermarket girl who goes partying in Ibiza

# Introduction

The Backstreets imprint has imitated the seventies 'Skinhead' novels with cheap fast tales of London street culture like Jonathan Brook's *Herbsman*, Two Fingers' *Junglist* and Geraldine Geraghty's *Raise Your Hands*. More young writers have been showcased by independent publishers Pulp Faction and their anthologies of new writers.

Over the past two years, club nights have also emerged featuring book readings. Jeff Noon's *Pollen* was launched at Manchester's Hacienda, with a DJ backing the reading. Meanwhile, a series of 'Arthrob' parties by Gnash have combined readings from the likes of Irvine Welsh and Hanif Kureshi, with DJ sets by Andy Weatherall and Richard Fearless.

*Disco Biscuits* is an anthology of nineteen stories which brings together this new generation of authors, as well as capturing the madness of the last ten years — from the sheer hedonism and excess of Mike Benson's 'Room Full Of Angels' to the anarchic comedies of Nicholas Blincoe's 'Ardwick Green' and Martin Millar's 'How Sunshine Star-Traveller Lost His Girlfriend'. In 'The State Of The Party', meanwhile, Irvine Welsh continues a tale of drugs and immorality on a Scottish council estate.

For one brief naive moment in the late eighties, in a field off the M25 at an acid house party or at an urban warehouse party, we all believed that things might change. Like our parents did in the sixties. And maybe for a short time things *were* different. Social norms and barriers did crumble — if only for a moment. Even football hooligans stopped fighting and started dancing (see Gavin Hills' 'White Burger Danny').

Raves *have* challenged the order of society — enough for them to have been made *illegal* anyway. No one ever outawed punk rock, yet here we are with a law that bans 'repetitive beats'. Steve Aylett's 'Repeater' captures the outlaw spirit of a generation taking to the roads, living in old ambulances and setting up sound systems for illegal outdoor parties. Meanwhile, Jeff Noon's 'DJNA' also challenges the Criminal Justice Act with a tale of a future Manchester where sinful dancing is outlawed.

# Introduction

Dance culture has now spread throughout the world, but its innocence has faded. In Douglas Rushkoff's 'The Snow That Killed Manuel Jarrow', the rapid descent of America's underground rave scene into commercialism and greed is symbolized by a raver lying dying on the dancefloor. Meanwhile, at the Mediterranean clubs of Jonathan Brook's 'Sangria' and the beach parties of Thailand in Alex Garland's 'Blink And You Miss It', all is not quite what it seems.

While the travellers have jumped ship for beaches in the Third World, in the late nineties Britain's urban youth have gotten into jungle and drum'n'bass with their manic breakbeats and mutant MCs. A true city soundtrack — booming from the open windows of Jeeps, vibrating up from the flat below, pirating the airwaves, bouncing round the concrete stairwells of council estates and filling sweaty clubs. One nation lost in bass. Two Fingers' 'Puff' is set in this scene, while Q's poetic tale of 'The Sparrow' gets down to the nitty-gritty of the new urban drug wars.

Why did I compile this book? I've been hooked on partying since I was fifteen and first slipped illicitly between Moss Side shebeens and indie gigs, triad casinos and reggae clubs. However, it was only after witnessing Manchester warehouse parties and the arrival of acid house at The Hacienda that it became a way of life. It was suggested that I write a history of acid house (and the mayhem that came after). But how can you capture the madness of the last decade in facts and figures? For all the record reviews and attempts to turn DJs and promoters into celebrities, dance magazines have failed to document what really happened, as rock and punk journalists did. After all, the *true* history is not about obscure white labels or DJ techniques or pop stars. It's about personal stories of messiness, absurdity and excess — best captured in fiction.

**Sarah Champion**

Nicholas Blincoe

'ARDWICK GREEN'

He was called Jackie Pye and smoked cigars. Chunks of ash fell on to the bar-top like rubble across a road. He wiped it to the floor with the edge of his hand and said, 'You're not making sense son.'

Andy tried to run through the concept one more time. 'What it is, it's like a slow wind down to the weekend. We keep the sounds really mellow through the whole afternoon — up till around seven-thirty. Then everyone gets off home, ready for work Monday morning.'

Jackie looked him over. The kid was sat at the other side of the bar, sat on two stools, one for his backside and one for his broken leg. Jackie regretted it, but he hadn't had a chance to ask about the leg yet. That might be a story worth hearing. So far, the kid hadn't stopped twatting on about his idea for a perfect Sunday afternoon.

Jackie still didn't get it. 'You want to hire this place for your disco?'

'Not hire it, no. I was thinking we split it. Like, you keep the bar, we keep whatever we make on the door.'

'Who the chuff's gonna come Sunday afternoons?'

'I reckon it'll be rammed. Like, maybe it'll take a few weeks but you know ... word of mouth, Mr Pye.'

The club was empty now, just this mad kid sitting opposite him, stretched out on a bar stool, scratching at a plaster cast.

3

Jackie flicked his old stogie butt into the sink, watching it settle among last night's dregs while he took a new cigar from his tit pocket. It was two-thirty now and the cleaner was still downstairs, sluicing out the member's lavvy. It would be another hour before the old cunt worked his way upstairs. The whole club looked like a shithole. Not that it looked a sight better clean.

'I tell you, son — the idea's cracked. Look around. You see what the place looks like? What it chuffing smells like? That's what daylight does to a place. They don't call them nightclubs for nowt. Who do you reckon could stomach it, if they weren't already beered up?'

'No no. It's a nice place this, Mr Pye.'

Andy was lying. He'd been told the place was old-style glamorous, but now he was here he knew his informant had to have been tripping. From the outside, the place looked like a giant double garage, off-white pebbledash thrown over it like an old sheet, trying to disguise the place as a coaching inn. The bow-shaped windows, studded with bulls-eye glass, totalled the ensemble. Inside, a passageway led past the lavvies and the members-only bar, past an old mechanical cig machine and on to a staircase. The dancefloor took up the whole of the first floor. Jackie Pye took up most of the space behind the bar.

'Is it chuff a nice place.' He swept his cigar hand across the room: the medieval beamwork, the wattle and daub walls, the DJ hut with its thatched roof, everything fake except for the dark beeriness and the standard wear and tear. 'What it is, is a nice fucking earner, pardon me. Least I do all right out of it and I can't see me doing any better if I open Sunday afternoons.'

Andy wasn't about to give up. He'd tried everywhere else in Manchester. None of them had got it, they'd just shrugged and said it wasn't worth hiring the barstaff for a Sunday afternoon. Now he said, 'You're wrong, Mr Pye. What I'm talking about is a chill-out club, you know. Like not mental or anything, just a place to get mellow and take the edge off the come-down.' He paused,

4

then said, 'So like, another thing if you're worried, there'll be no trouble with drugs.'

'I don't give a chuff about drugs, son. How did you hear about this place anyway?'

Andy pointed across the dancefloor to where Jess was sitting, semi-stoned, bumming his way round inner-space. 'He told me.'

'And who's he?'

'It's not him. I mean, it's his brother who knows the place. He used to come by before.'

Jackie Pye squinted into the dark. 'Conrad Stubbins?'

Andy wasn't surprised, there was a skin deep resemblance. 'Yeah, he's Conrad's brother Jess.'

'He doesn't say much, he tapped or something?'

'He's just helping me out, you know, 'cause of . . .' Andy nodded down at his pot leg . . . 'I can't drive.' Just looking at his leg, he got a rash outbreak that he couldn't begin to scratch.

Jackie stretched, letting out a sigh. 'OK son, I tell you what, I think you're a dick but seeing you know Conrad, I'll give it some thought. So if you fuck off, now, and give us a ring, say Wednesday, I'll let you know either way. How does that sound?'

Andy started nodding, collecting his crutches together and getting ready to stand. 'That's ace Mr Pye. Really. Ace.'

As he swung his good foot to the floor, he hovered and twisted, struggling to pull a roll of paper out of his back pocket.

Jackie said, 'The chuff's that?'

Andy spread it out on the bar-top. 'Artwork.'

'Arsewipe?'

'It's for the flyers. We'll hand them out round town. Outside the Hacienda and over Blackburn at the raves and that.'

Jackie Pye looked down at the postcard-size scrap of paper. The picture showed a field of red poppies against green grass, overprinted with the words: *Rest In Peace, The Weekend Stops In Ardwick Green*. Then the name of his club, *The Lamplighter*, and the date for Sunday week.

'Like I said, we'll do all the publicity. We'll get about 5,000 of these printed.'

Jackie shook his head. 'That picture won't do, son. You know we get good lads here, ex-servicemen and that, they're not gonna want to see some kids taking the piss out of poppy day.'

'They won't be around will they? Like, not up here. Not on a Sunday lunch.'

'Shouldn't think so. But ...' nodding back over to Jess '... there'll be a few of his brother's mates in the member's bar downstairs. Now piss off like I told you and I'll speak to you midweek.'

The boy started moving, swinging across the floor on his crutches towards the stairs where Conrad Stubbins's kid brother was waiting for him. Jackie dropped his eyes back to the bar-top, looking for his lighter.

It was true there'd be nobody dancing upstairs on a Sunday but it usually got pretty lively downstairs. With it being a club, The Lamplighter got those who wanted to make an afternoon of it and fuck the Sunday opening hours.

Just before the two kids reached the doors, Jackie called out, 'How's your Conrad doing anyway?'

The brother looked kind of startled but he spoke up. 'OK. Like, he's hoping to get parole any day now.'

Jackie nodded, said he wished him luck and let the boys go.

Once his cigar was lit, he began to think it over. There were plenty of older guys liked hanging out in a club Sunday afternoons so why should their kid brothers be any different? He didn't understood any of that crap about winding down, chilling-out and getting mellow. But he knew Sunday was the last chance to get really wasted before work started again. Maybe he'd tell the kid all right, just see how things went on a trial basis.

Under the Mancunian Way, following the desolate stretch of tarmac as it sweeps beer cans towards the Apollo Theatre. Or, coming crossways, from Ardwick Leisure Centre where Andy broke his leg, on to Brunswick Street and across the bottom of Plymouth Grove towards the infirmary, where he had it set in plaster. All the directions were set out on the reverse side of the flyer, minus the autobiographical asides. 'X' marks the spot where the two roads cross outside The Lamplighter, a flat-topped box squatting on a roughcast chunk of dirt grass. The heart of Ardwick Green. It wasn't the kind of locale Andy would have chosen but he wasn't going to let it ruin his DJ debut.

Come the Sunday, he arrived by taxi three-quarters of an hour before Jess and tried to get comfortable in the thatched-roof DJ hut. He had his professional slip mats skewered on the nipple at the centre of his Technics decks, one signed by Fabio and one by Grooverider, just to prove they were different people and not the same DJ using two different names. He had his cast resting on a stool and his crutches leaning against the back wall. Sitting sideways to the decks, he had to twist round as he practised on the cross-fader but he got a rhythm going, juggling the same three old school tracks until his first-night nerves settled: *Marshall Jefferson, Adonis, Frankie Knuckles*.

When Jess arrived, he came herding a pack of spaced-out acid teds ahead of him. A grin across his face so moronic his mouth wouldn't close. No doubt, he was monged but he kept it together with a kind of feverish energy. His mates had a whole lot less bounce, so immaterial they were practically transparent. Andy doubted they had enough energy even to begin to get mellow.

He waved Jess over, shouting: 'All right?'

Jess came up screaming, 'Double fucking top. What you reckon, you up for it?'

Andy nodded, he was in synch. He said, 'How was last night?'

'Fucking large, mate. We went to Fonzo Buller's place then up to Blackburn. I reckon we gonna get a big showing from there . . .' he pointed back to his crowd '. . . I brought these guys with me and I reckon we'll get hundreds more. Everyone who saw your flyers, they were really up for it. I tell you, you should have come too, helped spread the word.'

Andy shrugged. 'I got a broken leg.'

Jess had rung him up maybe six times between the end of the football scores and the beginning of *Blind Date*, trying to persuade him to come out to Blackburn. Andy let his answer machine deal with the calls while he hid behind the couch. He spent the rest of the night hunched over his turntable, clocking the bpm's of his records with a stopwatch and writing the score on the labels. Part of the reason was that he wanted to stay straight. The rest of it was that he couldn't face another night in Blackburn.

The last time he went, he remembered dancing through an industrial unit somewhere on the fringe of town, dawn seeping through a skylight while he went mental on the floor below. He was spinning round with his head upturned, imagining a camera tracking his movement across the compound floor. Slowly he began to grow aware of a metallic banging. There was a huge steel roll shutter at the end of the unit, big enough to drive a bus through. The banging was the sound of batons on the steel of the door. As the shutters lifted, it felt like the moment in *Close Encounters* when the bright smoky light seeps round the edges of the space ship doors. Andy began to feel the panic around him. He looked outside as the smoke cleared and saw nothing but blue and whites. Police cars.

From then on, it became a weekly roust. Wherever the parties were held, come dawn you got to walk this gauntlet of police cars and feel their eyes on you as you tried to focus and remember what you might be carrying. A double paranoia, not only the usual come-down but also the fear of being caught in possession. After the third time, Andy never went back. Whatever lie he had to tell, whatever weak excuse he had to spin, he avoided it. Maybe breaking his leg wasn't so bad, looked at solely from a Blackburn perspective.

Jess still risked it. Andy swore he just got off on the thrill. He'd once been arrested holding a quarter sheet of acid: maybe seventy-five tabs. He claimed he'd got away with it because even he'd forgotten it was there, tucked into the bib of his dungarees.

He even had a theory: so long as he believed he was clean, his pure aura convinced the cops. Maybe. But it took a special kind of karma to survive such a paranoid atmosphere. The people Jess had brought with him were proof positive, looking like psyche ward escapees as, one by one, they drifted to the floor on Bambi legs and tried to dance.

Somehow, maybe through an involuntary memory spasm, Andy mis-cued the next record, grinding the different beats into a Robochef blur. Looking out on the dancefloor he could actually see the confusion in the dancers' faces. He grabbed for the varispeed and started twisting it, feeling the veins standing on his forehead with the effort. As the two records dropped in together, the dancers lost their look of horror: but the really scary thing, nothing replaced it. They were drained expressionless. Blackburned-out and lost in its evil comedown.

Andy looked down at the record, calculating the number of grooves left to run. 'Listen Jess, I got to go.'

'What? Where? You going to the lav?'

Andy nodded. 'This track should last long enough but if I'm not back, just put on another record ...' he was half out of his seat before he thought '... and for fuck's sake keep it light.'

Jess's eyes were spinning at the same speed as the records, 'Oh yeah. No worries. I'm up for it.'

Andy set off, hoping Jess could be trusted. The idea was to keep it ambient, maybe a little Balearic. But Jess only functioned in excess of 150 bpm's and his idea of a smooth cross-fade was the jump-cut, one-twenty to one-ninety bang.

He was hopping down the steps to the toilet, his crutches under his arms, when he heard someone call his name.

'All right Andy lad? I heard you got a party going. I thought I'd come up for a boogie.'

A small guy with a big spliffy grin.

Andy said, 'Conrad. Fuck. When did you get out?'

Conrad Stubbins was fifteen when he first spent a night at the

Casino, whizzing on prescription pills he'd stolen himself. He was a couple of years younger when he developed a taste for amphetamine at clubs like The Twisted Wheel. Over his life, he reckoned he'd seen every kind of nightclub going. He knew what he liked but just about any place or tempo was fine by him. Not that he'd had a chance to do much boogieing the last few years. Andy had caught him on his way to the lavvy, just getting ready to freshen up. He shouted out: 'Yeah, I got out last night. Maidstone nick, this time. They gave me a National Coach ticket and told me to fuck off back North ... I said, My fucking pleasure.'

Andy was sat in the middle cubicle, the only one he'd found free. The lock was broken but he'd jammed his crutches against the door to hold it closed. He took a breath and shouted back, 'Yeah, well, it's good to see you.'

There were two lads wazzing up against the piss stones. Conrad caught them taking a sneak peek over their shoulders, a swift shuftie for the ex-con. He flashed them a grin and wandered over, taking the space between them. Standing there, unzipped, his business in his hand, he craned over to the right, made a long tutting suck sound, then over to his left. He gave that one a whistle.

The two lads shifted awkwardly but only one of them had finished: keen to zip up and exit while his mate was still in mid-stream. Conrad called him back, saying: 'Here, you know our kid? Jess?'

The lad nodded, a shade dazed and a mite uncertain.

'You been up Blackburn way with him?'

'Yes.' His eyes swivelling inside shadow cavities, rings so deep they came in graded colours blue through black. Conrad recognized the signs of comedown paranoia.

He locked on the eyes, nodding slowly with a smile, knowing he could just play the kid out; give him the slow snake eye while he took his time directing a steaming jet down to the piss gutter. The silence stretched out, the kid started shaking. Conrad finally said, 'I tell you, you're looking a bit fagged.'

'Yeah, well. You know.'

Conrad knew. Forty-eight hours maybe, stark staring awake with only ecstasy or acid to hold it together. He said, 'Me, I'm just starting. I took a couple of Es thirty minutes ago and just dropped a tab. Should be coming up nicely in a moment, what you reckon?'

The kid nodded, yeah, that sounded right.

Pisser number two was finishing, shaking himself dry and tucking himself back inside. He tried to sneak around Conrad's back and make for the door. It didn't work.

Conrad let out the last jet with a sigh and turned around. He shook the last couple of drops in plain view as he said, 'What about you. How are you, kid?'

He had them both now. One of them nodding, 'I'm OK', and the other just stone paralyzed.

'I got to say, looking at you . . .' Conrad kept his voice smooth and rhythmic, keeping time by shaking out his business, '. . . you both look like shit. What's this stuff you're wearing?'

They were dressed in sports clothes, but definitely not sports casual. One was wearing crappy jogging pants and a sweat top. The other had a hooded top, worn under dungarees. Both of them had mud-splattered trainers on.

'Me, I like to look nice. Matinique, Lacoste, Pringle. But maybe I'm out of date, what with being inside this last couple of years. What do you reckon?'

Actually, he was wearing Farah slacks but they weren't to know. They both nodded vigorously, 'No, you look all right.'

Like fuck he did. But until he got some new money together, he was going to have to wear his old clothes. The money he picked up coming out of prison had already gone on drugs. He folded his dick into the Farah strides — not a bad fit, he'd lost some weight in prison and Farahs only suited skinny lads — and walked towards them. They took a nervous step back but he kept coming.

One yard short of the wash-basin, he stopped and looked in the mirror. He could tell by his eyes he was coming up. The pupils were spreading like ink blots to cover the whole of his eye ball. He gave himself a good wide grin: that was pure spliff.

11

Looking at the size and style of his smile, he just knew old Jack Nicholson was a doper. No question about it. He brushed out the collar of his Lacoste polo top, picking at a fleck. The two lads shifted foot to foot.

He said, 'You not washing your hands you mucky buggers?'

All around the basin, the Formica top was crowded with beer glasses left over from the night before. The pissy dregs marking the bottom of each stacked glass, some stretching up to eight storeys high. Conrad let out a roar — *aaaarrrgghhh* — and swiped the lot on to the floor one handed. The two lads jumped a foot and ran for the door. Conrad's laugh following them out. He was already thinking, nice lads just a bit nervy. He'd met a few like them on the inside, they never seemed to shape so well to prison life.

All he wanted was a bit of space around the wash-basin. Smashing the glasses had been an impulse designed around his own amusement. Now he had a good clear stretch of Formica he could lay out a few lines. He dug in the flat front pockets of his Farahs for the wrap. He had four on him but he'd marked the outsides with a letter so he wouldn't get mixed up. BW stood for Billy Whizz. He untucked the corners to form a triangle and carefully opened the wrap. The gramme nestling along the diagonal fold greeted him like a crooked white smile.

Andy was sweating it out inside his cubicle. He heard the conversation, followed by the smash of the glasses. All he could do was pray Conrad would leave him in peace. Then the banging started, hammering at his door. Only the crutch kept the door in place. When that slipped, he knew he'd crossed the line. The man was standing there, grinning down at him.

'You got a credit card? I left mine at home.'

Andy's trousers were on the floor, spooled around his good ankle. The plastered leg was straight out ahead of him, naked except for the cast.

Conrad said, 'Fuck me, that's an awkward position. I tell you, I've never been able to take a dump unless I'm good and comfy.'

Andy hadn't been doing badly until the glasses started smashing. Since then, he'd been feeling a constipating spasm move up along his colon, gripping him tight.

Conrad carried on, 'I'll get it myself. Don't put yourself out.' He crouched down on the floor, frisked through Andy's trouser pockets and came up with a bank card and a twenty-quid note. 'I'll take the note too. I'm spent up and I got nothing to snort the bastard with.'

He started to leave but stopped, saying: 'Here, maybe this'll help ...' The Farahs had side pockets stitched army-style to each leg. Conrad fumbled through the left one until he came out with a bottle of Liquid Gold. '... have a snort of this, it'll loosen your ring.'

Andy made no move to reach for them. His hands were clamped to the side of the toilet bowl, as though he were in danger of floating upwards if he didn't hold himself down.

Conrad said, 'Second thoughts, I'll take a sniff myself first. I don't know how long you'll need it for.' He unscrewed the top of the poppers bottle, took a couple of huge snorts and rescrewed the lid. Two seconds later, he was screaming '*Waah-Aaarrrggh*. fuck ...' shaking his head. '... right to the fucking G-spot. Your shot, son.'

He leaned over and stuck the bottle right in Andy's face. Andy unclamped a sensitive hand and took it.

Coughing on amyl-fuelled laughter, Conrad said: 'Just give us a shout when you're done. I'll close you back in for now.'

The door swung to and Andy was trapped back in his cell, his leg straight out, a bottle of poppers in his hand. Pure fear throughout his whole body.

Conrad started work chopping down the speed, keeping up the conversation as he worked. 'I fucking love taking drugs in a lavvy. But, I tell you, you always got to take your time with amphetamine. There's nothing worse than snorting on a huge coarse lump. You want to see my nose. Over the years, the speed's burnt so much skin out of it, I got loose flaps up there you wouldn't believe.'

13

He laid out two fat lines, corrected a kink, and licked down the edge of the bank card before continuing: 'What I really hate is looking like some uncouth bugger. Finger halfway up my fucking nose, trying to prise speed bogies out ...' he shivered '... there's nowt fucking worse.'

Andy stayed quiet, hearing the lavvy door swing open and closed as another couple of lads came in.

Conrad just gave them a wink, 'Don't mind me.' They nodded back with tight little smiles. He noted, kind of humorously, that these two were the spit of the lads who'd just left. The exact same type of out-size muddy sports clothes, the exact same drug addled come-down looks on their faces.

He left them about their business as he rolled Andy's twenty into a tight tube. As he homed in on the start of his first line, he shouted: 'I'm going down.' When he reached the end he threw back his head and roared enthusiasm. The heads of the two new lads at the piss stones turned in unison.

'I told you two already, don't mind me.'

The heads snapped back, sharpish. Conrad finished the next line. This time, as he roared, he staggered slightly: feeling pulses of energy moving through his legs and seeping into his arms. Evidentally, the E was moving in to take control. He flexed out, feeling a rush towards his heart and remembered his amyl.

He kicked open Andy's door again. 'You finished with them poppers?'

Andy hadn't even touched the bottle. He just sat with it clenched in his hand, scared what might happen if he lost control for a second. As he passed it over, he somehow found himself saying, 'You finished with that twenty?'

Conrad said, 'Don't get funny with me ... you know you'll get it back just as soon as I'm done.'

He pulled the door back in place and found himself staring at the two new lads, zipping up and watching his and Andy's little scene in the crapper.

He lauched himself at them, grabbing them each around the

neck and pulling them down. With their cheeks nestled next to his, he said: 'Hey lads, lads ...' giving them a nuzzle '... I bet you're both mates of our kids and all? How about we all do some amyl, hey?'

He'd already decided, out of pure generosity, they were going to get the first shot. He unclenched their heads and uncapped the bottle, holding it tight to the nose of the left side lad. The kid thrashed back as he took the hit. Conrad jerked his arm and a thimbleful of amyl whipped in a spurt across the lad's face.

Conrad said, 'You'd best wash that off, it burns like fuck.'

As the lad staggered to the wash-basin, Conrad shoved the other's nose into the amyl bottle: 'Breathe deep.'

Conrad only released him once he'd got a good hard sniff. Afterwards, he noticed drops of amyl spooling off the edge of the lad's nostril.

He said, 'One sec ...' and used the edge of the lad's outsize sweatshirt to wipe the top of the bottle dry '... thanks, son. Best go and wash your nose now before it scalds.'

The two of them took turns to spoon water up into their brightened faces as Conrad readied himself for his next hit. The amyl whooshed over him, chemically combined with the E for a killer punch. Bright red, laughing like a fool in peace-love-and-intensity, he walked over to slap them on their backs, 'How the fuck you two doing, then?'

He still hadn't recapped the bottle ... only remembering as another spurt of amyl burst across the back of their necks.

'Oh shit.' From past experience, Conrad knew it would be a good few minutes before the liquid started burning but he'd got a load over his knuckles and thought he'd better wash it off immediately. He elbowed the lads out of the way and rinsed his hands. 'Sorry about that, clumsy as fucking fuck, must be getting a bit wrecked, eh?'

They were shaking their heads ... Its OK ... and making for the door. He stopped them. 'Wait up, you two. I got something I need a bit of help with.'

He fiddled in his leg pocket and brought out a couple of wraps. Pointing at the nearest lad, he said, 'You, what does that say?' He held up one of the wraps. 'My eyesight's going, I think it's the fucking acid. Can you see a letter there?'

The lad nodded, 'Uh-huh.'

'So whats it say?'

'It's an H.'

'Fucking A. You got a lighter?'

He had a clear plan. There was a piece of folded tin foil in his leg pocket, once he got it out and opened he emptied half the heroin into the groove of the fold. 'You, gimme your lighter and hold this steady.'

The lad did what he was told. All Conrad needed now was the twenty-pound note. He found it, still tightly rolled, tucked into the johnny pocket of his Farahs. Before he stuck it in his mouth he said, 'It's better with a piece of tin tube you understand, but this is all I got.'

He sparked the lighter under the tin foil, the lad holding it started sweating.

Conrad mumbled through clenched lips, 'Soz, I got your fucking thumb or what?'

The lad just gritted his teeth and Conrad turned his attention to the smoking trail of heroin. He tried to follow a steady course, chasing the vapour as he rubbed the flame around beneath the foil. Somehow, he got to the end, sucking hard as he said, 'Steady as a fucking rock.'

The lads stood there, one of them wringing out a burnt hand.

'So what about a round of applause.'

They started clapping.

'God love you pair of cunts, I know I fucking do.'

As they turned for the door, he stopped them again. 'Hey come on, it's a free fucking country and I'm not chasing you out. Have your wazz.'

They looked confused. One said, 'We been.'

'You haven't.'

'We have.'

'Look. I been fucking standing here all this time. You not fucking been, so go have a fucking wazz.' He grabbed them by their arms and pulled them back to the stones. 'Don't let any cunt come between you and a wazz, that's what I always say. So you get with it and don't fucking mind me.'

He kicked open Andy's door again: 'What you say, you cunt. Am I fucking right or what? Is this a free fucking country or what?'

Andy sat there shaking, Conrad slammed him in again.

'It's fucking right. So shove-the-fuck-up and give me the elbow-room to get my tackle out.' He elbowed his way between the lads, one of them twitching like a spastic and one of them even sobbing. 'What's your fucking problem? If your gonna start skriking you'll put me off my fucking stroke.'

They tried to look away. Conrad kept at it, urgently masturbating but unable to get harder than a half-erection, staring at his dick in disbelief. 'Jesus fuck, I don't know the fuck the fucking problem.'

He staggered backwards, slamming through the bog door on to Andy's lap. As he struggled upright he realized he'd started spraying piss — so much of it, it seemed to come out of more than one hole. He launched himself at the swinging cubicle door and made for the narrowing gap. As he powered through it, the lads running from the piss stones seemed to weave towards him like they were coming out of a fish-eye lens. There was nothing for it, the cunts had to be stopped. He swung at them.

His fist passed through them and continued, gathering weight as it speeded up, dragging him all the way around until he was punching through the next cubicle. Inside, a cowering little lad with huge wasted eyes started screaming and screaming, thrashing against the walls in terror. Conrad slapped him and staggered for the wash-basin mirror. He needed to know what was happening to him.

In the mirror, his head rose to meet him like a funhouse

17

clown. Its wide grin chewing through red lips. Total chemical audacity, spewing like a geyser. Around his head, mad screaming faces, wizzing up the walls and wazzing down the stones.

Jackie Pye finished inspecting the Gents and walked back to the dancefloor. Apart from the kid with the pot leg and Conrad's kid brother the place was empty. Looking at it now, you wouldn't credit the scenes going on earlier, pure bloody pandemonium. He'd seen nowt like it in years. Usually of a Sunday, all the members wanted to do was stay in the bar and get tanked. Today they'd all shifted themselves upstairs for a boogie. What with Conrad Stubbins just out of prison and his kid brother putting on this Welcome Home bash, they somehow got in the party mood. To Jackie's mind, it was a good job they did. The bunch of spaced out losers Jess Stubbins brought with him were good for nowt, too wasted to do anything except sit around the edges looking mardy.

All things considered, he had to say it hadn't gone too bad. Though there was still the matter of the bathroom. Eyeing the two lads sitting there, he knew they wouldn't give him any trouble.

He said, 'There's nowt I can do for you there. The basin's smashed, the stones are cracked. This all comes out of your end. Otherwise, throw caution to the chuffing winds, I'm happy for you to continue every week.'

Andy pulled the door takings out of his pocket and handed the wad over without counting. His weekend had definitely ended in Ardwick.

'Forget it, Mr Pye. It's not going to work out.'

He was lying across two chairs, looking at the mashed plaster and the fraying edges of his cast. Most of the damage happened as he tried to step across Jess's brother, frothing in the slippery piss across the lavvy floor. 'I've got to get back to the infirmary.'

Jackie Pye glanced over. 'I been meaning to ask. How'd you break your leg.'

Andy did it pulling a fakie, no more than two feet up a ramp. He said, 'Skateboarding.'

'Skateboarding?' Jackie Pye shook his head. 'Fuck me. I never pegged you for the reckless type. Normally, I'd have nowt to do with you but what the fuck ...'

Andy said, 'We've got to go.'

'Right you are. I guess Conrad's got your addresses. If there's any trouble about you turning up next week, he'll drop by. But I'm sure I'll see you same time next Sunday.'

Mike Benson

# 'ROOM FULL OF ANGELS'

as my stomach reached my throat I knew the dancefloor was the wrong place to be. I mean no matter what sort of state you're in you somehow know when things aren't going too well. and everything had been going so fuckin' beautifully so far that it was impossible not to notice the difference. everything was moving faster but I was becoming slower inside it. I could stand but my legs wouldn't dance anymore. I could only just nearly see. see with a suntan there's two problems. first of all everyone thinks you're feeling fine and second of all, no one wants to help you if you're not fine because you've obviously been abroad and they've not. although if you're pale and pasty looking everyone thinks you're fucked up and they're glad they don't look as bad as you. but they do. of course they do. they just can't see themselves. they presume they look the same as they did the last time they saw themselves in a mirror. and how can I tell anyone anything anyway when I know that if I open my mouth even a tiny bit i'm going to puke all over anyone or anything in front of me. so I keep my mouth shut as long as I can. i'm cool. I know what's going on. i've just got to get to a toilet or a corner or somewhere away from where I am now. and i'm getting past a blur of faces arms teeth scraped back hair and tight tops and I'm almost sure i'm going in the right direction and some fucker grabs me and hugs me and starts trying to dance with me. and she is fuckin' beautiful man. I know she is and I know she will be tomorrow and I know that if I go to

23

the toilet now i'll never find her again and if I stay I swear i'm going to vomit down her front so I play hard to get and hope to the god in her pants that she'll find me again and grab hold of me. I wriggle away from her with a tight downward smile and a two-eyed wink and wish i'd not eaten anything tonight today ever. I can hear thumping banging grooving pulsing sounds all around me. I can feel it feel me. i'm inside it as it enters me and if I could have I would have stayed with ... I pass a security man and ask through my teeth 'Toilet' and as he points through the crowd back to where i've just come from I open my jaw in sheer disbelief and watch his face drop as my stomach empties itself over his tight black T-shirt and his massive arm that's still pointing towards the toilet. I feel so much better now. my head's about three stones lighter and my face feels fresh even though i've just wiped ten buckets of sweat from it on to my vest about five times in the last two seconds. fuck. the girl. where is she? I go back to where I think I thought I hoped she was and I feel myself flying backwards. am I tripping? I have to ask myself because this feels like a true out of body experience and i've only had a couple of duff pills. as I bump into people around me I realize that i'm being pulled backwards by a force much stronger than acid. this is not a good trip. this is a journey back to that bouncer i'd just puked on. somehow i'd totally forgotten all about him. and he hadn't. so what the fuck do I do? first of all I tell him to fuck off and seeing as that doesn't work I say 'sorry man it's the pills in here. they've more scag than E in them.' which brings a smile to his face. he brings me up close to the smile on his face and laughs. the guy's a psycho but it could be working in my favour. so I try to lose my fear of physical torture and smile back at him with psycho sicko eyes. and thank fuck I pretended that I was about to puke again and he left me to it. now I can feel the rush i'd been holding down. my eyes are popping and my brain's bursting through the back of my skull and i'm ready to dance like a motherfucker and I see everything nothing at once and I don't hear music I feel it absorb it sense it become it hold it in my soul and thank it so much for being there. and i'm so glad i'm here and not somewhere else. there is nowhere in the world I would rather be than in this body at this place in this head at this time and si comes bouncing towards me rocking his arms in the air going yes yes d'you want half of this? and I go what? and he sticks half a blotter in my half-open mouth and we are fuckin' flying man and nothing but death can stop us. and no one tries to make conversation or look better than anyone else and I swear my eyebrows are going to float off my fuckin' forehead and acid mixes so well with pills as long as you're totally happy in the first place, and I can't imagine why anyone wouldn't ever be happy anyway. so i'm staying on because someone up in that box is dropping tunes from heaven and I swear this huge hot bright black room is full of angels.

we're in a car and i'm saying that that was the fuckin' best best beast of a monster party and someone says that we've not got there yet and i'm laughing my tits off and drinking beers with everyone else and they're all looking for tickets. are we? we are. we are going on somewhere and i'm a i'm I am a amyl. we've got amyl and we are filthy and the streetlights join up with each other. liquid light I say but some girl's screaming her head off beside me and the car stops and si goes it's ok mate we're nearly there and we're there and someone wants money. I pull my hand out of my pocket and I see a pink twenty in between the fingers and they don't look like mine but they must be. a thought flashes through my head but before I catch it it's gone and there's not that many people but the music's good. no the music's fuckin' hard it is kickin' and everyone here has everything they want and there's more rooms full of people on cushions smoking drinking chatting doing lines on the mantelpiece and we are here. every room has a new scene another set of decks another sound and air weighs more than me as I giggle across armies of arms legs lips and eyes. but that big room calls me back for louderharderfasterstronger things than mere social and physical pleasure. fuck knows what but i've got to be there really and the others are there and they must feel the same so we drink some vodka that fires through every inch of me until my toes have had some too. I see some guy in the toilet with his hand in his sock and pay twenty, split two pills in half and go looking for the others or trouble or both because no one's had enough yet. so I go back and buy one more for later. but i'll definitely save it for later because i'm not doing speed and katy left some charlie at ours last night so I have a wee line with frankie now anyway. frankie has a dedication to medication and proves it with some crystal powder in a bag for fives. we're wetting ourselves in there when sarah climbs over the cubical with a note rolled up stuck in her nostril. how can we refuse her? the whole place is full when we get out and I realize that i'm in a queue for the cloakroom. no wonder it's so fuckin' packed and we're getting ushered out politely into very bright sunlight and I wish I had her sunglasses so I whip them off her and she chases me across the street. how come you're still alive I say, looking back at the streaming traffic going in both directions. give me my specs back or i'll shag your best mate she says. did you say that? leave me your specs and i'll shag you, I say, hoping dreaming that that's what she means anyway. she snatches her sunglasses back and tells me there's a mad wee scene ten minutes down the road if we're hard enough. and we're in someone's back garden drinking mushroom tea deluxing to some delicious del mar with some very pierced up characters and their dogs. but they are cool as fuck with strangers so we fuck around there till it's cold and our jackets are on. they ask us to stick around and smoke their skunk but i've got to bite that extra pink pierced tongue once before I leave so I tuck a half behind si's teeth and he'll wait for a while while we slip out the front upstairs to a shocking blue tidy serene little corner all regency stripes and teddy bears and fuck man this is someone's little sister's bedroom and i'm not that bothered now. in fact intimate physical contact seems like the worst idea ever so we lick some of frank's powder anyway and i bite that tongue of hers once, just once, because i've got to and we go back downstairs and si's eyes are all over the shop. he just needs beer though so I head straight to a shop and can't talk for laughing. the old guy at the counter finds it funny for a while but the novelty soon wears off and si's on the floor tears streaming down his cheeks. I finally manage to hold it together long enough to ask for six stripe red six red stripe please. I know if I look at that guy's face again i'll lose it so I keep my head down and my hand covers my eyes because my ribs ache with laughter. we go back to that house but it's not there any more. but it was there. maybe it's the other way ... where the fuck? where are we anyway? and we're on the floor again, out of control pissing ourselves in front of a shiny red car sitting at the traffic lights. let's get a bus, says tanya. and this freaks me out because I didn't even know she was there. I haven't seen her all night and yet there she is standing with a tin of red stripe in her hand giggling her wee head off. i'm chuffed to see her and she sort of doesn't know what i'm talking about but neither of us give a fuck and we jump a bus back to hers to cane the rest of that charlie seeing as we love it so much. anyway there's more pills back at hers and they're pink sanyassi and it's either that or valium and that's better left till tomorrow. we've got six huge lines chopped right across two album covers, si's found a bottle of JD in the kitchen and I start fancying tanya which is a nightmare because she's got a huge boyfriend and the last thing either of us needs is each other so I breathe out and follow my nose along this never ending white line till I run out of air and carry on with my other nostril. now my head starts to rattle. all I want is more more is all I want. my brain is sharpish and the jack daniels takes the edges off. tan slaps in a banging tape and we are all fresh as daisies ready to go again.

Irvine Welsh

'THE STATE OF THE PARTY'

Crooky and Calum sat in a spartan but popular pub on Leith Walk arguing about whether or not it was a good idea to put something on the jukebox.

— Pump up the fuckin jukey Cal, your turn tae feed the beast, Crooky ventured. He'd just bunged in a quid and knew Calum had money.

— Wasta ay fuckin dosh, Calum said.

— Ah, bit c'moan ya cunt, pump up the fuckin jukey! Crooky implored. — Ah cannae handle nae sounds in a pub man.

— Hud yir hoarses. Some daft cunt'll pit somethin oan in a minute. Ah'm no wastin fuckin poppy oan a jukey.

— You're fuckin flush ya cunt.

Calum was about to continue the argument but his attention was arrested by the presence of a figure who shambled from the bar over to the corner of the pub, tentatively carrying a soda water and lime. Reaching his destination, this apparition just let his legs collapse and slumped down into the seat. He sat in a still trance, broken only by an intermittent twitch

— Deek the cunt thair man. That's wee Boaby Preston. Boaby! Calum shouted over, but the small, grey-fleshed figure ignored him

— Shut up, fir fuck sakes. That cunt's a fuckin junky. Dinnae want somebody like that in tow. Paupin cunt, Crooky said. — Nae fuckin passengers the night Cally, eh.

Calum scrutinized Boaby Preston. In the dirty, diminished figure

31

staring at the glass, he caught sight of someone else, someone Boaby Preston had once been. Childhood and adolescent memories bounced around in his head. — Naw man, you dinnae really ken the cunt. Sound fuckin guy. Boaby, Boaby Preston, he repeated. It was as if by saying his name often enough, Calum felt that he could somehow summon back the old Boaby Preston. — The stories ah could tell ye aboot that cunt ... BOABY!

Boaby Preston stared over at them. After straining for recall for a few moments, he then nodded a bemused, half acknowledgement. Calum experienced a depressing sadness at this lack of recognition and an embarrassment that, in front of Crooky, his familiarity had not been reciprocated by his old friend. Recovering from this setback he went over to Boaby. Crooky reluctantly joined them.

— Boaby ... ya daft cunt, yir no still bangin up ur ye? Calum asked with a weary compassion.

Boaby smiled slowly and made a non-committal gesture with one hand.

Uneasy at this reaction, Calum stormed into an anecdote. Surely, he thought, if he could whip up enough enthusiasm for old times, he might entice the old Boaby Preston to come out from his lair deep within the recesses of this parcel of jagged bone and gaunt, grey flesh which approximated him. — Ken whae ah saw the other day thair Boab? The boy thit stabbed ehs auld man cause eh widnae gie um the money fir a Mars Bar. Mind that cunt? Coke-boatil glasses?

Boaby said nothing, but grinned inanely.

Calum turned to Crooky. — This wis whin we wir wee laddies like, back doon the scheme, eh. Thir wis this cunt ... cannae mind ay the boy's name, bit eh stabbed ehs auld man cause eh widnae gie um the money fir a Mars Bar, fae the ice-cream van, ken? Well one time we wis in the Marshall, this wis years later like, me, Boaby here, n Tam McGovern, n Tam goes: that's the cunt thit stabbed ehs auld man cause eh widnae gie um the money fir a Mars Bar. Ah goes, naw, that's no the boy. Mind Boaby? Calum appealed to his wasted old friend.

Boaby nodded, the smile stuck to his face like it had been painted on

Calum continued — Bit Tam's guan: naw, that's the cunt. This boy's jist sittin oan ehs puff readin the *News* ken? Bit me n Boaby, we wirnae sure, eh no Boab? So Tam goes: ahm jist gaun ower tae ask the cunt. Well ah sais tae Tam: if it wis the boy, ye'd better watch, cause the cunt's fuckin tapped. Well Tam goes: fuck off, that wee specky cunt, n goes ower. Well, next thing we ken is thit the specky cunt's glessed Tam, cut the side ay ehs face open. Eh ran ootay the pub, we wir chasin eftir the cunt bit eh bombed away up the main road. Tae tell ye the truth, wi wirnae guan that fast, eh Boab? This wis yonks ago now though. Bit ah saw that cunt the other day; oan the 16 comin doon the Walk, eh.

Crooky was starting to get bored. Junkies bored him: pests, if in need; dull if their needs had been met. Certainly, they were to be avoided at all costs What the fuck was Calum playing at here? Auld mates or no, you couldnae play social worker tae a skag merchant, he thought in irritation. So Crooky was pleased when he noted a white guy with dirty brown-blond dreadlocks and a large hooked nose come into the pub and take up a stance at the bar. — Thaire's The Raven. Mibbee see if the cunt's goat any eckies, eh.

— Thir's supposed tae be somethin happenin at The Citrus the night, eh, Calum told him, turning from the impassive Boaby.

— Ye wantin an E if ehs goat thum? Crooky asked.

— Aye . . . no they doves but. Ah hud yin in the Sub Club in Glesgay last week. Yir up fir an ooir then yir fucked. Jist goes like that. Ah they weedjay cunts wir oan the Malcolm X's n aw, pure fuckin buzzin, n thairs me aw frustrated n comin doon.

A concerned frown moulded Crooky's face. — Aye, right. No wantin nane ay that.

He made his way to The Raven. They briefly exchanged pleasantries, then hit the gent's toilet.

Calum turned back to Boaby. — Hi Boab, listen man, really great tae see ya again. Mind whin it wis me, you, Tam, Ian n

Scooby? That wis some fuckin squad, eh? Dae anything, anytime. Ah'm no bein a borin cunt or nowt like that Boaby, bit it's likes, ah've been wi Helen fir four years now, ken? Ah'm still intae gittin out me face n that, bit no smack n that ken? Look at perr Ian now; deid likes. The virus, Aids n that, ken.

— Yech Ian ... Gilroy ... said Boaby. — Nivir really liked the boy, ken? he mumbled, an old grievance briefly animating him through his smack apathy.

— Dinnae talk like that Boab ... fuck sake ... the boy's deid! Dinnae talk like that ...

— Ripped me oaf ... Boaby slurred.

— Aye, bit ye cannae hud that against the boy Boaby, ken? No whin the boy's deid, that's aw ah'm sayin. Like ah sais, ye cannae hud nowt against a boy that's deid.

Crooky came back from the toilets. — Goat some acid, eh. Micro-dot. Ye intae trippin?

— Now, no really. Wantin an ecky, Calum looked uneasy. He was thinking of Ian, of Boaby, of how they had been. Boaby had put a lot of badness in his head. It would be stupid to trip feeling like this.

— C'moan Cally, thirs a perty oan the night; at this cunt Chizzie's. You ken Chizzie, eh.

— Aye, Chizzie, Calum said. He didn't really know Chizzie. He didn't really feel good. However, he wanted to get out of his face. — Like ah sais, ah'd rather huv an E, eh ... but well ...

They swallowed the micro-dots as surreptitiously as their haste allowed. Boaby, dictated by distress signals from his pain centres, hauled himself up and went to the toilet. He was quite a long time gone anyway, but it could have been months for Crooky and Calum, for by the time he came back, they were seized by a massive trip.

The pub mirrors distorted seeming to arc and form a strange bubble around them, cutting them off from the rest of the clientele who looked twisted, as if their images were reflected through warped lenses. This sense of isolation was briefly comforting, but it quickly grew suffocating and oppressive. They became aware of their body rhythms, the pounding of their hearts, the circulating of their blood. They had a sense of themselves as machines. Calum, a plumber, thought of himself as a plumbing system. This made him want to shit. Crooky had seen the film *Terminator* recently, and his vision became as through a red-tinted viewfinder, with lettering which spelt out alternatives flashing up before his eyes.

— Fuckin hell . . . he gasped.

— It's the end ay the world . . . or is it the start ay a new world, Calum asked, as he watched some strange creature crawl slowly across the floor.

*It's only a dog . . . a cat . . . you dinnae get cats in pubs but sometimes in country pubs in Ireland where they sit in front ay the coal fire but this yin must be a fuckin dug . . .*

— These trips man, how fuckin wild ur they, eh, Crooky shook his head.

— Aye, said Calum, n Boaby's jist fuckin banged up, the dirty wee cunt. In the bogs like. Look at um! Calum was initially grateful to Boaby for providing a focus, before he felt his blood coarse through fragile veins and visualized those veins popping under the bubbling power of the blood, like a turbulent river bursting its banks. — Goat tae git oot ay here man!

— Aye, lits git ootside, Crooky agreed.

It took them a while to actually manage to stand up. The whole pub was spinning round, people's faces were distorting wildly. At one moment all was light; at the next they seemed ready to black out, due to the awesome overload of the trip on their senses. Calum felt reality slipping from him like a rope which was being pulled through greased hands by an awesome force. Crooky felt his psyche peeling away rapidly, like skins on a multi-layered banana, believing that the process was changing him, stripping him down, altering him into some different form of life.

They got outside immediately, all but overwhelmed by a wall of sound and light. Crooky felt himself leaving his mortal flesh and shooting off into space, then snapping with great force back into his body. He glanced back down the street, a buzzing cacophony of strange but familiar sounds and a whizzing kaleidoscope of flashing neon; both producing a bizarre and overpowering interface. Roughly tangible through all of this was the solitary figure of Boaby whom they saw shuffling along behind them.

— C'moan ya junkie cunt! Calum shouted, then turned to Crooky. — Fuckin wasta ay space yon cunt! Despite his aggression Calum was glad that Boaby had tagged on as he did, providing a much-needed piece of reality orientation.

They made their tentative way through familiar, yet somehow alien terrain. Leith Walk looked like its old self, but only in short bursts. Then they were walking through Dresden after the bombings, the flame and smoke and smells of charred flesh around them. They stopped, looked back, and Boaby emerged from the fire, like, Crooky thought, the Terminator robot from the gasoline explosion. — Too fuckin risky . . .

Once again, Calum and Crooky felt themselves drift out off, then snap back into their bodies. Reality briefly asserted itself as Calum gasped, Ah cannae handle this man . . . it's like thirs some kind ay fuckin nuclear war gaun oan . . .

— Aye. They always droap the bomb whinivir you droap a tab. They dae it jist tae fuckin spite ye. Nivir mind Saddam-whit's-the-cunt's-face, Cally's dropped a fuckin tab, Crooky moaned.

Calum laughed loudly and therapeutically. It settled him down. Crooky was a sound cunt to trip with. No freak-outs with Crooky. This was brilliant.

They moved into a tunnel of golden light which pulsed and resonated as they looked on in bewilderment. — Fuckin no real ya cunt. How good is this, Crooky observed, his mouth open.

Calum could not speak. Thoughts came into his head. They were related to undefinable objects. It was as if he was a baby again and had rediscovered pre-speech thought. Rhymes and rhythms flashed incessantly through his head, but he couldn't say them, as these thoughts had no proximity to speech. It would all be lost when he came down. This secret mental language, this pre-speech thought. He began to feel terrible, deflated at the prospect of losing this great insight. He was on a threshold of some superior knowledge, but there was no way to break through. — We ken nowt, we ken fuck all . . . nane ay us ken fuck all . . .

— Take it easy Cal, c'moan man, Crooky implored. — All hands on deck. Look, wir nearly at Chizzies. Here's Boaby, for fuck sake. Boab! Stick in ya cunt! Ye awright?

— Ah cannae speak. Ah'm on heroin man. Heroin, Boaby slurred.

— Daft cunt. Should've taken one ay they microdots, eh. How good is this Cal?

— It's good . . . Calum said doubtfully. This was not acid. This was something else. He'd been tripping for years, thought he had seen it all; become blasé about the drug. Old fucked-up sages who now never touched the stuff because of that one-too-crazy trip had warned him: just when you think you've got the measure of it, you're hit with a trip which changes your life. They were right. Everything else he'd taken was just a preparation for this moment, and it was no preparation at all. Things would be different after this.

They walked on, with minutes feeling more like hours. They seemed to be constantly double-backing, it was like a strange dream where you appeared to be going one step forwards and two steps back. They would pass narrow roads with pubs on the corner. Sometimes it was the same road, the same pub, sometimes a different one. Eventually however, they seemed to arrive at Chizzie's stair door without recognizing any of the landmarks between the pub and their destination.

— Eh . . . ah dinnae ken which yin . . . Crooky tried to read the faded tags on the stair intercom system. — Thirs nae Chizzie . . .

— What's ehs real name? Calum asked, as Boaby boaked up some bile. It was important to get into the flat. Calum felt the presence of demons in the street. At first it had just been a suggestion. Now it was unbearable. — Jist git in, the demons ur oot here man.

37

— Dinnae talk shite, Crooky snapped. It was a thing they had when talking about tripping, about how tripping brought out the demons. That was fine after the trip, but they'd always agreed never to mention it on the trip and now this fucked-up cunt was ... Crooky composed himself. — It's eh, Chisholm, ah think ...

— Fuck, shouted Calum, jist press the fuckin loat! Press the toap yins! Whin some cunt opens git in the stair n follay the sound fir the perty!

— Aye! Right! Crooky did this and they gained entry to the stair. Their rubber legs carried them towards the sound.

They were relieved to see Chizzie standing on the top landing.

— Awright chavvy! Chizzie shouted — Good tae see yis! Good night aye?

— No bad ... wir really trippin likes. Crooky admitted.

— Whit yis fuckin like ya daft cunts thit yis are! C'moan in.

The flat appeared claustrophobic to Crooky and Calum. They sat by the fireplace drinking cans, looking into the imitation-coal fire, trying to blot out the party going on around them. Boaby went to the toilet and lurched back half an hour later, depositing himself in a pine rocking chair.

A square-jawed guy with a moustache approached Crooky and Calum.

— Awright boys. Raffle tickets fir sale. Club 86. First prize, Rover Metro. Second prize, two hundred pound hoaliday voucher fae Sphere Travel, eh. Third prize, Chrismiss hamper worth a hundred bar. Pound a ticket likes.

— Eh, ah'm no wantin any ticket ... Crooky said.

The guy looked at them with an expression of belligerent outrage.

— Chrismiss draw-aw, he snapped, swishing the book of tickets in front of them.

— Eh, aye ... Crooky fumbled in his pockets. Calum thought that he'd better do likewise.

— Chrismiss fuckin draw then cunt ... a pound a fuckin ticket fir a hamper or a hoaliday or a motor ... dinnae dae ays any fuckin favours!

— Eh, ah'll take yin ... Calum started to hand over a pound coin.

— Eh! One fuckin ticket! Moan tae fuck ya tight cunt! Chrismiss fuckin draaww! Club 86 Hibernian Youth Development ... yir no fuckin Jambo's ur yis?

— Eh naw ... ah'll take five! Calum shouted, with a sudden surge of enthusiasm.

— That's ma man! said the moustache guy Crooky reluctantly handed over two pounds.

— Ye gaun oan Setirday? Calum asked the man

— Eh? The man looked at him with hostility

— Easter Road?

The man stared at Calum for a moment and snook his head in an aggressive, surly manner. — Ah'm here fir a fuckin perty n tae sell fuckin tickets, no tae talk aboot fuckin fitba.

He departed, leaving Calum and Crooky feeling paranoid.

— Bevvy's the only thing for a trip like this. It's a depressant. Brings ye back doon, Crooky said, raising a can of lager to his lips. Calum nodded nervously and drank.

After about an hour they began to feel better, and got up and started dancing with some others. Somebody had put on a nice, trancey tape. Boaby was fast asleep in the rocking chair.

A wiry guy with a crewcut was shouting: — Chizzie! Pit ma tape oan! Ma fuckin tape ya cunt!

— Naw ... Finitribe eh, a skinny guy with hair in his eyes mumbled. Crooky thought he recognized the guy from somewhere.

Calum was starting to feel a bit paranoid again. He didn't really know anyone at the party and he began to feel out of place, as if he wasn't welcome. He sat down alongside Boaby.

Boab man, this is fuckin weird. Ah ken it's just the gear n that but thir's a couple ay cunts fae Lochend here n a think one ay thum's the bratay that radge Keith Allison, the cunt that chibbed Mooby ... that whole family man, total blade merchants ... ah heard the story that one time some cunt tried tae gless one ay they Allisons doon at the Post Oafice Club n eh jist took the gless oaf ay the boy, cool as fuck, and ripped the cunt's face open wi it ... ah mean, total psycho like, eh ... thir's that many things happenin in ma life right now Boab ... bad time tae take the acid ... ken Helen, like? Ken her sister ... Julia, ken Julia?

Boaby said nothing

— Ma fuckin tape then Chizzie ya cunt! The wiry guy with the crew cut screamed, but not particularly at Chizzie, and then started frantically dancing to the tape that was already on.

Calum turned back to the silent Boaby — It's no that ah fancy her Boab, ah mean no really. It wis just thit me n hur wirnae speakin n thair ah wis up the toon n jist sortay ended up in Buster's, n her sister Julia likes, well she wis thair wi some ay hur mates. Well the thing wis, nowt happened, no really. Ah mean, a wee bit neckin n that ... thing wis, ah wanted somethin tae happen. Ah did n ah didnae, if ye ken whit ah mean, eh. Ah mean, you ken how it is, eh Boab?

Boaby said nothing.

— See me Boab, ma trouble is thit ah dinnae really ken whit ah want oot ay life. That's whit it aw comes doon tae ... fuck this gear ... every cunt looks aw ancient ... aw decrepit likes ... even that Sandra lassie, mind hur thit used tae go oot wi Kev MacKay ... you legged her one time Boab, ya dirty cunt ... ah mind that ...

— Yill git fuck all oot ay that cunt, a skinny guy with black hair said to Calum. — He wis bangin up smack in the bog.

This guy looked horrible. He looked like something from a concentration camp; he was skeletal. As soon as Calum got a sense of this, the guy actually was a skeleton.

— Eh ... whaire's Crooky? Calum asked him.

— Yir mate? The skeleton's jaw rattled.

— Aye.

— He's through in the kitchen, ootay his fuckin nut. Bit ay a lippy cunt is eh no?

— Naw ... eh, aye ... ah mean, whit's eh been sayin?

— Too much ay a fuckin lippy cunt, eh.

— Aye ...

The skeleton departed, leaving Calum wondering how to get out of this nightmare.

— Hi Boaby, mibee wi should go ... eh Boab? No that struck oan the vibes here, eh.

Boaby said nothing.

Then a girl in a red dress came over and sat beside Calum. She had short blonde hair with brown roots. He thought that her face looked pretty, but her bare arms seemed sinewy and scraggy.

— You here wi that Crooky?

— Eh, aye. Eh, ah'm Calum likes.

— You're no Ricky Prentice's brother are ye?

Calum felt as if he had been electrocuted. Everyone knew his brother Ricky was an arsehole. If they knew he was Ricky's brother, they would think that he was an arsehole.

— Aye ... bit ah'm no the same as Ricky ...

— Nivir says ye wir, the girl shrugged.

— Aye, bit what ahm tryin tae say is Ricky's Ricky n ahm me. Ricky's nowt tae dae wi me. Ah mean, he goes his wey n ah go mine, eh. Ken whit ah mean likes.

— You're ootay yir face.

— They micro dots ... eh what's yir name?

— Gillian.

— They micro dots Gillian, no real.

— Ah nivir touch acid. Maist people that dae acid end up in the funny farm. They cannae handle it. Ah ken ay one guy did acid n went intae a coma ...

— Eh ... aye, Calum said nervously, hoping to change the subject.

— Hud oan the now, Gillian said, suddenly distracted. — Be back in a minute.

— Chiz-ay-ay! Git ma fuckin tape oan! The crew cut guy shouted.

— Aye Chizzie, pit Omlette's tape oan, Gillian agreed.

The loud guy called Omlette turned to Gillian, nodding in stern vindication. — See that, he looked at Chizzie who was rolling a joint on an album cover, and pointed back at Gillian. — Listen tae that! Git ma fuckin tape oan!

— In a bit chavvy, Chizzie looked up and winked.

Crooky came over to Calum. — This is too fuckin mad Cally ... there's you chattin up that Gillian n aw ya durty cunt ...

— Ye ken ur, like? Calum asked.

— Yir well in thair, an easy lay, Crooky smiled.

— She's awright, Calum said, slightly agog. — Seems a nice lassie like ...

— Filled mair jars wi abortions thin yir granny hus wi jam, ya cunt, Crooky sneered.

Gillian was coming back. Crooky felt a twinge of guilt as his eye caught hers and he smiled sheepishly before leaving them.

— Listen, Gillian said to Calum, ye wantin tae buy tickets fir the Christmas Draw? Club 86, she smiled, Hibernian Youth Development.

— Aye, Calum replied, before remembering that he had already bought some. She seemed so pleased though, he just couldn't refuse. He bought another five tickets.

— What wis ah oan aboot again? Aye, the guy who went intae the coma eftir the trip ...

Calum began perspiring. He could feel his heart beat wildly. He nudged Boaby gently, but Boaby fell out of the rocking chair and leadenly hit the floor with a heavy crash.

— Fuckin hell, Calum gasped, as Boaby lay prostrate.

People gathered round him. The guy with the moustache who had sold Calum the first batch of Club 86 tickets felt for a pulse. Then he opened Boaby's shirt and put an ear to his chest.

— Hi Geggs! Lit me in thair, Chizzie shouted, you've no goat ma medical trainin. C'moan Geggsie ya cunt!

— Hud oan the now, Geggsie waved him away. To Calum, Geggsie's hair across that sickly chest looked like ugly, rat-tailed tentacles that were draining the life from Boaby's body. Then Geggsie sat upright. — This cunt's deid. Your mate, he turned to Calum accusingly, as if it was Calum who had murdered him, — fuckin deid, eh.

— Aw fuck, dinnae muck aboot ... Calum said. Chizzie bent over Boaby's body. — Aye, ehs fuckin deid awright. Ah should ken: medical trainin Registered first aider it Ferrant's. They sent ays oan a course it Haymarket wi that St Andrew's Ambulance. Certificate, the fuckin loat, Chizzie said smugly. Then he sprang up. — Crooky! Sorry chavvy youse broat the cunt here. Ah'm no wantin the fuckin bizzies roond here man. Yill huv tae take the cunt away wi yis.

— Aw ... said Crooky.

— Nowt else ah kin dae chav. Try seein it ma wey. No intae any bizzies comin roond here, eh.

— Git the cunt ootay here! The guy called Geggsie roared.

— Wi cannae ... ah mean ... whaire we gonny take the cunt?

— That's up tae youse. Fuckin radges. Bringin a fuckin junky roond tae some cunt's hoose, Geggsie shook his head bitterly.

— Jist spoilin the fuckin perty, another voice opined. It was the guy with the blond crew cut, the one called Omlette. — Mibbee git ma fuckin tape oan now, then eh. Fuckin saw whit that yin did tae the boy, he laughed.

Crooky looked at Calum and nodded. They got on either side of Boaby, picked him up under his arms, and carried him out the flat and into the stair.

— Sorry aboot the wey this's panned oot chavvy. Yir mate thair, sound boy wis eh? Chizzie asked. Calum and Crooky just stared at him. — Listen mate, ah ken now might no be the right time, bit ah meant tae ask ye, ah'm floggin they tickets fir the Christmas Draw ...

— Goat thum, Calum said.

— Aye, well, right then, Chizzie said bitterly.

They began to take Boaby downstairs. Thankfully, he was light and small. Gillian and another girl followed them.

— Half the fuckin fanny's away wi these cunts, the guy called Omlette said bitterly, before the door slammed shut.

— This is too mad, the other girl said. — Is it cool for us tae come aye?

Crooky and Calum didn't respond. The worst of the hallucinations had gone, but their legs felt rubbery and everything was still a bit distorted.

— Ah want tae see whit they'll dae wi him, Gillian said.

— Whit ur wi gaunny dae? Calum asked, as they carried Boaby down the stairs. While Boaby was not heavy, it was as if he was a sackful of water, his weight constantly shifting. They adjusted their grip, and as they walked down the stairs Boaby's back legs trailed down the steps behind them.

— Fuck knows! Lits jist git away fae this fuckin place. Crooky snapped.


— Eeuugghh! Eeuugghh! Dinnae ken how yis kin even touch um, said Gillian's friend.

— Tsk, shut up Michelle, Gillian nudged her.

They got Boaby out off the stair and carried him down the dark, deserted street. His legs and feet dragged along, scraping his shoes at the toes and sides. Gillian and Michelle at first walked a few feet behind, then alternatively ran in front, or if they saw someone approach on the same side of the street, would cross the road and make parallel progress. — Ah've never seen anybody deid before. Gillian stated.

— Ah huv. Ma Grandad. Ah saw him laid oot. Michelle told her.

— Whae wis it that laid him oof? Gillian asked She visualized somebody killing Michelle's granded with one punch.

— The priest ... the church. Michelle said, in a strange, sad voice.

— Aw aye ... Gillian realized. Then she looked at Boaby. —
He goat any money on him?

Crooky and Calum stopped. — What dae ye mean? Calum
asked.

— Well, it's nae good tae him now. Better get him in a taxi or
something.

Calum and Crooky considered this for a while. Then Calum
said — The perr cunt's deid! We could git done fir murder! Wi
cannae git him intae a taxi!

— Jist sayin. Gillian said.

— Aye. Crooky snapped at Calum — The lassie's jist sayin.
It's cool Cal. Dinnae take it oot oan the lassie ...

Calum was ready to explode. This was Boaby. Boaby's body. He
thought of bonfire night. He remembered raiding other bonnies in
the schemes with Boaby. Boaby. Boaby Preston. He recalled playing
IRA and UDA with Boaby. He remembered shooting him and
Boaby playing dead, lying on the grassy bank alongside the main
road. When he got up, the back of his T-shirt was covered in
dog-shite.

Now Boaby wasn't playing dead and they were all in the shit.

— Ah'm no takin it ... THIS IS BOABY ... aw fuck ... Calum
moaned, then stopped suddenly, noticing a police car pulling up
alongside them. His thoughts turned from Boaby to himself. He
could feel his life disintegrating before him, as sure as Boaby's had,
silently in that chair, taken by the overdose, too junked to know
that he was slowly dying. Calum wondered about his girlfriend
Helen; whether he'd ever see her again.

A cop got out of the car, leaving his mate at the wheel. —
All right folks? He looked at Boaby, then turned to Calum and
Crooky — Yir mate looks like he's had a skinful.

Calum and Crooky just looked at him. The polisman had a
squashed nose with two large holes in it. His skin was the sickly
pink of uncooked pork sausage, and his eyes were dulled, slanted
and set far back, into a bulbous head. It must be the acid. Crooky
thought, it hus tae be the fuckin acid.

Calum and Crooky shot a glance at each other, over Boaby's lolling neck. — Aye Crooky said weakly.

Youse havnae seen any sign ay trouble, huy ye? Bunch ay nutters huv been fiilin in shop windaes.

— Naw, we've no seen nowt, Michelle said.

— Well, yir mate's no seen nowt by the looks ay him, the polisman looked contemptuously at Boaby. — Ah'd git him hame if ah wis youse.

Shaking his chunky head a couple of times, the cop snorted with disgust before departing.

— Fuckin hell ... we're fucked man! Totally fuckin fucked, Calum whined.

— That's an idea, Crooky said, what the polisman sais likes.

— Eh? Michelle asked. Calum looked incredulously at Crooky.

— Jist listen tae this. If we get pilled up wi his boady it's us that git sent doon. See if we could git um up tae ehs hoose bit ...

— Shite, Calum shook his head. — Better jist dumpin um.

— Naw, naw, Crooky said. — Bound tae be a polis investigation, ken?

— Ah cannae fuckin think straight, it's this acid ... Calum moaned.

— Mad takin acid, Gillian said, chewing a piece of gum.

Crooky watched the side of her face swell and ripple as she chewed.

— Ah ken whit wi should dae. Take um tae the Infirmary. The casualty. Tell thum eh passed oot, Calum said, suddenly animated.

— Naw, they kin tell ... time ay death ... Crooky told him.

— Time ay death ... Calum repeated in a ghostly echo. — Ah dinnae even ken the cunt really, well no that well. Ah mean wi wir mates donks ago bit wi drifted apart, ken? First time ah seen the cunt in years, eh. Junky now, ken?

Gillian pulled back Boaby's head. His skin looked sickly and his eyes were shut. She spread the lids open with her fingers.

— Euuggghh ... euggghhhh ... eugghhhh ... Michelle moaned.

— Fuck off! Calum snapped.

— Ehs deid fir fuck sake, Gillian dismissed him, closing Boaby's eyes. She took a compact from her purse and began dabbing Boaby's face. — Make um look less creepy. In case wi stopped again likes.

— Barry idea, Crooky nodded approvingly.

Calum looked across the dark blue sky, the dead, dulled tenements. The burning streetlamps only seemed to emphasize the lifelessness of the ghostly city that surrounded them. There was one shop light though, that beamed ahead. It was the all-night kebab shop.

— Ah'm starvin, Crooky ventured.

— Aye, said Michelle, me n aw.

They put Boaby on a municipal bench which lay under some trees at the entrance to a small park.

A'll leave Boaby here wi you Cally, n we'll go owen get some doners. Crooky said.

— Hud oan bit, Calum started, but they were moving across the road to the kebab shop.

— Stay cool Cally, dinnae strop oot oan ays. Be back in a minute, Crooky explained irritably.

Cunts, thought Calum. This was a bad move, him left on his jack. He turned to Boaby. — Listen Boab, really sorry aboot this man, like ah ken ye cannae hear ays . . . it's like Ian n aw that auld crowd . . . nae cunt kent aboot the virus n that Boab, every cunt thought ye could only git it fae shaggin, back then, mind? It wis like only poofs in London, accordin tae they adverts, no junkies up here. Some boys like Ian, they wir only oan it fir a few months Boab . . . jist bad fuckin luck Boab . . . ah took the test, efter Ian ken? Clear, Calum observed, blankly pondering the implications. For the first time he realized, it didn't seem to matter.

A drunkard in a smelly overcoat approached them. He stood staring at them for a bit, seemingly rooted to the spot. Then he sat down beside Boaby. — VAT's the thing nowadays, he mused. — VAT my friend, he winked at Calum.

— Eh? Calum said irritably.

— A rerr baked tattie it that shoap it Cockburn Street son, a rerr baked tattie. That's whair ah eywis go. That shoap at Cockburn Street. Nice people workin in thair, like, ken? Youn ones like yirsel. Students. Students, ken?

— Aye, Calum rolled his eyes in exasperation. It was cold. Boaby's neck felt cold.

— Philadelphia, the city ay brotherly love. The Kennedys. J F Kennedy, the drunk said smugly. — Philadelphia. Brotherly love, he wheezed.

— Boston bit, Calum said.

— Aye . . . Philadelphia, the drunkard croaked.

— Naw the Kennedys came fae Boston. That's whair they came fae . . .

— I FUCKEN KNOW THAT SON! DON'T FUCKEN PREACH HISTORY AT ME! The old drunkard roared into the night. Calum watched his spittle splash against Boaby's face. Then he nudged Boaby. — You'll ken! Tel yir fuckin friend here! Boaby slumped against Calum who pushed him back upright, then pulled on his body to stop him from sliding against the drunkard.

— Leave the boy, ehs fucked, Calum said.

— Ah kin tell ye whair ah wis whin John Lennon wis shot . . . the man wheezed.

Calum shook his head in derision. — Wir talkin aboot the fuckin Kennedys ya tube . . .

— AH KEN THAT SON, BIT AH'M FUCKEN TALKIN ABOOT JOHN FUCKEN LENNON! The drunk stood up, and started singing. — So this is Cris-mehhsss and what have we done . . . a very merry Cris-mehhsss and Happy new yeh-ur . . .

He moved unsteadily down the road. Calum watched him vanish into the night, his voice still audible after he was out of sight.

The others returned with the kebabs. Crooky handed Calum one. He still had a spare one in his hand. — Fuck! he spat between his teeth. — Ah forgot that cunt wis deid, wasted a fuckin kebab! He looked at the spare kebab.

— Oh aye, fuckin selfish ay the cunt tae go n die like that, Calum glared at Crooky. — Waste ay a kebab! Listen tae yirsel Crooky ya cunt! Boaby's fuckin deid!

Crooky stood with his mouth open for a bit. — Sorry man, ah ken he wis a mate ay yours.

Gillian looked down at Boaby. — If eh was a junky, eh widnae huv wanted it anyway. They nivir eat.

Crooky considered this. — Aye, that's true, bit no aw the time though. Remember Fat Phil Cameron? Eh Cal?

— Aye, Calum nodded. — Fat Phil.

— The only cunt ah've ivir kent whae goat intae smack n pit weight oan, Crooky smiled.

— Bullshit, Gillian scoffed.

— Naw, it's true though, eh Cal? Crooky appealed to Calum.

Calum shrugged and then nodded in acknowledgement. — Fat Phil used tae take ays shot, then go radge fir a sugar fix. Eh'd head up tae The Bronx Café n buy a huge bag ay donuts. Ye couldnae git near they fuckin donuts n aw. Better chance ay gittin the cunt's skag oaf um thin one ay they donuts. He goat better though, goat cleaned up ... no like poor Boaby. Calum looked at the greying corpse of his friend.

They silently finished their kebabs. Crooky took a bite out of the extra one, then slung it over the hedge. Looking at Boaby's body, Gillian seemed sad for a bit, then she put lipstick on the blue-tinted lips.

— Nivir hud a chance, Calum said. — Boys like him. The cunt goat in too deep, ken? Thir wis that many ay they boys, good fuckin guys n aw, well, some ay thum, bit jist like any other cunts, good n bad in every crowd, ken ...

— Mibbe ehs goat Aids anyway, Gillian said.

— Eeuugghh ... Michelle screwed her face up, then looking thoughful said — What a shame. Imagine how ehs Ma must feel.

Their deliberations were disturbed by noises coming from down the street. Calum and Crooky tensed up. There was no time to run or manoeuvre. They knew that the owners of the voices, maniacally screaming a medley of drunken football songs at each other, were just indulging in a spot of practice for the time when they could vent their aggression on some external force.

— Better nash, eh, Calum said.

Calum saw the dark demons come into full view, illuminated by a shining moon and sparkling street lamps. How many there were he could not be sure, but he knew that they had fixed him in their sights.

— HI YOUSE! One of them shouted.

— Who the fuck ur you shouting it? Gillian sneered.

— Shhh! Calum hissed. — Lit us handle this. He was panicking. Fucking daft slags, he thought, it's no thaim thit gits the fuckin doin. It's us. Me.

— HI! ANY AY YOUSE CUNTS SEEN THE FUCKIN POLIS? One guy shouted. He was tall and powerfully built with dark greasy hair and blazing eyes devoid of reason.

— Eh, naw . . . Crooky said.

— WHAIRE YIS FUCKIN BEEN? The greasy-haired guy shouted.

— Eh, a pairty, Crooky nervously told him. — . . . The mate's flat in that, eh.

— That yir fellay, doll? Another guy with a pork-pie hat said to Gillian, while looking Calum up and down.

Gillian stood silent for a moment. Her stare never left the face of her questioner. With a harsh contempt in her voice she said. Might be. What's it tae you?

Calum felt a simultaneous eruption of pride and fear. Magnified by the acid, it was almost over-whelming. He felt a muscle in his face twitch wildly.

The guy in the pork-pie put his hands on his hips. He bent his head and shook it slowly. Then he looked up at Calum. — Listen pal, he said, attempting to sound reasonable through his obvious anger, if that's yir burd ah'd tell ur tae watch ur fuckin mooth, right?

Calum just nodded. The youth's face had distorted into that of a cruel gargoyle's. He had seen that image before; on a postcard of Notre Dame Cathedral in Paris. The demon had been looking down on the city, crouched high up on a ledge; now it had come to Earth.

— What's this cunt goat tae say fir ehsel? The greasy-haired guy looked at Crooky and pointed to Boaby's body. — Eh's goat fuckin lipstick oan. YOU A FUCKIN POOF, PAL?

— Eh, the boy's . . . Crooky began.

— LIT THE CUNT SPEAK FIR EHSEL! HI PAL, WHAIRE'S IT YIR FAE? the greasy-haired guy asked Boaby.

No response was forthcoming.

— WIDE CUNT! He lashed out and slammed a fist into Boaby's face. Calum and Crooky relaxed their grip and the body fell heavily to the ground.

— EHS DEID! EHS FUCKIN DEID! Michelle screamed.

— Eh fuckin well will be in a minute, the greasy-haired guy said, pointing down at the body. — C'MOAN THEN YA CUNT! YOU N ME! SQUARE FUCKIN GO'S! GIT UP YA FUCKIN CUNT!

He started booting at the corpse.

— CUNT'S FUCKED! SEE THAT YA CUNTS! He turned triumphantly to his mates.

The pork-pie hat guy upturned his palms, then extended his hand to his greasy-haired pal. — One fuckin punch Doogie, cannae say fairer thin that, he curled his lower lip and half shut his eyes. — Took the daft cunt oot wi one fuckin punch.

The guy called Doogie, swollen with belligerent pride, looked at Crooky and Calum. — Whae's next?

Calum's eyes furtively scanned around for potential weapons. He could see nothing.

— Eh, wir no wantin any bother . . . Crooky said.

The guy called Doogie stood immobilized for a second. His

51

face contorted as if he was trying to assimilate a barely digestible concept.

— Fuck off ya radge! You're a fuckin arsehole son, Gillian said.

— WHAE YOU FUCKIN TALKIN TAE? He roared.

— Dinnae ken, the label's fell off, Gillian said chewing steadily and looking him up and down with contempt.

— IT'S FUCKIN ... IT'S FUCKIN BURDS LIKE YOU THIT DESERVED TAE GIT FUCKIN RAPED, SLAGS WI A FUCKIN MOOTH! Doogie had never been dismissed in this way by a woman before.

— HOW THE FUCK WID YOU KEN ABOOT ANYTHIN! YOU NIVIR HUD A FUCKIN FANNY THIT WISNAE YIR MA'S IN YIR LIFE YA FUCKIN PRICK! AWAY N SHAG YIR POOFY MATES UP THIR FUCKIN ERSES! Gillian screamed like a banshee; no fucker talked to her like that.

Doogie stood hyperventilating, seemingly rooted to the spot. His face distorted in uncomprehending disbelief. It was like he had seized up. — You dinnae ken ... you dinnae ken nowt aboot mee ... he moaned like a wounded animal, pleading and raging at the same time.

For Crooky, the distortion of the guy's face was magnified twenty-fold by the acid. He felt a surge of raw fear which transformed into anger and he ran at Doogie, throwing punches. In no time he was overpowered and beaten to the ground where Doogie and two others began kicking lumps out of him. At the same time the guy with the pork-pie hat exchanged blows with Calum who was then chased around a car. He pulled at the aerial which came away in his hand and he whipped the guy with the pork-pie hat across the face with it, opening up his cheek. The guy screamed with pain but mainly frustration and anger as Calum rolled under the car. He felt some boots in his side as he crawled into its centre and safety, but to his horror, he felt somebody getting under with him. He started kicking and punching, flaying out in a frenzy, before he realized that it was Crooky.

— CAL! IT'S ME YA CUNT! FUCKIN COOL IT!

They lay breathing heavily, bonded in a state of abject terror, listening to the voices:

— BREK INTAE THAT FUCKIN CAR! START THE MOTOR! KILL THE CUNTS!

Fuck sakes, Crooky thought.

— Gang-bang the slags! A fuckin line-up!

Aw fuck . . . but they daft cows started it, they caused everything, Calum thought.

— Aye, jist fuckin try ya cunts! That was Gillian.

Gillian, he thought, Cannae let them touch her. — Lit's git ottay here!

Yea-ehs! They thought together. Go. Jist fuckin go. Please.

— Git the cunt thit Doogie decked!

Daft cunts.

A consensus quickly formed around this. From under the car Crooky and Calum watched the gang kicking Boaby's body around.

One guy stuck a lighted cigarette against the prostrate figure's red lips. Boaby didn't move or respond in any way.

EHS FUCKED! THAT'S ENOUGH! one voice shouted, and they stopped.

They panicked and departed hastily, one guy in a blue jacket shouting back at Michelle and Gillian: Youse fuckin boots say anything aboot this n yis ur deid! Right!

— Sure, Michelle voiced sarcastically.

The guy ran back and struck her across the face. Gillian stole across and punched him in the mouth. She made to do the same again, but he restrained her by grabbing her arm. Michelle had pulled off her high heel and, in a tearing, upward sweep, tore the jagged seg of its point across his cheek, up into his eye.

The boy staggered back in pain, stemming the blood with his hand. — Fuckin slag! Could've hud ma fuckin eye oot! he whined, before moving away with increasing speed as they came slowly towards him, like two small predators circling a larger, wounded animal.

— YOU FUCKIN DIE YA CUNT! MA BRARS'LL FUCKIN KILL YE! ANDY N STEVIE FARMER! THAT'S MA FUCKIN BRARS YA CUNT! Gillian screamed.

The boy gave a frightened, bemused look and turned to run after his pals.

— GIT OOT FAE UNDER THAIR YA CUNTS! Gillian screamed at Crooky and Calum.

— Nup, Calum said weakly. It felt good under the car. Crooky, though, felt as if he ws being buried alive, like he was sharing a coffin with Calum.

— Thir away, Michelle said.

— We're sound here. It's the acid . . . aw this shit . . . cannae hack it. Youse jist go hame . . . Calum rambled on.

— AH SAIS GIT FUCKIN OOT! Gillian shrieked, her voice scrapping on their raw nerve-endings.

Compliant with shame and fear, they wriggled out from under the car. — Shh, Calum moaned. Yill huv the polis here, eh.

— Eh, nice one. Eh, thanks girls, Crooky said.

— Aye. Well done, Calum agreed.

— That prick hit Michelle, Gillian pointed at her friend, who was putting her shoe back on and sobbing wretchedly.

Crooky's bushy eyebrows knotted in pity. — We'll git the cunts eftir, eh Cally? Git a squad the gither. Couldnae huv hacked swedgin oan the acid bin ken? They wirnae hard cunts. Fuckin wankers Mind you, ah thoat ah wis fucked whin thay goa ays doon, bit thay wir kickin each other mair thin me, the daft cunts. Ah'll git they cunts though. See if it hudnae been fir that acid, eh Cal, Crooky said

— Mad tae take acid, said Gillian.

They looked over at Boaby. His face was bashed in at one side, like his cheekbone and jawbone had collapsed. Calum thought again about the time he had pretend shot Boaby in Niddrie, as a child, when Boaby had played dead. — Lit's jist go, he said

— Cannae just leave um, Crooky ventured, shuddering. That could've been ma face, he thought.

— Aye, wid better go. The polis'll git they bastards fir it. They killed um really, Michelle said tearfully. — Everything dies, thir's nowt naebody kin dae aboot it . . .

They walked away from the body in a silence puncutated only by Michelle's sobs, through the night, towards Crooky's place in Fountainbridge. Crooky and Calum staggered wearily on ahead. Gillian had a comforting arm around Michelle, a few yards behind them.

— Thinkin aboot Alan? Gillian asked her. — Time ye goat him oot ay yir system, it really is Michelle. Ye think he's sittin greetin aboot you right now? Huh! She sneered. — Ye should jist git the first guy ye see tae screw yir fuckin brains oot. That's your problem, ye need tae git laid.

— Ah loast that joab in the bank thanks tae him . . . Michelle whimpered. — A good joab. The Royal Bank.

— Forget him. Start enjoyin yir life, Gillian said.

Michelle gave a hostile pout then forced a smile. Gillian nodded at Crooky and Calum who were still lurching on ahead. The two women started laughing. — Which one do you fancy? Michelle asked.

— Nane ay thum really, bit ah cannae stand him wi the eyebrows, Gillian pointed at Crooky.

— Naw, he's awright . . . Michelle said, It's ehs mate, that Calum . . . ehs no really goat any erse oan um.

Gillian considered this. Michelle was right. Calum didn't really have much of an arse. — As long as he's got a fuckin cock, she laughed, flushing with a hormonal itch.

Michelle joined in with her laughter.

Gillian kept her stare on Calum. He was quite skinny, but had both big hands and big feet. Those three factors together surely, she thought, made it odds-on that he'd have a big cock.

— Right, well you fire intae him n ah'll fire intae his mate.

— Suppose, Michelle shrugged.

\*        \*        \*

Irvine Welsh

They went up to Crooky's flat and sat beside the fire. Gillian was on the couch massaging Calum's neck. He was coming down from the acid and her touch felt good. — Yir awfay tense, she said.

— Ah feel tense, was all Calum could say. Ah wonder why, he thought, recounting the events of the evening. Ah feel tense, he sniggered.

Michelle and Crooky were crouched together on the floor, whispering to each other.

— Yi'll probably think ahm a slag or that, jist say if ye do, Michelle said softly to Crooky.

— Naw ... Crooky said, doubtfully.

— Ah used tae work in the bank, the head oafice, Michelle said in self-justification. — The Royal Bank. She emphasized the 'Royal'. — Ken the Royal Bank ay Scotland?

— Aye, it the Mound likes, Crooky nodded.

— Naw, this is the Royal Bank, that's jist the Bank ay Scotland you're thinkin ay. This is the Royal Bank ay Scotland ah used tae work fir. The Head Oafice. St Andrew's Square.

— The Royal Bank ... Crooky acknowledged. — Aye ... The Royal Bank, he repeated, looking into her dark eyes. She looked beautiful to him; those eyes, her red lips. The lipstick. The visuals from her lipstick, even coming down. Crooky realized that he loved women who knew how to wear lipstick and he thought that Michelle certainly came into that category.

Michelle sensed his desire. — You n me through thair then, she said, nodding urgently at the door.

— Yeah ... sound ... the bedroom. Aye, the bedroom, Crooky smiled, raising his bushy brows.

They got to their feet, Michelle eagerly. Crooky tentatively, and crept across to the door. Crooky caught Calum's eye and puckered his lips and fluttered his brows as they departed.

— That leaves you n me, Gillian smiled.

— Eh aye, Calum said.

They lay out on the couch. Gillian took her coat off, and draped it over them. It was a large, brown imitation fur. Calum liked the way she looked in her short red dress. Her arms seemed OK; he realized it must have been the acid.

Gillian was aroused by the hardness of his body. She couldn't make out whether it was muscle or just large bones under the skin. She began touching him: rubbing his crotch through his jeans. He felt himself go hard. — Feel ays, feel ays well, she said in a soft low hiss.

He began kissing her and twisted his hand down her cleavage. Her dress and bra were so tight he couldn't expose any tit without his activities causing her to wince in discomfort. So he disentangled his hand and ran it up her thigh, getting his fingers inside her pants. She pulled away from him, springing from the couch, but only to undress. Gillian ushered him to do the same. Calum got his clothes off quickly, but his erection had gone. Giliian got back on the couch and pulled him to her and he grew hard again for a bit, but he couldn't sustain the erection.

— What is it? What's wrong? she snapped.

— It's just the acid . . . it's like . . . it's like ah've goat a girlfriend, ken. Helen. Ah mean, it's like ah dunno if wir still the gither like, cause eh, well, wuv no been really gittin oan n ah've moved oot, the flat n that likes, bit wir still sortay seein each other like . . .

— Ah'm no wantin tae fuckin mairray ye, ah just want a shag, right?

— Eh aye. He ran his gaze over her nakedness and got hard without feeling himself stiffening.

They pulled the coat over their naked bodies and had a shag. It was based only on a grinding, genital interaction rather than any deep psychic communion, but it was hard and intense and Gillian came quite quickly, Calum shortly after. He felt pleased with himself. At one stage he had wondered whether he'd be able to hold on for her. He could do a lot better than that. It was the acid, Boaby, all the shit in his head. He could do a lot better, but this wisnae bad in the circumstances. he thought happily.

Gillian was content. She thought that she wouldn't have minded getting there again, but at least he managed to keep it up until she'd come. It was OK, it had cleared things out a wee bit.

— That wisnae too bad, Gillian conceded, as they fell asleep.

Later Calum felt Gillian moving, but he pretended to be crashed out. She got up from the couch and started to get dressed. Calum then heard whispering conversations and realized that Michelle had come into the room. This made him feel embarrassed at his nakedness under the coat.

— How wis your night? Calum heard Gillian softly ask Michelle.

— Shite. He didnae ken whit tae dae. Like a fuckin virgin. Couldnae git it up. Kept gaun oan about the fuckin acid ... Calum could hear Michelle dissolve into tears. Then she asked, with a sudden eagerness: What was he like?

Gillian struggled into her dress, then considered, for what to Calum's ears seemed like a very long time. — No bad. A bit ay a grunter like ... aw perr Michelle ... it didnae happen fir ye ... ah should've gied ye him, she gestured with a thumb at Calum.

Michelle rubbed her tearful eyes smearing some thick eye-liner around the sockets. Gillian went to speak but couldn't get a word in before Michelle started talking. — It's just thit wi Alan, well, it wis brilliant. At the start it wis brilliant. It goat crap later oan, when eh wis wi that fuckin hoor, bit at the start ... nothin could beat it.

— Aw, Gillian said softly. She would mention Michelle's eyes later. She turned to Calum. — Hi Calum, she shook him gently. — Ah'm gaunny huv tae wake ye. Ah need ma coat. We're oaf now.

— Eh, right ... Calum said. His brain felt like it had been pickled, and his body seemed to have been battered all over but at least he was back down from the acid. — Lit ehs git ma keks oan well.

They went behind the couch. — Will no look, honest, Gillian said.

This sparked off a laugh from Michelle which Calum thought had a disturbingly predatory harshness to it, particularly with her dark eye sockets, but he pulled on his pants, then his jeans and handed Gillian the coat.

— Well, eh, cheers then . . . Michelle, eh Gillian. Eh, Gillian, ye goat a number? He asked tentatively. Calum didn't know whether or not he wanted to see her again, but it seemed a good idea to at least offer. He thought that Gillian was a bit of a nutter.

— Yir no gittin ma number. You give ays yours, she said, passing him a pen and a piece of scrap paper from her bag. It was a voucher for the Club 86 Hibernian Youth Development Christmas Draw.

— Did ah flog ye one ay they raffle tickets? she asked.

— Aye, ah boat five, he replied, writing down his number.

She looked at Calum, then turned to Michelle. — That wey if ah want tae see you, ah kin. Ah dinnae like laddies hass in ays oan the phone: Come oan oot Gill-i-ihhnnn, she imitated a creepy, insipid voice. Then she went over and kissed Calum and wrapped her arms around his naked torso. She whispered: You're gaunny fuck me again, really soon. Right?

— Eh, mmh, he muttered incoherently. — Eh, aye. Calum remembered at that point a nature programme he'd seen where the female praying mantis ate the male praying mantis's head during sex. He watched Gillian departing with Michelle and could certainly imagine her french-kissing praying mantis style.

Alone in the front room Calum sat watching morning television and smoking cigarettes. He rubbed at his penis and balls and smelt Gillian on his hand. He thought of Helen and Boaby and started to feel depressed and lonely. Then he made some tea before Crooky came in.

— Good night? He asked Crooky whose face was split by a hatchet-wound grin.

— The best mate, the best. That Michelle man; The Royal Bank, whoa ye cunt ye! Takes it aw fuckin' weys! She was fuckin gantin oan it, bit Crooky wis up tae the joab.

— Gie her the message, aye? Calum asked, ashen-faced.

— Ah fuckin split hur right up the middle man. The Royal Bank'll not be able tae sit on a bicycle seat or eat a good meal fir a long time eftir that! Crooky here, he drummed his chest with his

index finger. — Ah'm well in credit at the Royal Bank! Ah only
made one withdrawal, but ah pit in quite a few fuckin big deposits,
if ye catch ma drift. Wir talkin high interest n aw! Ah should've telt
hur, ye want any ay yir mates sorted oot, take the address doon n
send thum up tae Crooky ... He's simply the best ... do ... do ...
Crooky burst into song, thrusting his hips ... He's beh-rah thehn
all the rest ... he's beh-rah thehn eh-eh-ne-one, thehn eh-ne-one
ah've eh-eh-vah met ... he's simply the best ... do ... do ...

Calum left Crooky to his dancing. He couldn't be bothered
slagging him off. A sadness had gripped him, Boaby relentlessly
intruding into his thoughts. When had Boaby really died? Sometime long before last night.

— What aboot you Cal? How wis it wi that Gillian? Crooky
suddenly asked, with a smirk on his face.

— No up tae much really, ma fault likes. The acid, ken?

Crooky shot him an expression of theatrical disdain. — That's
a poor excuse Cally ma man. Take Crooky here, he pointed at
himself. — Or tae gie um his official title: SIMPLY THE
BEST. Nae amount ay drugs kin knock this boy oot ay his
stride. That's whit sorts out the highly-skilled time-served men
fae the also-rans.

— Suppose yuv either goat it or yuv no. Calum acknowledged
wearily.

— That's it Cal, natural talent. Aw the coachin manuals in the
universe cannae instil that.

Calum was thinking about Boaby, and about Gillian. — Ah
once saw this documentary aboot insects, n thir wis this prayin
mantis, ken they big, radge insects?

— Aye ... fuckin evil lookin cunts, eh.

— The lassie prayin mantis eats the laddie prayin mantis's heid
whin thir shaggin ... ah dinnae mean the lassie prayin mantis n
the laddie prayin mantis ... ah mean, like, male n female, ken?

Crooky looked at Calum. — What the fuck's that tae dae wi
anything?

Calum bowed his head and put his hand up to it. It seemed to

Crooky like he was trying to cover his face. When he spoke his voice seemed urgent and breathless. — We ... saw a boy ... Boaby ... we saw Boaby die ... it shouldnae be like this, it shouldnae be like nowt's jist happened ...

Crooky slid on to the couch beside Calum. He felt stiff and awkward. He tried to speak a couple of times but he was gripped by a paralysis. After a long silence he looked at the telly and asked: What's this shite?

Calum lifted his head up. — Breakfast telly. Aw we need is breakfast now, eh.

— Aye, aye, aw right ya cunt! Ah'll go doon fir some rolls n milk in a bit. Then Crooky looked at Calum, glad that the tension between them had ebbed. — Wonder whit'll happen about last night?

Calum thought about Boaby, about how you never ever could tell that arrogant little cunt anything, how he always strode along with that petulant twist to his lip, as though the world owed the stupid wee fuck a living. — Fuck knows. Nowt tae dae wi us though. We jist say we thoat thit Boaby wis fucked; we tried tae help um doon the road, eh. Gillian n Michelle'll vouch fir that. We jist huv tae say thit we goat chased by they boys. They'll be the ones tae git done.

— Bit Boaby ODed, Crooky said.

— Bit it serves they cunts right. They nutters, they might've killed um. Whae's tae say? It's thaim or us, n it's better thaim.

Crooky watched the sunlight come up from behind the tenements opposite. The city was coming back to life. The demons he and Calum always talked about were in retreat; the guys at the party, the gang of nutters, Boaby, Gillian and Michelle, the Royal Bank, even. Especially that slag The Royal Bank. It was just the acid. He should've fucked the slut though, she wisnae bad looking, he thought bitterly. The nightmare was over now though. The sun was here; they were still here.

— Aye. Crooky agreed, better thaim thin us.

Calum thought that he heard a car pull up outside. He

was convinced that there were at least a couple of sets of
heavy footsteps coming up the stair. Paranoia, he thought, it's
just the residue of the acid he told himself, just the come-
down.

Gavin Hills

'WHITE BURGER DANNY'

Danny MacGuire pops back into my life at the beginning of summer '88. It is about two a.m. Saturday morning. The revamped Mud Club has just turned out. Word has of a warehouse party round the back of London Bridge station. I follow the crowd on to the top deck of the nearest bus, where they are all trying to skin up what looks like the crumbs of an oat-cake. And up the stairs shines Danny glorious. He is off his tits.

The buttoned label on his Stone Island jumper is half undone, flapping at half mast down his arm. Out the side pocket of his Ball jeans sticks a single red rose. He's grinning ear to ear. As he sways towards us, his black floppy fringe is windscreen-wiping his face.

'Loving it!' he screams, acknowledging me with a pointed finger.

'All right Danny, how's tricks?' I enquire in the strange whining mockney accent I adopt when talking to prime geezers or taxi drivers.

'Fucking blinding mate, fucking blinding! Happy as fuck.' With that he slumps into my lap. Not something one expects from a well-known soccer hooligan.

It must have been three or four years since I'd seen Danny. Truth is, I didn't really know the guy well. I'd spent a couple of weeks at the White Cliff Bay holiday camp on the Isle of Wight with him and few of his mates some summers back and kicked around a little with his crowd in my formative years. I'd bumped into him a few times since then at football. He went to borstal I went to art college. That was it.

Danny had a big rep though. He was one of Arsenal's top boys. A Gooner since the under-twelve's. People knew Danny and his Archway firm. He didn't look *all that*. He wasn't a big bruiser type. Probably couldn't even fight properly. He was sharp though, with a lot of front. Always with the mouth, always 'giving it the big' un' as they say. Yep, he didn't give a toss. He had the balls and wit to be Lord of his particular flies.

Danny was always very good at being the centre of attention, top dog, so to speak. That night was no exception. Bug-eyed and brainless, Danny was an eye-opener. Sociability hadn't always been his strong point. It pleased me to see him so placid.

'Good to see you mate, good to see you!' he shouts.

His legs straddled across mine, he pats me on the head and starts wittering. 'You're all right aren't you? Good to see you. No, it's great isn't it? Right result meeting up with you. Good to see you. Honest, mate. Havin' a laugh, yeah?' then 'Gooood ta see yoou!' he shouts again. This time in the manner of some two-bob game-show host. I make the mistake of laughing.

Danny sees fit to go into full cabaret mode.

He launches into a strange song reminiscent of what I believe is a Cockney classic called 'The Umbrella Song'.

'Tooo-raa-loo-ra-loo-ra, Tooo-raa-looo-raaa-looo-raaa, in tha moorning!' he serenades in finest pub-singer tones.

'Tooo-raa-loo-ra-loo-ra, Tooo-raa-looo-raaa-looo-raaa, in tha mooooo-rning!!'

As he continues the song becomes more manic and more incoherent. 'Toooo-raa-loo-ra-loo-ra-loo-ra-loo-ra, Tooo-raa-looo-raaa-looo-raaa, in mooooo-rning!!!'

His friends find this endearing and amusing. I find it psychotic. He's off his face. A resident of Planet La-la. Lying across my lap unaware of anything save his *joie de vivre*. I'm aware of Danny boy though — a hooligan legend. Once ran fifty Mancs armed only with a life-size cut-out of Michael Parkinson. Grabbed it from outside the Nationwide in Holloway Road then swung it round his head knocking out all comers.

Useful man though, Danny. Didn't mind him lying trolleyed on my lap. It was fair enough, seeing as I'd leaned on him on more than a few occasions, randomly flashing his name about if I'd wanted to impress dodgy acquaintances or escape potential trouble.

When the singing stops, Danny pulls the rose from his pocket and informs, with his usual charm, that he's 'Teefed it off some cunt who had basket full'. He waves it about a bit then pulls off the petals. He becomes transfixed with the texture of the petals on his fingers. He squidges the rose between thumb and index finger. I stare at the petals trying to see what Danny sees. Yet I am simply pissed and slightly stoned.

He's gone. Eyes askew, face munched up, saliva dribbling from the gap at the side of his mouth where a cigarette has just fallen out. I'm now babysitting the Attila of Archway. He is in ecstasy. An unusual sight that's about to become all too common in these 'sick' times. He's as 'happy as fuck' and he keeps telling me so.

Up until this point it hadn't occurred to me that Danny and I could be going to the same place. Never seen Danny on the club circuit. But the bus stops at London Bridge and we all bundle down the stairs and get off. Danny pours along the street. I'm thinking he could be a liability but somehow he knows where to go straight away.

'Clink Street, yeah? Yeah, you coming, yeah?' he drawls. I nod. '. . . Fucking blinding mate, fucking blinding!' his arm rests upon my shoulder.

As we walk through the newly yuppyfied wharf buildings of the South Bank we start to hear the thump of a bass beat. Danny stops by a dry docked old Scud and fumbles through his pockets, eventually finding the one with the small plastic change-bag full of white pills.

'Top ecstasy mate. White Burgers. Fucking blinding!' he announces to the world in general.

I'm thrilled. Somebody selling ecstasy is still a genuinely unusual sight and Danny suddenly becomes very popular. X, as it is still known by its non-users, is a rarity. Some blue Texas-legal lozenges had been going around on and off since about '84. They were daring, they were decadent, they were always supposedly available from a friend of a firend. They were thirty quid. Now X was down to twenty.

Some sense of lucidity grabs Danny in his dealer role. 'Twenty quid each or three for fifty. Pucka, I promise you.'

Friends purchase. I go to purchase. He shakes his sweaty head. Danny simply slips a small white burger in my mouth. I raise some saliva and swallow.

Previously I'd only done a quarter round a friend's flat. We sat, we watched videos, we talked, laughed, then went down the pub for a giggle. Nice, special even, but nothing to give up your day job over. (Not that any of us had them.) Things were going to change that evening. *My mate* Danny MacGuire would suddenly become a *good fucking bloke*. What a diamond. White Burger Danny.

So to the warehouse. Clink Street, no name just an A-Z reference. A legend in the making. Danny knows the bouncers and gets us the squeeze. 'Millwall' he says by way of explanation.

The venue is dark, a series of small rooms sporadically lit by coloured lightbulbs. The scene is bedlam. Happy crowds swing from rafters and hug in circles. Girls role around on the ground oblivious to the floor's glue of garbage which sticks to their baggy Chipie dungarees. And the music. *Acid man, acid-man, acidman, acidman, acidman, acidman, acidman. Tweak, tweak, tweak.*

I want to go mental.

Time passes. How I love the music. I'm dancin'. How I love Danny for just being there. Danny's dancin'. Dancin' like Charlie fuckin' Chaplin. Life is good. *It's all turned out nice again.*

68

I explore. Christ it's good. A shabby South London shit-hole. A run-down old dock building. The loos overflow with piss and there's no bog roll or door. Wasted waifs straddle the bowl trying to unload their contribution to the Southwark shit-mountain. The windows are smashed on the upper floors. Glass lies as ice on a moulding carpet. An acid casualty scraps his hand with a dagger of glass, watching the blood as it trickles out.

In one room there is a huge hole in the wall where a crane arm once lifted the pillage of the Empire out of the Thames. Nutted clubbers dangle their feet out of this crumbling gash, mesmerized by the forty-foot drop below them. Every now and then they pretend to throw each other out. This is a very funny game: more join in throughout the night.

On the dance floor people swap flashing plastic space guns for robots and pass around texture toys like squidgy balls and a snot-like Playdoe called Slime. There's no bar. Cans of coke and cartons of Ribena are dished out of a bin full of melted ice and fag butts at £2 a time.

A queue has formed parallel to the refreshment queue. Here eager ravers can get a sniff of poppers and a neck massage. It's gratis and, as is commented on every ten seconds, boy, are they grateful.

A young thin black man in a bandanna approaches me. He's tripping his nuts off. He points at his Smiley badge. 'We've been unhappy too long. The time has come to smile!' he says in Oxford English, then disappears to find 'My dog, my dog, gotta find my dog.'

I return to Danny who is slumped by a speaker. He offers me cigarette. I accept the offer even though I don't smoke. It burns like an Olympic torch in my hand for what seems like an age. I'm starting to rush. I wave it in circles before my eyes. The amber glow impregnates my brain. I'm in a heaven unknown. Joy shakes me. The speaker ploughs the sounds through me. I'm 'up' big time.

'*Work it to the bone, bone, bone. Work it to the bone. Gotta work, to the bone, bone, bone.*'

There is nothing like a visit to the acid house to make you feel at home. Radiant girls come and kiss you, the boys to chat and hug. It was as if the veils of pretence and reservation had fallen and truth was allowed to dance naked. Quite literally on some occasions. There were few stars, only extras, and we all had speaking parts. Well, gibbering ones at least.

*Everyone* is dancing. No place for wallflowers. *My head is in a spin, my feet don't touch the ground.* I'm finally part of something important: my own fucking head. Christ I love it. Thank you Danny, cheers. Sweet. Oh it's good. I want to spend the rest of my existence in the blur of ecstasy. It's such a good crowd. Everyone's mad.

Thud, thud, thud. Bang, bang, bang. I can feel it now. I never knew how good life could be. Shit this is good. Why haven't I come here more often? Blinding. Fucking blinding. I remember thinking it, thinking it in full 3D: *the eighties have been shit and this is fucking excellent.* The release was orgasmic. No, *better.*

Dawn comes up and I sit with Danny on the stairs of the fire escape. The bouncers are there; the Boys are there. White Burgers are being chomped like Polos. I suck another. Soon I am in a mirage. All I survey is water colours. Faces flow. Conversation pours nonsensical. I am not alone in this delusion. I soon realize I have entered an ICF psychoanalysis session.

There's a group of about twelve lads. Well, men really. Boys, top boys. London's leading hooligans. They've spent the best part of the last ten years chasing and occasionally stabbing each other. So many games, so many fights. Here they were: Chelsea, ICF, Bushwhackers, Yids and Gooner Danny, all reminiscing, all stroking each other and snuggling up. They rambled their memories like senile old soldiers.

And after each incoherent tale of a pub done over or 'off' at

Euston came hysterical laughter. How we roared. Because after each little adventure story someone would pipe up with the words 'Fuckin' stupid really wasn't it?'

And, it was dawning, *of course* it was.

'I remember waiting two hours for West Ham in Plaistow Tube,' chirped up Danny '... about a hundred of us sitting on the platform for two fucking hours. ICF eventually come steaming down the steps, throw some fucking CS gas and one of those smoke grenades. No one can see a fucking thing, everyone's choking. People fall off the platform. There's bodies ...' his eyes roll to the heavens then drift back in focus '... there's bodies everywhere. By the time the smoke clears there's fucking Old Bill everywhere. I end up getting nicked for having pocket fulls of Fruit And Nut swiped from the Choccie machine ...' He pauses, laughs and everyone has a giggle.

'Fuckin' stupid really wasn't it?' they all comment. It's the funniest thing in the world.

'I was fucking there you cunt!' pipes up Tony, the slim weasely guy skinning up in the doorway.

'... That was twenty quids' worth of fucking gas too! And we'd walked all the way there from practically Mile End. Fuckin' stupid really wasn't it?'

We continue to chortle. Our entertainment then stretches to sticking Rizzlas on each others foreheads and emptying bottles of milk over our heads. Don't ask.

The atmosphere goes cold when Chelsea Mickey informs Millwall Jonno that what was *really* fuckin' stupid was the time he stabbed his mate Henry in Shakes, Victoria, in '84. Apparently you can still see the stains of his blood on the pavement by the taxi queue.

There's a strange gurning stand-off between two less-than-handsome faces. Mickey eventually starts laughing and they both call each other cunts. By now everyone is monging out completely. Here we are, among the thugs who've swapped the splash of claret for the taste of White Burgers. For a few brief moments on a few brief occasions, acid house was like that. Altogether, all out of our skulls, in no-man's-land.

I don't remember how I got home that morning. I think I walked. I just remember thinking, 'Fucking blinding, Danny, fucking blinding.' Thinking about what happened to him later, I think there was some strange inevitability about it. I reckon he was fortunate in a funny way, fortunate to have at least had those days. He'd have been a real sad case allowed to grow old as was.

For hundreds of years the likes of Danny and the likes of me and you, rarely experienced joy in their life. They grafted then they died early — from disease, childbirth, war and plain poverty. Most people, even as we leave the twentieth century, can make little of their lives except make do and mend. So thank heaven for the pills.

After Clink Street, for the next year, all our crowd dined regularly on White Burgers. Everyone knew everyone. We were hoolies, homos and just plain hedonists. As the months flew by, consumption got higher and clothes got sillier. From Shoom to Spectrum, Super Nature to Sunrise, we were filled with hope. Heady nights listening to 'Dreams of Santanna' in some strange chemical factory on the Isle of Dogs. Piling down Clapham Common Pond on a Sunday to circle dance with our regular gang of nutters. Prancing around some distant service station after hours of searching for the 'big one'. Talking to Northerners for the first time without taking the piss (much).

I didn't see Danny again until the beginning of summer '89. We were driving around somewhere south of the M25 Leatherhead turn-off. Lost and trolleyed in England's green, pleasant, and highly policed countryside. It was the time of the big crackdown. A few of the Sunrise parties had made the *Sun*'s front page. All hell let loose with the police setting up a special squad just to stop raves. It was all very silly, but lots of fun. The sense of achievement when an event actually went off was as good as the feeling of the drugs. Well, almost.

On that night we were caught between a Boy's Own barn dance somewhere near Gatwick and a World Dance 'two million K rig bouncy castle' rave at some pit of a farm near Crawley. There was a little convoy of cars snuggled up in an unsuspecting Esso garage.

Danny's there. Bowling around the forecourt shouting some loony garbage and throwing around pilfered confectionery that he's just swiped from the garage shop. His hair is tied back in pony-tail, his face pitted but tanned. He's got on what can only be described as kaftan top, track-suit bottoms up and a criminal pair of Kickers — very Balearic!

I get out of the car. He clocks me and throws me some con-traband Rowntree fruit pastels. After the minimum of small talk, a bag of goodies is produced. Es are flogged to all my little posse of imbeciles. We then talk a little more. The MacGuire winter had been spent importing quality hash from Morocco via the rail network, which was free thanks to a host of stolen Inter-Rail cards. Ibiza had come with the spring and a lively trade bringing in Es to and fro from Berlin.

Danny was living large and obviously having the time of his life. 'Beats getting your ear cut off in Stanley Park,' is how he put it.

My lift follows Danny's slightly trashy BMW and it eventually finds the World Dance event. We're on about the fifth possible venue sight. Speed has enabled this one to be finally encamped before the police arrive. It's basically a slope of set aside with an adjoining farmhouse-cum-commuter home. The promised bouncy castle has yet to be inflated.

'Ostriches Come Dancing' it said on the flyer. I never knew what that meant. I think it was something about getting your head out of the sand and listening to varied music. Fine by me. I'd been listening to Weatherall play Carly Simon and Pete Shelley at Queens Yacht House every Sunday for the last six months.

We were all well up for it tonight. A far away field filled with a funfair. The cars streaming in from all over. Then the music starts playing. It's on. Great stuff. About ten thousand plus punters, the music's mad and the White Burgers are stronger than ever. Mud, drugs and mayhem. Happy days.

Danny tells me he likes the eclecticism of the music, fishing for a more meaningful chat. I attempt to raise the level of our conversation but with his usual flair for idiocy Danny then jumps on top of a nearby motor. He proceeds to dance along the roofs of the adjoining parked-up cars that now surround the muddy area which, for the purpose of the evening, is a dancefloor. He jumps along denting panel work and smashing the odd window. Quite a feat really as some are pretty far apart. It's his own form of percussion. I can't say it made me feel comfortable. Fascinating none the less, and *very Danny*.

The bouncers take an initial interest then, 'cause it's only Danny', let him get on with it.

Danny then joins in the whole rave deal, standing on top of some Pykie's Burger Van dishing out his own musical madness. The crooning Danny mixing in with Sueno Latino 'Tooo-raa-loo-ra-loo-ra, Tooo-raa-looo-raaa-looo-raaa, Too-ra-li-ay, Tooo-raa-loo-ra-loo-ra, Tooo-raa-looo-raaa-looo-raaa, in the moorning!' A crowd gathers, clapping and cheering. How sweet. Nutter that Danny.

I later see him in a pair of plastic rabbit ears at the head of a conga. I join in at the back. They're playing Les Negresses Vertes and then some bug-eyed guy gets on the stage and shouts 'All we want is hardcore techno!' Danny can't oblige. The shocking thing is that this major Acid Ted on the stage has over half the crowd roaring approval for him. They want it too.

(I always think that I lost a bit of my youth at that point. I realized the club I'd joined a year before had now changed. The pleasure had moved from the party to the polemic. Boundaries had been formed.)

I'm on about my third White Burger and decide all I want is something different. I want to be somewhere else, preferably at the Boy's Own do, but that isn't possible. I sod off and sit in Danny's motor, one of the few unvandalized cars in the area.

Entertainment is provided by listening to Glenn Miller tracks on Radio 4. Things perk up. Truth is, all music's fucking great when your on your third White Burger and have just necked a can of Tennants. 'Brown Jug', 'In The Mood': I was in the mood all right. Top mood. Most fun I ever had in a field in Sussex. That weekend.

I'm sitting blissed out and all of a sudden the car fills with a flashing blue pulse. Someone dressed as Thora Hurd is tapping at the window asking me to move the car. I haven't a clue what's going on. I can't find the car keys. I fumble around trying to work out what to do. Eventually I let the hand-brake off and roll the car on a mindless journey with the help of some panicked strangers. I push for ages until there's enough space to allow, what I now realize, is a van with a flashing blue light, to pass me.

The following hours are spent with me slumped at the wheel of a BMW, attempting to skin up one last joint and stashing all the rest. It's obvious that the police are raiding and I've gone completely para and necked all the drugs on me thinking I'm about to be arrested by Thora Hurd. Meanwhile' Danny has lost his rabbit ears, his way and apparently his car. He goes around going ballistic on people because he thinks his car's been stolen. Oops.

As the morning light illuminates what is obviously a land-fill sight, Danny finds me and his car. His hands are covered in blood. He's smashed the window of another BMW to break into what he thought was his car. Time to go home.

The place is swarming with Old Bill. Somebody has managed to OD behind the decks. It was an ambulance that had come up behind me freaking me out. The bouncers had added to the evening's fun by kicking it off with the police who'd come to help, so things are getting heavy. It's not good. I can't find the car I came in. They've pegged it hours ago.

I make a rational decision. I ditch Danny and start walking the thirty miles home. Along the B roads of sunny Sussex I tread a weary path, eventually copping a lift off some low-lifes as far as Gatwick airport. On arrival I make my way to the shopping experience that is the Gatwick Village, find a spare sofa and sleep. This is when it all went a bit Pete Tong.

I'm out cold, lounging between pensioners off to Madeira and Suburban Sadoes 'ere we go to Magaluf. I'm woken by Security Guards who ask me my business. I inform that I'm waiting for friends to pick me up. I sleep.

I'm woken by some policemen who grill me for my name and address. I sleep on.

I'm woken by being thrown on the floor by three armed policemen who spread-eagle me and tell me not to move. I realize I'm covered in a load of Danny's blood and fit the description of a desperado. *And* I'm still tripping. They search me thoroughly. They find something in my sock. A feeling of panic comes over me. I'm major paranoid. It's really fucking scary. I'm trying to look innocent but guilt is flowing through me like bad acid. It's ecstasy in reverse. The rush of terror surges.

'What are these then?' asks an Officer.

I look down. Am I still tripping, or what? 'Fruit pastilles,' I reply.

And indeed they are, I'd shoved a couple down my socks in the darkness thinking they were lumps of dope. Thank fuck for that. It takes six hours in a police station for this to be confirmed. I can't even raise a smile in the cell. I'm sweating like a rapist and feeling very shit.

When finally released I have to bunk the train up to London and am subsequently hectored once again. By the time I get home I'm hallucinating all kinds of things. Last White Burgers I ever did. Do your head in those things. Never touched fruit pastilles either since then come to think about it.

Truth was, that wasn't the end, It wasn't even the beginning of the end. It was just the point when I realized that it wasn't inevitable that a night of ecstasy was a guaranteed good time. I was awakened from the fun of a world of secret fulfilled desires to the grey knowledge of the universal.

The next day Danny left a funny message on my answer phone. I didn't ring back.

'Fuckin' stupid really wasn't it?'

There's a footnote. A couple of years latter, as the blizzard of cocaine started to hit London, Danny fell under the first avalanche. He was put inside for dealing. Came out briefly. He was moody-as-fuck the few times I bumped into him. Got to see his beloved Arsenal win the championship though.

Then I saw his picture on Thames news. He was banged up big-time for stabbing to death the landlord of The Cocksure pub in Sommerstown. He believed the guy had grassed him up for using the saloon bar to distribute charlie to half of London. He hadn't: his Mum had.

On June the 9th 1995 Danny MacGuire was found hanging in his cell in Brixton Prison. The judge recorded a verdict of suicide due to manic depression. The pain of life had hit him and he'd taken the only known cure. It's a loss, must have been bad for his family, but the guy had killed somebody and I can't put my hand on my heart and say it's a complete disaster. Life was only going to be downhill for him. It could be argued he did the right thing.

I'll remember him as White Burger Danny, happy once, as he lay across my lap on the bus, crushing the petals of a stolen red rose. For a moment he'd ridden sublime on the seraph-wings of ecstasy. Then come back down to earth with one up each nostril and the thrust of a kitchen knife. From Gooner to goner. Lost it big time, but lived it full. He saw, but blasted with excess light, closed his eyes in endless night. Still owe him fifty quid, now I think about it. Right result really.

Martin Millar

# 'HOW SUNSHINE STAR-TRAVELLER LOST HIS GIRLFRIEND'

This is the story of how Sunshine Star-Traveller, DJ, astrologer and delver into the secrets of the universe, lost his girlfriend. It was, as he explained later, due to a dire combination of dreadful cosmic alignments, inescapable karmic doom, and the endless chaotic reverbrations brought about by the merest touch of misbehaviour on his part.

Reviewing events afterwards, Sunshine Star-Traveller, or Sunny, as he was known to his many friends, was unable to fathom exactly why things had gone so wrong. The night had ended so badly that he could only shake his head in bemusement, and ponder sadly on the cruelties of life once your stars aligned themselves in a malevolent manner. Once this happened, Sunny knew there was nothing to do but wait for it to pass. Even a spiritual person like himself was bound to suffer.

'I only hope,' he says, shaking his head, so that his hair dances around his waist, 'that it's a temporary set-back. If I've plunged into one of these nine-year cycles of destruction, I'm going to be very depressed.'

The unfortunate events had occurred at Cool Tan in Brixton, where Sunny had been booked to deejay at the two-till-five morning spot. Sunshine Star-Traveller was becoming a popular DJ in South London, securing himself several favourable mentions in dance magazines and the invitation to remix some tracks at a Brixton

81

studio where the recording equipment was nicely complimented by a peace garden, and statues of Buddha.

He is pleased with the results, and has with him a test pressing of the best track. This test pressing is very important because his girlfriend, Starlight, is due to perform her well-known 'Spinning Dance of the Chakras' at Cool Tan while Sunny is playing. He has done this remix specially for her, and she has spent some time rehearsing, getting her movements in perfect alignment with the music. Her 'Spinning Dance of the Chakras' is performed on a rope high above the crowd, and it's a spectacular affair which brings joy to all who see it, and endless days of peaceful vibes, at least according to Starlight.

'Be sure to play the right track while I'm performing,' says Starlight, as they pack up to leave. 'I don't want to find myself halfway up a rope and you playing the wrong music. My chakras won't stand for it.'

They go down with with Gus and Azrobel, a couple who help by carrying records, doing this entirely for the purpose of getting in free, which is fair enough. Many people would contrive some reason or another for getting free into the weekend raves at Cool Tan, which were popular events. Cool Tan, the squatted and rather desolate remains of the old dole office in Brixton, was used during the day as alternative art gallery, vegetarian café, drumming workshop and suchlike, and at the weekends as a place for raving. So people now danced where their older brothers and sisters had once stood miserably in line to sign on which, as Sunny points out, is strong evidence that the world is moving towards a new age of peace and harmony. Starlight agrees. As her contribution to this new age, she busies herself with ensuring that everyone's chakras are in good running order.

Sunshine Star-Traveller, Starlight, Gus and Azrobel fight their way in about midnight. There are more people there than can fit in the building even with the back doors open and another rig playing in the car park, so getting in is not easy. Even with Sunny hammering on the doors screaming 'Let me in, I'm deejaying tonight', it takes an hour or so, and even then they have to climb in the front window while the doormen struggle to keep back the extra hordes trying to follow them through.

They dump their records behind the decks, and look around. It's packed, with a lot of dancers, and thundering trance shaking the crumbling old walls, and lasers picking up the dust and the smoke, illuminating the heads of the crowd, and reflecting off the silver bangles in their dreadlocks, and the rings in their ears and noses and lips, and even their tongues, if they open their mouths at the right time. People roll joints in corners, and a makeshift bar sells water and cheap cans of beer, and it's all very friendly, as is to be expected.

'When are you playing Sunny?' ask two young women, friends of his.

'In an hour.'

They seem pleased. Starlight doesn't. 'Stop flirting with Anne and Tulip,' she says.

Sunshine Star-Traveller protests his innocence. 'I wasn't.'

'Yes you were,' retorts Starlight. 'I know you told Tulip you once made love beside a pyramid in ancient Egypt in a previous incarnation. Gus told me.'

Sunny gasps at this shocking treachery on the part of his friend. 'I was merely relating a true historical incident as told to me by my past life cards,' he blusters.

'You were merely trying to get her into bed,' says Starlight who, despite her yin-yang tattoo and necklace made of daisies, is not really a woman who stands for any nonsense. She departs to prepare her act. Sunshine Star-Traveller looks round for Gus to berate him for letting slip such important mystical secrets to his girlfriend, but Gus and Azrobel have disappeared. The two main planks of Gus and Azrobel's relationship are an astonishing capacity for drugs, and never having any money at all, so they are now casting their net widely among friends and aquaintances to see what they can find.

Starlight checks that her rope is firmly in place. She has a word with the lighting engineer, making sure that he remembers his insructions. Satisfied that everything is ready for her 'Spinning Dance of the Chakras', she heads back to the decks which are mounted on a low stage supported by beer-crates. Gus and Azrobel have returned though Sushine Star-Traveller is missing.

'Where's Sunny?'

Gus shrugs. Starlight glances at her watch, which is yellow with flowers, to match her hair.

'He's due on now.'

Starlight is puzzled. Sunny is serious about his deejaying. For him not to show up on time is unheard of. She begins to wonder if he might have come to harm in some particularly dangerous part of the old building. Only last week Azrobel had slipped on the stairs and banged her head, though it hadn't done her any harm. She decided she'd better ask the two women at the decks if they wouldn't mind playing a little while longer.

'Would you—'

At that moment one of the pair slumps to the floor.

'I guess that's the end of our set,' said the DJ's companion, and starts helping her friend out the back for some fresh air, leaving their last record playing.

'Damn it,' says Starlight. 'Where's Sunny? He's due on now.'

Sunshine Star-Traveller has a watch with flowers which matches Starlight's. Despite this he has lost track of time, because he is at this moment having sex in the women's toilet with Anne, one of the girls he had strongly denied flirting with. Now the toilets at Cool Tan, which was after all built as a dole office and not a nightclub, are not the fashionable sort of place where both sexes mingle to do their make-up in front of the mirror. The women's toilet is a small, grimy row of cubicles on which the doors have long since disappeared, being replaced with thin plastic shower curtains. There is of course no way of locking the curtain, and anyone in the cubicle runs a continual risk of being interrupted. Which means that it can only be described as risky for Sunshine Star-Traveller to be having sex with Anne in the toilet at this moment. Many people know Sunny, and if the matter becomes public knowledge, Starlight is bound to hear of it, and she won't be pleased.

There are three cubicles, and progress in and out of two of them is frequent and uninterrupted, but the large queue of women outside, sensing that something is amiss in the third, are already muttering in frustration. Sunny and Anne are lost in the enertaining business of contorting themselves in the confined space. Rather like a tantric position in one of my yoga books, thinks Sunny, with satisfaction. Eventually, however, the mutterings of discontent outside grow more audible.

'What's taking them so long?'

The voiced protests bring Sunny back somewhere close to the real world, and he remembers that he's meant to be deejaying soon.

'Perhaps we should leave,' he whispers.

'To hell with them,' whispers Anne. 'What are they complaining about? There are two other cubicles.'

Meanwhile downstairs, things are starting to go wrong.

'I'll look for Sunny,' shouts Stralight. 'You take over the decks.'

'What d'you mean?' retorts Gus, feeling the first twinge of panic.

'You'll have to take over,' screams Starlight.

'Me? I can't do it.'

'Yes you can, you're Sunny's helper.'

'I only carry the records, I don't know how to work this thing.'

'Well how difficult can it be?' says Starlight, motioning to the double decks. 'You're always saying it must be easy doing what Sunny does. Just keep things going and I'll look for him. Quick, before the record ends.' She brushes aside Gus's objections and shoves him and the semi-conscious Azrobel onstage.

'But don't play that record till I'm up the rope,' warns Starlight, pointing to the test pressing. 'And look after it, it's very important.'

Gus looks despairingly at the equipment in front of him, and the hundreds of dancers on the floor, and starts to sweat. The lights, heat, noise, stress and drugs start to bring on hallucinations, which he heroically fights down.

'What'll I do?' he wails to Azrobel.

Azrobel decides that this is a good time to sit down and stuff her dreadlocks in her mouth.

'Well thanks for your help,' snarls Gus, with some feeling. He realizes he's trapped. The reputation of the Sunshine Star-Traveller Techno Rig depends on him. At the time when Sunshine Star-Traveller should be doing a well practised segue into the start of his set, there is only Gus, a box of records, and half a spliff he's picked up off the floor. So he does the best he can which is to whack the first record he finds on to the vacant deck. He waits for the music to begin. It doesn't.

'What now?' he cries out loud, to what is beginning to seem like a pitiless universe.

'Hit some buttons,' suggests Azrobel, in between chewing her locks.

Gus hits a button. Nothing happens. He hits another one. Again, there's no result. He bangs his fist down in frustration. The record starts to spin. Encouraged, he starts hitting more buttons and pulling faders at random and as he does so the start of his record and the end of the last one seem to merge in a miraculous combination of sound and tempo giving a blast of energy which rocks the crowd. People cheer as the Sunshine Star-Traveller sound system roars into action in a fine manner.

'Not bad,' says Gus, as more people force their way on to the dancefloor.

'I knew this DJ stuff couldn't be that hard. Sunshine has obviously been lying to me. He's like that you know. Always trying to make out he's smarter than he is.'

From the floor, Azrobel grunts her appreciation. Gus hunts in the darkness for another record to play, while Starlight carries on the search for her missing boyfriend.

Her missing boyfriend is currently arranging his clothes in the cubicle. As brief sexual encounters in toilets go, it's been pretty successful. Now they'll have to walk out past the queue outside which could be mildly embarrassing, but not too serious.

No one could prove I'd been fucking in here, thinks Sunny. I could have been comforting a sick friend, or helping her with her contact lenses.

He peers out of a tiny crack in the curtain, then shrinks back against the ancient cistern, horrified.

'My girlfriend's out there at the front of the queue!'

Anne giggles.

'It's not funny! We can't walk out of here right past Starlight. Events of cosmic significance would inevitably follow.'

By which he means that Starlight will probably give him a good slap in the face, and never speak to him again. This distresses Sunny, because he likes Starlight, even if he does forget occasionally that he's going out with her.

'I'm meant to be at the turntables now.' There is no means of escape. The tiny window behind him is too small to crawl through. 'I'm doomed.'

'Just wait till she goes into another cubicle,' whispers Anne. 'Then we'll slip out. Incidentally, was that as good as the time we made love beneath the pyramids?'

Downstairs, after his fine beginning, Gus is having problems. The first problem is people coming up and shouting unintelligable requests for records he's never heard of, and the second is his ignorance about what he's actually doing. He gets another record on the deck but is unaware that twelve-inch singles are often pressed at thirty-three rpm. Having a sort of folk memory that singles are always at forty-five, he starts it off at the wrong speed. He's dismayed at the appalling noise that follows. He's used to a lot of very fast beats but this just sounds ridiculous.

'What the hell is Sunny doing with a record like this,' he complains, and whacks the needle into the middle to see if it sounds any better. It doesn't. The crowd bay in protest at the horrible noise.

'This ketamine is affecting me badly,' says Azrobel, from the floor. 'Everything sounds funny.'

'That was last week,' shouts Gus, still struggling with the decks. 'Well it's still affecting me.'

Gus deperately picks up another record and slings it on the vacant turntable. To everyone's relief, it starts at the right speed. The crowd in Cool Tan, a genial group of people, would be quite willing to forget their temporary inconvenience and get on with dancing, had Gus not at this moment dropped his spliff on the record, causing a huge lump of burning ash to send the needle scittering wildly over the record, and making a really terrible noise.

·He yanks the stylus back and rectifies the situation as best he can, but he knows he's losing losing the crowd.

'This acid is really kicking in,' says Azrobel, stumbling to her feet. 'I just saw that record smoking a joint. I'm going outside for some fresh air.'

Gus, having finally got a suitable record playing at the right speed, is pleased beyond measure when he bangs his toe into a bag of cans stashed under the decks.

'There are times,' he reflects, 'when water just isn't enough,' and he starts pouring lager down his throat, and over his combat jacket and boots.

'Do something!' pleads Sunshine Star-Traveller, still cornered in the toilet. 'Rush out, grab Starlight, and get her away.'

'Will you dedicate a record to me?'

Sunny is staggered at the irrelevance of this. Here he is, trapped in the most desperate situation of his life, only a shower curtain between him, his lover and his girlfriend, his sound system going to neglect and ruin downstairs, and this person is rambling on about dedicating records to her. It isn't even as if they know each other all that well. He controls his irritation, and promises to dedicate a record to her. Anne stumbles out of the toilet, pretending to be unwell, and drapes her arms around Starlight's neck.

'I feel terible. Take me outside for some fresh air.'

Downstairs, many people feel terrible. A monstrous electronic humming is piercing eardrums all over the dancefloor. Gus, with some vague recollection of his small childhood record player, knows that earthing problems can cause humming and is frantically scrabbling about the back of the turntables searching for loose wires. The dancers, starved of music, grow restless, and hurtle abuse.

'I'm doing my best,' screams Gus. 'Isn't there a sound engineer somewhere?' But if there is sound engineer anywhere, he is no longer to be found. Gus manages to break the small light on the turntables, plunging him into further gloom.

'The Sunshine Star-Traveller sound system is certainly having an off-night,' is the general opinion on the dancefloor, and some people depart to the car park where a reggae sound system is playing beneath the stars. Starlight, back from taking Anne outside for fresh air, elbows her way over to Gus.

'Why are you destroying my boyfriend's reputation?' she demands. 'Play a record for God's sake.'

The humming stops, for no apparent reason. Gus crashes a record on, and sends up a prayer for it to play properly. The prayer is not answered.

'What's gone wrong now?' he screams, and starts hitting buttons and pulling faders, and wondering if he should flee the scene before the crowd lynch him.

Perhaps his prayer is answered, after a short delay. He miraculously gets things right and the music starts. Starlight angrily lights a candle to replace the damaged light.

'Can't you do better than this?' she demands. 'The crowd are laughing at you. It will be very bad for the Sunshine Star-Traveller image if you don't pull yourself together immediately.'

'It's all that dumb Sunny's fault. Where is he?'

Starlight confesses that she can't find him.

'I'm worried. He might have got over exicited and climbed

on the roof to raise his arms to the full moon — he does that sometimes — and fallen off.'

Gus hopes that if he has fallen off he's seriously injured himself, but refrains from saying so.

'I'll go and look for him again. Meantime, try and do better. And whatever happens, be sure to play the right record when I'm up the rope performing. If that goes wrong I'll kill you.'

Starlight departs. Gus is taken aback. This is a side of her character he's never seen before.

'It's all very well her going around with a big yin-yang sign tattooed on her shoulder and claiming to perform a chakra dance for the peaceful reunification of the world,' he complains, 'but when it comes right down to it she's threatening to kill anyone who spoils her lousy performance. I shouldn't be suffering this. Where the hell is Sunshine Star-Traveller?'

Sunshine Star-Traveller, again trapped in the strange and mysterious web of cosmic coincidences, is at this moment having sex with Tulip in the women's toilets. Tulip is, of course, the second of the young women he had claimed not to be flirting with. He's not quite sure how this has come about. One moment Anne had hurried off, dragging Starlight away with her, the next Tulip had burst through the curtain.

'Eh hello,' said Sunshine Star-Traveller.

'Why Sunny,' said Tulip. 'How clever of you to wait for me here.' And after that it just sort of happened.

'You were right,' proclaims Tulip with enthusiasm. 'I can remember doing it just like this beside the pyramids, three thousand years ago.'

Sunny is vaguely aware that this isn't all that good an idea as he is at this moment meant to be deejaying downstairs, but as he has previously implied to Tulip that they are in the grip of an inevitable cosmic cycle of sexual gratification, he can't really think of a way out of it. Sunny is weary, but feels unable to refuse.

Downstairs Gus is putting in the worst deejaying performance in living memory. The problems he has with the headphones alone are enough to give him nightmares for weeks afterwards. People are shouting abuse, and promising they'll never again go near any event at which Sunshine Star-Traveller is playing. Some of them seem on the verge of violence.

'Which just goes to prove it's not true about ecstacy always putting you in a good mood,' reflects Gus grimly, and struggles on.

Azrobel appears beside him. 'I feel better. I've come to help.'

'Good,' says Gus. 'Starlight's due to perform soon. If that goes well, we might escape with our lives. Hand me the record.'

'What record?'

'Sunny's special mix for Starlight's performance.'

Gus holds out his hand. His hand remains empty. He turns round, and reels in shock as he sees that the record is not where it should be.

'Where is it?' he screams.

Azrobel is now facinated by her toes. She starts talking to them in a conspiratorial manner

'Where's the record?!' pleads Gus.

'The special record?' said Azrobel, dreamilly.

'That's right, the special fucking record, where is it?'

'I buried it,' replies Azrobel, and turns once more to her toes.

Gus's despairing cry reverberates through most of the building, though it doesn't quite reach Sunshine Star-Traveller and Tulip, presently rearranging their clothes in the toilet.

'The queue's gone, there's no one outside,' whispers Tulip, peering through the crack in the curtain. 'I don't care anyway, just so long as we don't meet my boyfriend.'

'Boyfriend?'

'Yes. Patrick. But don't worry, he's probably dancing downstairs somewhere.'

Sunny has a troubling memory that Patrick is about eight feet tall, but tries not to dwell on it. All he has to do is hurry downstairs, reclaim the turntables and make sure Starlight's 'Spinning Dance of the Chakras' goes well. Yet for some unfathomable reason, twinges of paranoia are now playing round the edges of Sunny's normally placid mind. He feels tense, strained even. Almost as if he had something to feel guilty about. So when Tulip and he depart swiftly from the cubicle into the now empty toilet, he is quite unable to cope with the sight of Starlight's distinctive yellow dreadlocks coming his way. He yelps in fear, grabs Tulip's arm and leaps sideways into the nearest empty cubicle.

Unfortunately — and this is where Sunshine Star-Traveller really begins to realize that the stars have it in for him — it is not empty.

'Why hello Patrick,' says Tulip to the figure sitting in front of them.

'What are you doing in the women's toilet?' splutters Sunny.

'What are you doing here?' demands Patrick furiously. 'With my girlfriend?'

Sunny just can't think of a good explanation. His nerve cracks and he flees. Outside the toilet Starlight, still searching, is questioning people as to Sunny's whereabouts. Unable to face her, Sunshine Star-Traveller leaps for what was at one time the dole office manager's office, and disappears out of the window.

'Wasn't that Sunny running in there just now?'

Starlight hurries into the office and peers out of the window. 'You're right.'

'What's he doing on the roof?'

'Looking at the full moon,' explains Starlight, and sighs. 'That's why I love Sunny so much. He's so spiritual.'

She leans out and calls gently to him, intimating that while she appreciates the beauty of his soul, and his need to pay homage to the moon from a good vantage position, he really should be getting downstairs as it's almost time for her performance. Sunny, hearing his girlfriend shouting at him, fears the worst. He loses his grip, and falls off the roof.

Gus and Azrobel, meanwhile, having one of those lovers' tiffs which happen even in the gentlest of relationships. Gus is screaming 'Why did you bury the record you ignorant bitch' and trying to get his hands on his girlfriend's throat, while she fights him off with a plastic bottle of Irish spring water.

'Help. Help, I'm being attacked by a madman!' cries Azrobel, and beats him over the head.

Gus realizes that this is getting him nowhere. He forces himself to be calm, no easy matter with the amount of substances rampaging through his body, and tries persuasion.

'Please tell me where you buried it.'

Azrobel can't remember.

'Starlight's due up the rope in five minutes! She'll kill me if I don't play he right music. Please try and remember.'

Azrobel again becomes interested in her toes. Gus fights down another strong impulse to leap at her throat.

'Why did you bury it?'

'You said it was important. I was keeping it safe.'

Gus has to admit there is some kind of logic in this.

'Good,' he says, in a placatory manner. 'Well done. It was a fine idea to bury the record. I'm very pleased with you Azrobel, for keeping it safe. But please try and remember where it is.'

Azrobel ponders for a while. Four minutes, thinks Gus.

'In the car park,' says Azrobel finally, and looks pleased with herself.

Gus slams another record on and takes off at a sprint. It isn't until he reaches the car park that he realizes the incongruity of Azrobel's statement. How could she have buried a record here? It's covered in concrete. There's a reggae sound system, and a lot of dancers, and not a few tired figures resting from their exertions inside, but no obvious place where anyone could bury a record.

'Did you see a women burying a record out here?' he demands, grabbing the nearest person, who bursts out laughing, as do her friends.

'Gus is in a bad state tonight,' say some people who know him, and smile indulgently as he hunts futilely for the test pressing.

'Is Azrobel all right?' asks a friend, as he scurried past.

'Yes, why?'

'I saw her crawling around over there by the drainpipe a while back. She was acting funny.'

'Aha,' thinks Gus and races to the drainpipe in question. There, tucked behind it, is the precious disc. With one minute left, Gus scoops it up in triumph. At that moment Sunshine Star-Traveller falls off the roof on top of him and they collapse in a heap.

'What are you doing?' demands the terrified Gus, severely shocked.

'No time to explain. Who's at the decks?'

'No one.'

'No one? You might at least have covered for me,' complains Sunny. 'What's that you're holding?'

Gus looks down.

'Bits of your record,' he says sadly. 'It broke when you landed on it.'

'Aaargh!' wailed Sunny. 'You moron, you've ruined it, what am I going to play for Starlight?'

Gus is not pleased to be abused by Sunny, after all he's done for him, and tells him so. They proceed to argue. Suddenly they remember that not only is no one at the decks, Starlight is due up the rope for the fabulous 'Spinning Dance of the Chakras' in about thirty seconds.

'I'll get you for this!' screams a voice from above. It's Patrick, looking upset.

'What's that about?'

'I'll explain later,' says Sunny as they flee into the building.

'Starlight's not very pleased with you,' reports Azrobel, as they appear.

'She's waiting at the rope to start performing. She says to tell you she's annoyed at you for deserting her. There's a time for staring at the moon, Sunny, and a time for playing records.'

The last record is coming to an end. Starlight, waiting impatiently in the middle of the floor, sees Sunny at the decks and begins her ascent. The lighting man focuses a big spotlight on her. Sunny starts scrabbling frantically for some piece of music which will do for the chakra dance.

'What's been going on here?' he cries, finding his records in a hopelessly confused state as a result of Gus's fumblings, and Azrobel's sudden desire to take every sleeve off and use them to build a pyramid. As the last record fades, Starlight ascends the roof and poses dramatically in the spotlight. She hangs rigidly from the rope with one arm, so that her athletic prowess is obvious to all.

'She's going to kill us for changing the music,' mutters Sunny. 'I can't see a thing. Who broke the light?'

He takes out a white label he's just received which is pounding trance with some bits of Indian chanting here and there. Judging it to be fairly suitable, he puts it on and hopes for the best.

Unfortunately, the best does not happen. The white label which Sunny has selected from his carefully arranged record box is not the one that should have been there, due to the drug-demented Azrobel shuffling them about. As Starlight begins her famous 'Spinning Dance of the Chakras' for the furtherment of world peace and universal harmony, what actually plays is a hideous, tinny, techno version of the theme-tune from the *Magic Roundbout*. Sent to Sunny from Lithuania, this nightmarish record has laid neglected and forgotten in the back of his box till now. The watching multitudes, expecting something rather more spiritual, burst out laughing as the unfortunate Starlight spins dramatically to the ludicrous electronic accompaniment of the *Magic Roundabout*.

Starlight stops spinning. She descends the rope with dignity, stalks over to Sunny, climbs on stage, and attempts to strangle him with his headphones.

Anne now appears at the side of the stage. 'Have you dedicated a record to me yet?' she asks, and smiles very sweetly at Sunny.

'What were you doing with my girlfriend in the toilets?' roars Patrick, fighting his way through the crowd.

'What has been going on here?' yells Starlight, and carries on the attack with the headphones.

Which is how Sunshine Star-Traveller lost his girlfriend, and a great deal of his credibility.

It is some time before he can show his face again, and Starlight refuses ever to speak to him again, for making her look foolish. It's also the end of Gus and Azrobel's relationship.

'I can't believe you would attack me in public,' she tells him later. 'I refuse to go out with a man with such violent tendencies. Starlight is going to teach me her "Spinning Dance of the Chakras" and we're going to India together.'

As Sunny explains to Gus afterwards, it's just amazing the terrible luck a person can have if their stars get into a bad alignment, 'According to my past life cards, mine are in their worst conjunction since the twelfth century.'

'It's nothing to do with your stars,' retorts Gus. 'If you hadn't insisted of fucking in the toilet instead of doing your job, none of this would have happened.'

Sunshine Star-Traveller dismisses this.

'It was entirely down to bad luck. If that record I played had been anything except a techno version of the *Magic Roundabout*, it would have passed off OK. Starlight thought I was making fun of her. I'm a victim of the stars. Possibly even a chaotic rip in the fabric of the Universe. Once that happens, there's nothing you can do about it but wait for it to pass. Even a spiritual person like myself is bound to suffer.'

Michael River

'ELECTROVOODOO'

The flyer made no mention of an address or even a phone number. There was only a single electroglyph, the double-coiled symbol that meant *transformer*; and the words: EAT ME.

Wilmot slipped it back into his pocket. The river gusted a warm freight of industrial odour. He leaned as far as he could over the railing and tilted his face into the wind, closing his eyes, feeling it tease flecks of skin away. The air carried a faint trace of music.

A boat on the river sounded its horn and hands clapped on his shoulders, hauling him back.

'Shit — !'

His friends laughed; Nat and Jiffy and Coral K. 'Spooked you good,' crowed Nat.

He shrugged out of their grip. 'Real funny.'

'Sorry we're late,' said Coral K. She pushed skinny dreads back from her face and smiled. 'Tubes and stuff.'

'Sure, it's OK.'

'Has everybody got a flyer?' asked Jiffy. 'Yeah? Then let's do it.'

They crumpled the flyers in their hands and stuffed them in their mouths. The shiny card shivered on fillings like tin foil and tasted putrid, like fish gone off. Wilmot choked but forced himself to chew the card to a sodden pulp and swallow.

Nat ate two. 'Just to be on the safe side,' he explained.

'On the *wild* side, you mean.'

'Whatever.'

They sat and dangled their feet over the embankment wall. A layer of rubbish undulated over the river as far as they could see: plastic bottles, tin cans, fragments of polystyrene, plastic bags billowing like jellyfish. The tide was low and a burned out car rested half submerged on the opposite bank.

'Look!' said Coral K. 'A cow!'

The cow floated belly-up, its legs oddly stiff, until the current turned it over; then the bloated carcass just did a lolling somersault and floated on as before. 'You don't see them too often these days,' she said a little wistfully.

Wilmot's vision blurred for a moment; for a while more he thought nothing was going to happen. Something shifted. There was a barely perceptible change, like an optical trick, a silhouette reversed.

'I see it! I see it!' shouted Nat.

Jiffy scowled. 'Sure, man, we all see it. Let's go, huh?'

Wilmot looked around in wonder. The signs were around them, as plain as anything. Written on the walls and in the water. Letters coiled in barbed wire, reflected from neon signs. As if the world was no longer given, but written.

They dropped one by one down a short ladder to a path running under the wharf, a dank vault between striated green joists. Fine damp moss-hair scattered cold droplets on their heads. A helicopter droned by high overhead, probing the humid air with a blurred beam. They ran across a flat strand of slime studded with small stones and washed-up bottles, and found an entrance.

It was a plain metal door recessed into soot-blackened bricks. Though it looked locked solid with rust, it swung easily open to Nat's push. An iron spiral wound into the earth.

Their boots clanged on the treads and set the shell reverberating. A turn around the spiral and the only light was a spectral glow reflected from somewhere far below. The rumour of music grew heavier with every step down, swelling up from a whisper to a hammering roar, until all other sound was made subservient to it.

Wilmot stumbled on to flat ground, almost running into Nat.

'We're here,' said Nat. 'This is it. This is it.' His eyes were glazed and there was a glow through his bottom lip.

Wilmot frowned and stuck out his tongue. He twisted it out as far as he could and strained to see, until black spots flitted before his eyes: the tip was luminous, pulsing with an eerie luminescence.

Coral K poked her own glowing tongue at him and laughed. She said, 'This is your first time, isn't it?'

'Yeah.'

'You get used to it. Kind of. Come on, we'll be left behind.'

Nat had already disappeared beyond a corner. They followed him and entered a high brick-walled space. Amp ziggurats towered upwards, shuddering as they released their grim ecstatic music, beautiful and broken, conjured up by DJs moving almost invisibly through a dense labyrinth of consoles. Lavalamps dangled on strings from the vault, turning slow pendulum swings, and in their shifting red light people were dancing. They filled the place from wall to wall. Many of them carried tribal markings, the slick gravure of tattoo on their bodies. Their hair was all the rainbow hues of plastic, cropped and plaited, twisted into mutant dreadlocks. They danced a jolting dance, galvanic limbs swaying in the air without inhibitions, and their panting tongues glowed bright.

Wilmot took a breath; inhaled a heady musk of sweat and happiness.

He worked his way in, although at first the crowd would not accept him. He had to force passage through a tough meniscus, as if the other dancers sensed he did not belong. Light and smoke flashed overhead. He waved his hands in the air without conviction. But the bass started speaking to him and he forgot everything else. It felt like everybody there was sharing one consciousness, like turning into some kind of hivemind. This mind only understood one thing, only thought one thought: and that was rhythm.

Nat had a theory: 'Like, where does music come from, right? Out of the body. Heartbeat, breathing, stomach pumping food; they've all got their own bpm. That's just the lowest level. The whole planet is built out of different rhythms — yeah, Gaia knows about bass! Real music, true music, *deep* music dances to Her pulse.'

Wilmot watched hands moving through the air around him, maybe some of them his own. He got lost in the crowd and music. He danced for an hour or two or three and when he slowed down he drifted out to the edge and Jiffy caught his arm.

'There you are,' said Jiffy. 'Want to come down the trance-hall?'

Projections played over the ceiling of the trance-hall: images of environmental collapse: floods, skeletal forests, scummed-over lakes, cracked lake beds and oil-slicked shores. People sat or lay on the floor, trancing out or talking softly.

Coral K and Nat were there already, lying with their heads almost in contact and talking. Wilmot sat by them. He ate more *gno*, not painted on a flyer this time, but baked into pills. It still tasted bad.

Nat was saying, 'Their voices come to me sometimes, in the night. Like my dreams are tuning into some broadcast frequency.'

'All knowledge is broadcast,' said Coral K.

'*Things are as they are because they were as they were.*'

'Hey,' said Wilmot. 'What are you guys talking about?'

Nat grinned. 'Ever hear of St Rupert? A great man, a great scientist: though we don't hold *that* against him. That was him speaking: *Things are as they are because they were as they were.* He's the one who discovered that once a thing has been done once, it's easier for it to be done again.'

'There was a monkey living on an island in the Indian Ocean,' said Coral K, 'who worked out a method of breaking open shellfish by banging them between coconuts. Within weeks, other monkeys on islands hundreds of miles away had discovered the same trick.'

'It's like the idea exists and is floating around, waiting to get picked up. He called it *morphogenesis*. That's what *gno* is, a morphogenetic enhancer. Compounded out of guarana and planarium worms and who knows what else.'

'Jesus. No wonder it tastes like shit.'

Coral K's hand touched Wilmot's. 'Gaia is dying and there's nothing we can do about it. It's too late. But the *idea* of Gaia still exists, and like any idea, it will be easier to use a second time. That's what we are trying to do; kick-start Gaia's successor.'

'Who we call *Mechaia*,' said Nat.

Wilmot frowned. 'But how can we do that?'

'Transference,' muttered Nat and looked away.

'Wait and see,' whispered Coral K. 'You'll see soon enough.'

Wilmot felt her hand lying lightly on his. He lay back and slit his eyes so the projections were only amorphous shapes, ambiguous. The *gno* brought him a vision.

> *I see the machines arising.*
> *I see them swarming out on to the streets;*
> *fridges waddling clumsily,*
> *CD-players perching in pylons,*
> *TVs basking in the sun*
> *and vacuum cleaners swimming sinuously the silted river waters ...*

He sat up with a start. 'Say, when Gaia dies, when we bring Mechaia to life, will there be a place for us?'

'People don't deserve a place,' said Nat. 'We fucked up. We had our chance. This is the only little bit of good we can hope to do. Plus, it's fun.'

'Oh. But will their world be any better than ours?' he

persisted. 'Will they read the signs we have left, avoid our mistakes?'

'Nobody knows that,' said Coral K.

The word came whispered around: 'The Undergod is here!'

Nat jumped up. 'The ceremony,' he said. 'Come on.'

The trance-hall emptied out. Wilmot lost his friends somewhere in the main hall. He slithered through to get as near to the front as he could. Fragmented images burned across the ceiling. The sour scent of *gno* was on everybody's breath. He glanced; all he could see were eyes glistening and tongues glowing across the dark, pulsing bright and fading.

The Cable stalked out of the wings and they sprang out of traps. They wore clingfilm cauls, they were scarified and bleeding. White welts and red glistening fresh cuts in rough designs, spidery electroglyphic circuits. All the crew were there: the Inductor and Telegram Sam, Ray-X and Mother Baud, the Raster Man ... and one other, who waited still in the dark unseen, whose hands whispered over the decks: the Undergod.

With their hands glowing pink in washing-up gloves, they danced around squeezing out lines of detergent, laying a complex circuit diagram on the stage floor. When they were done they took up station around the edges and waited.

Everybody waited. *Somebody will be chosen*, thought Wilmot. He closed his eyes, imagining an invisible hand seeking over the crowd, singling him out and descending ...

Somebody screamed.

He was a young man, maybe eighteen, maybe younger. The people nearest to him lifted him to their shoulders. He surfed over the heads of the crowd, hands reaching to touch him however fleetingly. He spiralled to the centre as if sucked into a whirlpool.

Wilmot saw the skein of veins lying over the back of his slender wrists; blue and violet through the skin ... his narrow eyes, and how the corners creased when he smiled ... the snub ring piercing his right nostril ... his violet rayon shirt, reflected light sliding on it like surf, opened one button at the neck ... six or seven straggling hairs clinging to his clavicle ...

Wilmot felt a surge of love for him. He caught hold of his lapel as he surged past; its cool trace left his fingertips tingling.

Scrap by scrap his clothes tore away until the hands deposited him naked on the stage.

The Inductor welcomed him. Others of the Cable pulled covers away to reveal an assemblage of jury-rigged components, of cut-up and rewired domestic appliances. They bound his arms behind him with electric flex, wrapped it tight around him, coil after coil, and strapped him into their weird machinery. He opened wide his mouth to receive the electrodes.

They wired him up, pinching his flesh with electrode clamps.

The Undergod threw the switch.

*Flash.*

His whole body spasmed. He shouted, spitting blood. Red flecks spattered the front circle of the crowd, and a wave of revulsion rippled back; but also a chorus of baying yells, urging him on.

*Flash.*

Sparks danced in his mouth, spun off his nose piercing, dazzled across the glistening masks of the Cable. Vital energy fed across into the Cable's circuitry. A TV screen lit up like an old diode set, a white dot that zipped out into a horizontal line, that flared up into a wobbly rectangle of static seethe. Out of the silverfish void emerged flashes of colour, premonitory crackles, static jabs leaping off the tube. It seemed there was an image trying to form, maybe a face, lips moving. Wilmot strained to hear words under the static.

*Flash.*

As the lifeforce drained out of him, the boy's spasms grew weaker. Blue smoke wisped from his skin.

A toaster capered across the stage, lolling tongues of fire, barking like a dog.

The boy gave a final, strangled joyous shout — and the equipment blew out in a shower of sparks, hot rain over the front circle. The toaster tipped, clunked on to its side. The TV picture collapsed to a dot. The power failed and the music squealed down into silence.

'It is not to be, not this time,' a voice murmured close by.

Wilmot turned to see who spoke but could make out nothing in the dark. He tried to find a way out. Hands pushed against him, fingers probed his face. He lost all sense of direction. His own breathing sounded louder than the ringing of vanished music.

'Wilmot? Is that you?' Somebody caught his elbow.

'Coral K?' He caught his breath. 'That was kind of spooky,' he said into her ear. 'I mean — well, kind of spooky.'

'It's OK,' she said.

'Does it have to be like that?'

She brushed his forehead gently with her thumb. 'We have to coax out the ghosts in the machine, find a catalyst. There is no time left to be squeamish.'

The power came back. Sinking globules of oil turned and quested for the surface of their lamps. The Inductor and Ray-X stepped over the detergent, disconnected the body and dragged it away. The music returned to normal; the crowd surged up over the stage, some slipping on Fairy Liquid and laughing.

Wilmot held out his shivering hands. His skin was dotted with sweat like scattered sequins.

'Come on,' said Coral K.

Light swimming like a congregation of amoebas over everything, and everybody's eyes shining, everybody's tongues glowing. He was filled with secret knowledge. He knew that soon the police would arrive, tipped off somehow; piling in with lights flashing and truncheons flailing. And the gathering would break up, flee, scatter into the sleeping city, find their homes and wait for the signal to be sent out. Then they would assemble once more, and another would be chosen.

Kevin Williamson

'HEART OF THE BASS'

It was all Streamer's idea, see. He says, Yeah I'll get everything sorted, man, so don'tcha worry. True to form he hires a car with a dodgy ID and says, OK my furry crew, let's go wild wild wild in the cunt-ree. He thinks this is so crazily put that he cracks himself up and not for the last time.

We've all noticed how Streamer has been acting kinda stranger than usual lately and we've been wondering about his hair. Streamer had this corkscrew afro perm tumbling down around his shoulders and then one day, say, four or five weeks ago, Streamer turns up with a bizarre-looking baseball cap on his head. It's a black leather Nike number with a sort of Foreign Legion-type flap which covers the back of his neck. He says it's for environmental protection. Sunburn mutates yer DNA, says Streamer. Gives you all sorts of skin cancer. Because of the ozone layer, right? Says he heard it on the radio. This, right, is coming from the George Hamilton IV of Wester Hailes. Anyway, we reckon Streamer's hat is more daft'n'mental than environmental but, well, no one has seen him without it on since he got his hair cut, not even at the sweatiest nights of Joy and Taste. And since Streamer isn't the sort of person who allows people to mess with his apparel even when he's well luvved up no one knows what this new haircut of his actually looks like. I mean, we can all see from the sides that there's been a fair bit of shaving involved but as for up top, well, it's anyone's guess. Maybe he shaved it all off on an impulse and now hated the look. I dunno.

Anyway, everything was supposed to've been arranged. By Streamer. But what he forgets to do, right, is to buy enough magic beans for everyone. He flips a cassette into the motor's crappy tape machine and casually drops an atomic bomb into the general company. Yeah, I'm well sorted, he says, how about youse?

Now I look at Susie and Susie looks at Roberto and Roberto looks at Sleepy Sue and Sleepy Sue kinda shrugs and I look back at Streamer thinking, Fuck you, man, you was the collector, the guy. We thought this was all tied up. Like pre-arranged.

It's Saturday night and getting late, see, with another forty miles of pitch-black April roads to negotiate before Loch Fyne. I think, Streamer's done it again. He's fucked up our night. We're not going to get there till after midnight and anything that's going around will have gone around. I'd been nipping his head on the phone about time being of the essence but he was determined to fanny around chasing up some iffy deal that may or may not have been Streamer-type bullshitting. I'm seething and want to say so but bite hard on the pink one. See, the trouble with Streamer is, well, he's never wrong, right? And when pressed he's liable to sporadic outbursts of the noble art at the slightest slight. I say nothing and stare morosely out the window.

So what have you got then? asks Roberto, breaking the tense silence — except for the music — and trying hard to play down low the niggle in his head.

A couple of lovey-dovey hearts, laughs Streamer.

No one else does.

And what about the rest of us, asks Sleepy Sue rather abstractedly. She's sitting there like the mother goose that's just laid a golden egg, which in a way she has. A small but effective temgesic one.

Fucksake children, says Streamer with a mock-posh accent, does one want ones *nappies* changed, huh? Streamer sneers and swerves past a Mercedes at a hundred plus. Did you see that?

No problemo for the Streamlined One. He's well chuffed with his derring-do.

Roberto mutters and stares accusative at me as if it's all my fault or something. I just shrug and roll a fat one thinking thank fuck for the shitey tartan techno on Streamer's cassette deck. Anything's got to be better than listening to his bollocks tales of drugs and shagging.

We drive onwards and upwards through snow-capped muesli mountains and Susie rests her head on my shoulder and whispers, It's gonna be a bastard long drive. I nod and light up the jay. I'm more worried about getting to Loch Fyne in one piece. Roberto notices Sleepy Sue has gouched off into limboland beside him so he slides his hand up her T-shirt and makes the word FUCT ripple around like shimmering waves on a Lycra shore. Sleepy Sue's quite attractive in a dozy sort of way and Roberto's totally into her but she never lets him get too near. She says two Taureans together is a recipe for disaster. Roberto once said to me — when he was aled up — that he wouldn't mind a bit of bull-fighting with her cause she gives him the horn in a big big way.

Streamer is roaring at the road and cursing the motor for its bad handling of tight corners. But he grins back at us and says the first pill's coming on nice. Fuck.

I put my arm round Susie and give her a big hug. She's a babe.

But hey! credit to the guy. He gets us to the cottage alive, in one piece even, and wow! the place is jumping. Yesss! We all cheer up considerably, kiss Tom Wilson's cheesy bounce goodbye and stumble out of the Escort stretching our cramped legs. Roberto sings, *What's the story, Hibees glory!* and we all laugh. Little things like that say, Don't worry, the evening's gonna turn out just fine. Maybe . . .

A girl comes over to greet us wearing nowt but a Zulu mask and a pair of fluorescent yellow beach shorts. Groovy groovy people! she shrieks. Where *are* you all from?

Portafuckinbelly! yelps Roberto, in Capital City Scotland! — obviously in the mood for some inter-city jest.

Cool, says the Groovy Girl. Anybody needing anything?

Aye, says Streamer. I'm needing a pish and this cottage looks a right fucking urinal if you ask me. In despair Susie covers her face with her hands. She's seen it all before. The Groovy Girl turns abruptly and goes back into the house, stopping momentarily outside the door to shake her large breasts — which incidentally are painted into red, white and blue circles like targets — at a guy staggering out to be sick.

Nice party, reckons Streamer, his face lit up like the Blackpool Illuminations.

Inside the cottage, which is all decked out like a club, me and Roberto score some Snowball 96s which nearly an hour later are doing fuck all. The girls on the other hand have swallowed a black dot each that they've scored from one of the DJs. They wander about contentedly, muttering to themselves about how romantic it is to be in the countryside away from it all.

Never mind, I says to Roberto, trying to shake off Streamer, at least the sounds are the biz. Nice and hard. Just the way *WE LIKE IT, WE LIKE IT!* The two of us are singing like hyenas at animal closing time. There's some mad things happening all around us and I'm wishing this E would kick in. I reckon we've been sold a dud, I say to Roberto. What d'ya reckon?

Looks like it. You up for a trip? he asks. It'll be better than fuck all and since we're here for the duration ...

Alarm bells. Me and trips just don't go. But, like he says, we're here for the duration. What the hell. We wander through to pay the DJ a visit.

Five minutes later we're about to settle down in the kitchen with a jay, having necked the black dots, when the biggest fucking rush comes rolling over me and I feel my legs buckle and I think, aw shit. The ecky had been lying dormant, burning away on a slow fuse, and I think of that insurance ad on the tele where the husband starts singing, *'there may be trouble ahead ...'*

I could see some synchronized swimming coming from Roberto's direction. He must've been hearing the same song as me. Altogether now, he grins, in an hour or two when the dot kicks in we're gonna be FUCKED.

Susie leads me out into the garden away from the craziness which is beginning to do my head in. Wow, she says, look at the sky.

There are no clouds but the stars are something else. They're all joined by silver filaments creating this amazing spider's web effect. It's beautiful. Awesome. We just stand there on the shore of the loch holding hands like a couple of, well, star-struck lovers I suppose. I tell her how much I love her and we kiss. And hug. And kiss.

Behind us in the cottage the DJs are really getting wired into some crazy jungle sounds. The drum'n'bass vibe is floating gently across the water towards the mountains on the other side of the loch. People are staggering around saying cosmic shit and this guy stands beside us complaining about how you never get really big Yorkie bars anymore. Thur no fir truckers any mair, he says, thur fir fuckin' taxi drivers. And we're both cracking up like it was funny or something.

I says, When I was a kid we never got anything to eat apart from totties. Monday to Friday we had boiled totties for our tea. On Saturdays we went to my uncle's chip shop and we got a bag of chips for a treat. And then on Sunday, for our Sunday dinner, you know what we got?

What? he says. A Yorkie?

Naw. Fuckin roast totties, man.

The three of us get them acid giggles that start to hurt after a while but are almost impossible to stop.

You know what? I says, trying to get my breath back. I never even tasted pasta or rice till I was eighteen and left home. I comes down to Edinburgh, right, from the Highlands like, and discovers fast food shops. Unbelievable, man. All them new foodstuffs. So I phones home all excited to tell the old dear about the city, and know what I says? I says, Ma, you'll never guess what kinda food they've got down here? She says, What's that son? And I says, Baked totties, Ma, they've got fuckin' baked totties down here!

The Yorkie guy goes, Get tae fuck man, that's just total pish, but he's got the giggles bad. Susie's trying to swig from a beer to try and put a brake on the laughter but she just ends up spraying the beer all over place. Aw fuck, I says, this is just fuckin' mental, lets get back into the heart of the bass.

Susie drags me round to the back of the cottage where it's quiet. She lifts up her dress and I see she's wearing nothing underneath. Come on, she says, fuck me, quickly, do it right now, *pleeeez*. My whole body is instantly erect and sensitized in a way I never knew was possible and behind us are trees and I'm inside her, jeans at my ankles, and I start spelling out the word pleasure to myself. P-L-E-A-S-U-R-E. Fuck.

Above us there's an outdoors sodium lamp which seems to drench us in a cone of yellow light and sex has never ever felt so good and Susie is beautiful in a saintly kinda way. She's moaning softly into my ear how much she loves me and I look down and Jesus, she's fucking me real hard now, aw yess, and fuck, wait a minute ... She's fucking me? I look down again and Susie's got this big stiff cock which she's ramming into my pussy and I can feel her inside me, she's really hurting me, and I'm loving every second of it. What the fuck ...

I'm seated in the kitchen and things are getting really out of control. I'm sure I hear somebody whisper, Watch out for the black dots, man, they're fuckin' lethal. I turn round and say, Who d'ya think you are? Wavy fuckin' Gravy or what? But there's no one there.

Out the corner of my eye I see Susie shooting the breeze with Streamer beside the sink. They're flirting, I know they are. I look away and watch Roberto and Sleepy Sue hugging each other by the door like there's no tomorrow. Sleepy Sue is saying, Roberto baby, you think I wasn't awake back there in the car — you're a bad person, aren't you? Roberto's grinning like the feline crazy from *Alice In Wonderland*. I knew they'd get it together eventually and I feel so happy for them I start to cry. So I slip a pair of sunglasses on.

Streamer and Susie are looking over at me all conspiratorially, and fuckin' hell, I just don't believe the guy. He's got his zip down and is holding his cock in his hand. It's as stiff as a broom handle. Susie's stroking it with her fingers while looking over at me all coy. Naw, naw, naw. I'm not having this. Not after what she was saying earlier. No way. I'm going to claim the bastard.

I get up and try to walk towards them but two things sort of happen that put the skates under Plan 9 From Outer Space. One: the room telescopes out and I decide miles are too far to walk; and two: although I stand up straight, my arse is still on the chair. I quickly sit back down and reconsider the terrain which is now fuzzying up with thick black smoke.

It's daylight isn't it? I ask Sleepy Sue.

She shrugs. Dunno. Could be. She's wearing the sunglasses I had on earlier. I check my face with my hands to make sure they're gone.

Susie comes into the kitchen. Where have you been hiding? she asks. We've all been dancing ourselves into a frenzy through there.

I was with you, I says. Out in the garden.

I don't think so. Not for hours. I thought you were out in the garden with Roberto?

I stare at her in panic. Eh?!? No way.

Someone's pointing at me and smiling and it suddenly occurs to me that something has happened of such an immensity I want to crawl under the table and die. Everyone knows.

They've all seen us haven't they? I ask Susie in a hoarse whisper. Everybody's been in on it. Was it all planned? A big acid joke on the ecky head, eh? I'm getting hysterical.

What the hell are you on about? says Susie looking a bit worried.

I rush out the front door and the morning sunlight hits me like snow blindness. When I get focused I see there are people sitting around in little clusters, chilling and smoking, and not really saying very much. But they're all looking at me. They all know.

I go down to the water followed by Susie and say nothing. I just clam up and stare at the oyster beds that last night looked like a pack of nippy wee bearded dogs. We sit on a rock and look out across the water.

You really freaked last night didn't you, Susie says, and puts her arm around me. It happens, don't think about it. And you weren't the only one. That Streamer stunt really fucked up a lot of people. No one's ever gonna forget that in a hurry. But I must admit, I thought it was hilarious.

I didn't want to mention the sink incident. It was probably just . . .

Aye, Streamer really did it last night, she goes on.

I stare at her blankly and she looks kinda surprised and asks if I can remember anything about what happened.

Nope, I says. I seem to remember everyone screaming and then a sort of void.

You're joking! You don't remember Streamer taking off his hat?

Nope.

Wow, she says, her face all lit up. It was unbelievable. Streamer gets the DJs to turn off the music and grabs the mike saying he's got something to show everyone. So everyone gathers round in the living room and Streamer gives everyone a pair of plastic glasses which he says to hold in their hands until he says otherwise. Then he stands up on a chair and *Hey presto!* whips off his baseball cap. And you know what the mad bastard had gone and done?

I shake my head, prepared not to be surprised by anything Streamer might have done.

Well, he's had all his hair shaved off and gotten a blurry green and red tattoo done all the way across his skull right down to the back off his neck.

A blurry tattoo, I says. What kind of tattoo?

Well, that was the sting. He then asked everyone to put on their glasses and would you believe it, the mad bastard'd only gotten a huge 3D tattoo of his brains done all over his head. Everyone started screaming and freaking out and you just seemed to disappear into a puff of smoke. When I found you, you were standing by the sink, holding a broom in your hand, talking gibberish.

What? No kidding? I smile from ear to ear, Aw, Jesus, I love you babe. Susie's looking at me uncomprehending but I mean it.

We sit in silence chilling for a while, getting our heads in shape. It will be time to leave soon and Streamer will drive us back to the city in his own inimitable kamikaze way. He'll be sat in front of us, his hands gripping the wheel, his Tom Wilson tapes doing our heads in, with his stupid tattoo and his stupid jokes.

Ach, but so what. The Sunday morning sun is just beautiful and a million silver reflections on the loch glisten and then vanish as if in some artistically co-ordinated dazzling light show. The word PERFECT begins to ... naw ... no more words.

We stand up and hold hands. To our left, out in the middle of the loch, three brown geese fly slowly, so very slowly, just inches above the water. We watch them take an eternity to cover what only seems like yards. Their slender necks are extended like serpents' tails and their powerful wings beat soundless and graceful, in rhythm with each other, in rhythm with our souls, and in rhythm with the world.

Jonathan Brook

'SANGRIA'

# I

It's so hot even the roaches are feeling lazy. They wait for my leathered foot. Rather get turned to paste than scrape around in the heat. I can understand it.

I'm moving very slowly across the square. There's no wind from the ocean. It's three in the afternoon. I've been sweating since I woke up, two hours ago. Juan's truck is outside the club. There's a girl sitting in the front, smoking a cigarette, leaning out of the window with it. Juan doesn't like cigarette smoke.

'Hi.'

'All right?'

She's about twenty. Fresh bait for the tourists, tight T-shirt and shorts. She isn't tanned yet.

'Juan in there?'

'I think so, yeah.'

I don't recognize her. He probably picked her up from the airport this morning. A kid with bleary eyes arriving at three a.m. on a charter ticket you can get for sixty. Then the ride into town and all the lights flashing off the sea, the heat, the scent from the hills, the promise of work in one of his clubs. It doesn't look too bad at night.

'See you later.'

'Yeah.'

It's cooler inside. The air-conditioning purrs. The decor's tacky but expensive. Juan spent thirty grand on black marble for the stairs. He shipped it over from Italy. He got his brother to rip out the floor and spray this weird blue shit all over it with a huge pump, a vast cake gun. In an hour the stuff was set. You could crack nuts on it. I know. I saw it all. I was here when they finished the renovations. They flew me over a week early, full wage for sitting around the hotel pool, staring up at the sky, wondering what the fuck I was doing here.

I push around the edge of the bar. The copper top's shining. I can see my face in it, flabby and greased with sweat lines. In the back room Juan's leaning on a huge wooden tub. Pat's sitting on a chair. They're both laughing. Pat waves at me.

'All right Danny?'

'Pat. How you doing? Hiya Juan.'

'Hola Danny.'

He's stripped his shirt off, thrown it across a naked rocking horse. The room is a store room for all the junk he's used in his clubs. There are piles of bottles, crates and boxes, huge tins of olives and cooking oil, lights, tools, lumps of wood, crap everywhere. At the back there are some windows and a balcony, hanging over the ocean.

I can see drops of sweat in the rug on his chest. The skin's clammy, like his face. He's thick-set, turning to fat round the gut, going into middle age. Pat just sits there smiling. Juan's holding a steel paddle.

'What the fuck's that in the tub?'

'I'm making drink, boy.'

'Oh yeah?'

'Have a look.'

I step over to it. It's full of a wine-red liquid, stained chunks of fruit and dark shapes floating around in it.

'You want a taste boy?'

'Fuck that.'

'Go on, it's good. Sangria boy.' Juan grips the paddle, reaches down to the floor and passes me a glass. I stare at the Sangria.

'Nah.'

'Go on.'

I dip the glass, rinse it and lift it out half full. I hold it up to the sunlight. The Sangria looks like coagulating blood. They're staring at me. I take a sip. 'It's not too bad.'

'Told you.'

'No, you can taste the orange in it, and vodka ...'

'Juan just pissed in it,' says Pat.

'You what?'

'He pissed in it. Can you taste that?'

Pat puts his head back and howls. I empty the contents of the glass into the tub. 'You fuckers.'

'Kidding Danny. We was only joking about it when you walked in. I told Juan it tasted like piss.'

Juan drops his pants and takes out his dick. He's smiling at me. He lifts a fat stubby brown dick up to the rim and shoots a curve of piss into the tub. Pat starts laughing again.

'You guys are fuckers.'

'Yeah.'

Juan finishes and dresses himself. 'Is funny, yeah?'

'Yeah.'

'All those pricks they get hot and buy my Sangria. So, they drink my piss, funny.' He starts stirring with the paddle.

I work for Juan, on an island, in the ocean, off the coast of Africa.

Juan is a millionaire. He owns clubs and restaurants all over the island. He takes lots of coke. He goes out with a Swede who has a water gymnastics team. I went to see them at a marina last week, a massive, white-stone, multi-level aqua park by the sea with guys in tuxedos handing out flutes of cheap champagne. There were four Swedish girls with his girlfriend, doing swimming tricks in a central pool, formal, like it's art. But there is no art here. The place was full of pissed businessman. Three Germans started shouting for the girls to strip. Juan got mad. If I hadn't been there to calm him down he would have taken them up to the mountains. A bad idea to fuck with Juan because he takes people up there and they don't come back. I don't go in for that shit. Now and again I have to warn someone off, take them down to the beach and scare them, that kind of thing. I deal with the tourist side. Juan looks after the locals.

I've seen Juan with the Chief of Police. They're buddies. They grew up in some shit-hole village together. Juan didn't know what a toilet was until he did his national service. Back in those days there were no police, just guys that used to carry guns to kill the wild dogs that hung out all over the mountains. That's how the police force started. Juan's friend was a dog killer with a badge.

I just help out, pick up the DJs they fly in, hand out the flyers to the girls, keep Juan happy with any problems. There's some competition now from other clubs so I'm supposed to keep an eye on them. But there's money enough for everyone. The island's covered in kids who want to dance and get trashed.

I've been here for four months. I've got used to the roaches. My pad's fucking crawling with them. I always knew that when the roaches didn't bother me anymore I should quit, but there's nothing to go back to. There are too many people in England. The place is saturated.

Pat stretches his arms and gets up from the chair. The sun is coming in through the windows, lighting up the sea-horse tattoo on his forearm. He's a professional party bum, been on the tourist trail for years, Greece, Thailand, Morocco, India, working for guys like Juan, whoever needs a link man to set up clubs, fix DJs, all that shit. He's tanned through and covered in a mane of blond hair.

'It's this guy down at Fantasy, Alfredo, you know him?'

'Yeah.'

'That's what I was ringing you about. Have you been down there this week?'

'No.'

'It is fucking rammed. The place is packed.'

'I haven't been down there for a while.'

Juan drops the paddle in the tub and starts shouting. 'This fucker. He is making twice what I have here. I want you to find out how he does this and stop it.'

Pat slaps me on the shoulder, waves at Juan to go back to his paddling. 'What he means is, we know the guy's up to something. We're not saying like, go and burn the place down or nothing, what we know is he's got some kind of scam going.'

'I don't know what you're trying to say.'

'I mean he's got a scam going. He's flown some guy over. A hypnotist.'

'What?'

'A hypnotist.'

'You want me to check out a hypnotist?'

'Perfect.'

'What's he called?'

'Charles.'

'All right. I'll go and see him tonight.'

'Danny, just find out what he's doing and put him off.'

When Juan started, the club was nothing but a black disco pit that made money. All he needed were a few bouncers with Alsatians to break up the knife fights. It was an alcohol frenzy, open till eight a.m. Then his friends at the police building, a dirty box in some dry scrub at the edge of the town, they told him the place was getting a little heavy. The tour reps were complaining about their charges coming back with holes in their chests, pink bloody froth messing up the hotel lobbies. When the tour reps whine, the police move in. The mayor and all the politicians live over in Marbella. They need the tourists back home to pay for their yachts. A few phone calls and they're getting nervous so the police say tone it down.

This Juan does by modernizing the place and hiring a covers band, a hotel lobby act to keep the police sweet. They do the evening crowd, fat Woolworth shop girls, gangs of mechanics and bus drivers, plebeian desperadoes from all the nowhere towns in

England, the odd local, a friend of a waitress, all in their shorts and damp T-shirts, sipping beers, smoking cheap cigarettes.

And in the evenings the raves. They're more sophisticated than the early club nights he was putting on. He got Pat in to organize DJs from back home, co-ordinate the drug supplies and work on the promotion.

At one a.m. Juan turns the air-conditioning off and the dancers arrive. Their eyes are already blank from whatever chemical shit they could buy in the square or they get furtive with Pat or the dealers Juan uses. Then the great dance begins. The room becomes an organic mass, they strip in the heat, the air gets thick with smoke and flashing light. In an hour they've regressed a thousand years, an atavistic slide, following the screamed messages in the sound from the speakers, in the wash they free themselves, the great pretence until they need another hit. Brain coma, body is everything, movement, believing they have found some kind of escape, the poor fucking dupes. All the promises are empty. There is no 'other side' to be taken to, no 'higher consciousness' to be reached. Only Juan in the back room pissing in the Sangria.

It's just me, Pat, some dickhead DJ, the bar-staff and a thousand tripped-out schmucks approaching salt deprivation muscle spasms in the heat. Or maybe it's the strychnine in the stuff Juan's been selling, tightening up the stomach and giving them the lift.

The drug is like the music. It's of uncertain content and uses poison as a base, a doppelgänger for the real emotion, strychnine for the lift, battery acid residue for the zing, largactil for the down, it's hard and chemical, synthetic, manufactured. It says it's spiritual but there is no heart to it, just a hard metallic vibe. It is nothing but an action, all designed to make Juan a lot of money.

Their muscles ache, their eyes and ears bleed, they pass out and defecate unknowingly. I see the wrecks. I help Pat cart them out to the beach and drop them in the surf. They feel fine the next day. They're only kids doing what they're told to do and that is to follow the herd to the rave.

There is no art here. This is a land of pie and beans, Bernard

Manning videos playing loud in the bars, plastic palm trees and skittering roaches, girls from the Midlands in bikinis outside the clubs getting felt-up by anyone they think they can get in, earning their commission. They spend it on sulphate so they can stay awake all night, watching the street battle between the Moroccan and British drug dealers.

I know more about the hypnosis angle than Pat and Juan imagine. I've been watching the kids in the club. I can see the music fucking with the Alpha waves in their heads. I know about that stuff. They're manipulated by so many mediums now, the media, the TV flip into sedation, fast-picture subliminal control. What happens in the club is the most intense Alpha-wave manipulation in current use. Drug someone and condition them with repetitive perception stimulation and they will do what you want them to do. Here, the victims are happy to be taken, it's what they crave. Like the roaches in the heat when they want me to step on them, their heads are so fucked up.

## 2

It's two in the morning and I'm outside Fantasy Island. I couldn't sleep this afternoon. The guy downstairs was beating his sister again. I killed a bottle of gin and crushed roaches. It got so hot today my fridge broke down. I reached in to get some water and it was an oven, all the food was trashed and it stank. I haven't eaten.

I can just hear the waves above the beats from inside, voices drifting up from the beach. The club is full. Outside there are groups of kids hoping to get in, ugly girls in pastel outfits, burnt red skin from the afternoon out on the sand, their podgy bare arms sticky with sweat. The guys are ruddy-faced with empty eyes, dragging hard on cigarettes, leaning on the wall, trying to breathe.

The club doors are open but there's a chain across the entrance. They only do that when people are starting to faint inside, it's so busy. I know the doorman so he lets me in. I push my way into the bar room. The club is heaving, there's no space and everyone's drinking, sinking shots, tumbling through the Sangria at a fiver a go. I understand why Juan's unhappy.

'Danny, let me get you a drink.'

Alfredo's a bit younger than Juan, more the suave, greasy businessman than the gangster I work for. He came home when he saw how much money the clubs were making out of the tourists. I think he made his money running blow out of Morocco, the switch game. Alfredo would hire two boats and two crews of dumb hippies. The crews think they're the only ones in on the deal, they don't know about each other. The first boat pulls in and Alfredo's waiting with Mohammed Shabour, the biggest dealer on the coast. He used to be the Sultan's bodyguard. He was an executioner before that, chopping through necks with his scimitar. I've met him a few times. He's one of those guys who laughs a lot and slaps you on the back all the time but I kept thinking of the Sultan with his hovering thumb, Mohammed waiting for the down sign.

The first crew comes in and they think they're big time. Alfredo gives them some good blow and in an hour or two they're all blasted. They stack five tons of shit henna gear on to the boat and then they sail off into the sunset. Two hours later the second boat arrives and they get the good stuff on board, ten or twelve tonnes. The next day the first boat is sailing into port and the customs people are there waiting for them. Alfredo's made a call. While the customs guys are calling their wives and passing round some very old brandy in their celebrations, the second boat comes puffing into harbour. It's an old trick.

I haven't been here long but I've seen a lot. I was pretty much down and out in the lust for life stakes before I came out here. London had sucked me dry, but here there's nothing but making the buck, it's finished me off. The place is full of runaways and losers who earn a parasitic dollar off the tourists, serving the needs of the club owners, myself included. And it's blatant. I marvel at the self-deceit of the blank-eyed tourist clubbers. They want to believe that this is a land of sun and good vibes. I guess if the belief is strong enough then it's true for them. Sometimes I see myself as the deluded one. I'm outside the world. But I can't think like that for too long. The vice is concentrated here, crushing, everything is shoddy and artificial, plastic, powdered beer, tits out for thirty notes, dancing round the disco halls, cat-eyed dealers out of Walthamstow and Moroccans who'd rather go to prison here than return to the open-sewers of home, selling their asses to the Swedes.

I should go back but I nearly fell to pieces there. This place is too unreal to get stressed about, I can take the ride. And the cheap gin numbs the realization of what I am, what I do here.

'I'll have a Remy.'

'When it's free you take the good stuff.'

'Of course.'

He leads me back to a private room. There are a few tables, men and women scattered about. They're mostly locals, Nationale boys or town hall people coming in for their sweet stuff paybacks.

'I want to talk to this guy Charles.'

'Yes?'

'I'm interested in hypnosis, I hear he's interested too.'

'He's the fucking best man.'

I could have hung around the club and waited for the guy, got him fingered by one of the staff. But I see no reason to fuck about like that. Alfredo knows me, if any shit happens it'll come my way eventually anyway. He doesn't mind me being direct. I watch him smile, sipping from one of the fat glasses that a teenager in a bikini has placed on the table.

'What do you want to ask him?'

'I'm curious about a few things. Just wanted a word.'

'All right, I'll try you out on him.'

Alfredo gets up and moves to the back of the room. There

are two men in the shadows. Alfredo leans down to one of them and the guy stands up. He's thin, withered, in a black suit. He's got a bald shiny head, gleaming with sweat under the spot lights. They come back over. The man moves very slowly, studying me. When they reach the table I see the fur on his face. He's bearded, a thick, black smudge of hair. He looks the part. I have to suppress a chuckle.

'I'm Danny.'

'Charles.' He stretches out his hand. I stand up and take the proffered shake.

Now it gets weird. Charles grips my hand so hard I think my fingers are going to crack. He starts shaking my arm up and down so my whole body is wobbling. Then he pulls me towards him and his eyes open up. He pushes his face into mine and starts yelling.

'Just sleep. Just sleep.'

He's leaning in on me, trying to push me to the floor, still gripping my hand, induce the 'down' sensation — downward movement can lead to the trance. But I'm covered. I know my shit. I focus and break away from him. Charles smiles.

'The revolutionary handshake technique. I've yet to perfect it. I only have a sixty per cent success rate at the moment.' He sits down at the table and pulls out a cigar.

'How can I help you?'

'I want you to lay off the subliminal shit in the club.'

He doesn't react. He's very cool, cuts the butt and takes a few seconds lighting the stick.

'I know what you're doing, Charles.'

'No you don't.'

'You're putting verbal commands under the music. I saw the dancers. They look more moronic than usual. And they're drinking.'

'So negative a view. I'm being white.'

'You're filling up the club, that's all.' Now he puts an elbow on the table and leans forward, staring at me. His right hand is still at the side of his chair. I see him flick a digit, a pulse, he repeats it. 'You can stop that shit as well.'

'You know you're the first person I've met here who believes in it, knows a little about it.'

'I've come across it before. Don't do any more rhythm shit on me, all right?'

'Why are you so tense? Alfredo's happy with the changes I've made.'

'I work for someone who's not.'

'So I have to convince him to be reasonable.'

'That won't be easy.'

'And what if I'm doing something positive for them?'

'I don't get you.'

'What if I'm giving them something they can't find in the music. You don't know exactly what my message is do you.'

His voice is soft and refined, lazy, has the remnants of a public school lilt. I sip some of the Remy and start again. 'Things are simple in this place. You'll see that in a week or two. Everyone has to make money from the tourists. The clubs share out the punters. Alfredo knows he shouldn't be pushing it. At the end of the day the man I work for and the man you work for will be slapping backs and swapping anecdotes about orgies on the beach. They're locals. Ultimately they stick together. I'm trying to avoid any friction in the meantime. Just tone it down.'

'I'd like to know what you think about the music, the people who come out here.'

'That doesn't matter.'

'I'm curious.'

'I think they're fools.'

'And what do they think of you?'

'I'm inconsequential to them. If you're not on the party train then there's no point wasting time on you.'

'You feel excluded?'

'I don't have their hope.'

'You're trapped Danny. This thing that happens here, it's a

wonderful development. But you're blind to it. For the first time, all these people are in harmony.'

'I don't believe that. I believe it's a myth that provokes some warped contentment within them. A myth they can break into easily, with no effort.'

'You think it's false.'

'We're talking as though there's an object to discuss here but there isn't. It's a vapid event, a lie, all of it, these kids listening to your messages, getting stoned. It's just the money machine. The club scene is just part of the superstructure stretching up from the base. On the base you have the man I work for and others just like him. This is just a money deal.'

'You're so bitter.'

'I've seen it in England. It's no different. It's a manipulative-style con.'

'There's so much more than that. I agree with some of what you're saying but there are more subtle currents of change which are important. Some people have achieved something. That's what I'm doing here.'

'With your hidden lines. What are they? "Have another drink", "Spend money", "Bring your friends". Your subliminal shit is just the same message the club girls are peddling outside, except they use flesh to get into the punter's brain. You're just more sneaky.'

'I'm saying a lot more than that.'

'Like what?'

'I'm grooming them. I'm going deep into the id, planting seeds. I have direct access to their minds.'

'But you're white?'

'That's right. I'm not taking them out back and fucking them.' He leans back in his chair, threads his fingers together and goes on with the speech. 'I'm on a crusade. The music's pure. It's corrupted by some but it can be anything we want it to be. Sadly the dark is less restrained and hesitant than the white. The feelings in the sound have been used to make money, it's true. But I'm fighting back. I'm supporting the music with positive messages, affirmations. They're walking out of this club feeling better than they ever have done. And that mood that you might describe as false is no less genuine than anger or lust or any other emotion they may have.'

'Why here?'

'It seemed the perfect laboratory. There are no regulations or restrictions here. I need somewhere to do research, develop the techniques. There are many questions of balance and approach. Then I'll begin recording the music, distributing it.'

'You're interesting, Charles, but you've forgotten the economic position here. The freedoms you've described are accompanied by some drawbacks.'

'The man you work for?'

'Yes.'

'I can control that. I'm a master of suggestion, shaping someone's ideas so they meet mine, without upsetting them, without damaging them, not manipulation but instruction.'

'Juan'll be too busy breaking your legs to be responding to any suggestions.'

'Juan's probably a fool. You could be so much more than his messenger.'

'Maybe. I don't have your ambition though, do I?'

'No.'

'I can't decide if you've anything to say or if you're just a psycho. I suspect the latter. I do know that you don't have the right to fuck with these peoples' heads.'

'But they want to be influenced, they crave it. That's why they come here. The influence is in the music already. You've studied them. You know it's a fact. They don't even want to be themselves anymore. They're bored with their own heads.'

'I'm tired. I have to get back.'

'You're in pain. You're negative. If you'd let me show you what I'm doing ...'

'I'm going. I'll see you around the town and maybe we can

talk then. Just tone it down and everyone's happy, just cut the take a bit.'

'I'm not sure I can.'

'It would be better for everyone.'

I get up from the table. The Remy's gone to my head. I need something to eat. 'I'll see you around Charles.'

'I hope so. Soon. I'd like to know more about your opinions on this.'

'I'm too far gone for that, Charles.'

'You're alone, Danny. Let me come out with you.'

'No. You stay here and work on your affirmations.' I start through the room and back into the crowd.

They dance like painted savages. The music has been stripped down so there is nothing but the beat, the first instrument of the world, the calling drum, firing the emotions, spurring them on to war or sorrow, the communal throng as one emotion, as one drive. I can feel Charles in my head. He's underneath the sound somewhere, barely audible but his voice is in there, planted in my brain. I make it to the door and crash out into the square.

3

I head over to the main centrum. There's a German sausage bar there. Two gay guys from Dortmund ran away to the sun to live in peace and tolerance, opened up a Bratwurst stall in the middle of the club area. It's a long silver bar, no walls or a roof or anything. It never rains here. I chew on a sausage. I'm miserable.

I could get on with Charles. He's the only person I've met here who might be a friend. But it's not going to work.

I should see Juan and tell him it's sorted. Alfredo will take the hint. But I'm feeling sad and desperate. I don't want to go back to the roach pad and I don't want to see the fat money man I work for. I wander off from the sausage stand and drop into Lycra's bar to get drunk.

She runs a little bar between two clubs, a few tables and some palm trees. I take a seat at the end of the pink paved enclosure she governs and watch her wind her way through the table tops to take my order. She's liquid, undulates.

'Hi Danny.'

'A gin please. English.' She smiles and goes back to the bar.

I've come here every few nights since I arrived. I love watching her. It's as close as I get to desire. There's lots of sex here but I can't do it. I can't go through the party talk, the make-'em-laugh rigmarole, the slap and tickle verbal jousting.

She brings my drink and a freebie cocktail that tastes of strawberries. All the workers are out in the night, peddling, teasing, playing the games. There's a boom from the clubs. The dancers are finding their release, the blissful avoidance they've tried to term a culture. I keep thinking about what Charles was trying to say, his alternative, the messages he's sticking into the sound wash. I have no faith.

You run out of things to reject and then you can only hate yourself. It's easier to play along with it all, the smiles and the enthusiasm. I had that once, earlier in my life. But the things I admired were tangible or significant. They were to do with skills, abilities, not something always out of reach like the club scene. It's so abstract it's nothing. But it's me that's lost out. I grew older and lost faith. I'm alone with Lycra, a thousand years away from asking her to sleep with me, to wake up with her in one of the beach huts with a wall of glass and the sun coming up over Africa, honey skin, morning talk. I'm only 2D. I can feel the blood pushing around my body but I can't connect with this place, the people here.

I have three more gins then I take a bottle back to the roach palace. I crash out on the sofa, wake up at seven to puke up the sausage, spraying the roaches in the acid wash from my stomach.

## 4

'Alfredo called me last night.'

'Yeah?'

'He's mad. So's Juan.' Pat is standing in my doorway. I'm buzzing with the hangover. It's four in the afternoon and it's so hot I feel like I'm bathing in lava.

'Fucking hot today.'

'Forty.'

'Come in.' I pull on some shoes and a shirt. Pat is on the sofa in the living room when I pace through. It's a studio layout. The kitchen's along one wall. 'Want some coffee?'

'Nah.'

I mess with the machine and pour the grounds into a cone. Pat looks over and sighs. 'What did you say to the freak?'

'I told him to slack off a bit.'

'Alfredo's shouting war.'

'That's crazy. I did nothing, just asked him to lose the monopoly.'

'You know what the guy's doing don't you, the hypno shit? Alfredo said you know all about it.'

'Yeah, yeah I know the scam.'

'Good.'

'Huh?'

'Juan wants him for the club. Juan doesn't fucking understand it and neither do I so you're gonna have to be the link.'

I rinse a cup and pour out the coffee. I drop a chunk of chocolate in it and fill it up with milk. Then I walk through to the room, sit down, take a long slurp and light a cigarette. There are packets of cigarettes all over the coffee table. 'Juan wants him? You mean he wants the hypno?'

'Yeah. We've been round there this afternoon, offered him some money to come over to us.'

'What did he say?'

'He said he's going to work all the clubs on the island. Came out with some funny shit.'

'Ha. He's a spiritual man, Pat. Spreading his message.'

'You what? Give us a cigarette.'

'Juan doesn't want that does he, him working around?'

'No.'

'I thought he'd be happy with my suggestion. It makes sense for him to stay with Alfredo but give us some of the crowd back.'

'So why didn't you turn up last night to tell us?'

'It was too late, I was sleepy. I think I must have known this was going sour on me. Why does he want him for the club anyway?'

'Because he's seen how much Alfredo's making. He went down there last night. The Hypno's a fucking golden goose. Anyway, it's bad fucking news, lot of bad feeling. We're gonna have to sort it.'

'Like what?'

'You talk the Hypno into doing Juan exclusively and I'll make peace with Alfredo.'

'I don't think he'll do that. He's seen a market for his wares.'

'Just fucking talk to him.'

Pat looks nervy. He's probably been up with Juan all night, doing coke, making plans, talking about their empire, two dumb fucks raking in the cash and me and the Hypno suddenly linked as a greed solution. 'All right, I'll go see him.'

'I'll run you over there now. The guy's out taking the sun at his hotel, stretched out like a lizard. He's weird man, does my head in.'

'Let me have a wash, yeah?'

'Make it quick. Juan wants him to start tonight.'

## 5

Charles's out by the pool, frying his back. The hotel's at the edge of town, under the rim of the brown hills that slope up to the mountains. It's very hot here. I ask Pat to get us some beer and sit down under a shader next to the hypnotist.

'Hello Charles.'

'Hello.' I can't see his face, it's wrapped up in a towel. When he speaks the words are muted. 'How are you today?'

'I'm hungover. I'd rather not be here.'

'I imagine that applies to wherever you are, Danny.'

Pat arrives with two beers. He gives one to me and puts the other next to Charles. 'I'm going over to get Juan. I'll be back in ten, yeah?'

'See you then.' I take a long sip of the beer. 'Charles, I think you should strongly consider getting a taxi to the airport. I'll call one for you.'

'I'm not going anywhere.'

'You should leave for England on the big metal bird in the sky. Before Juan gets here.'

'Why's that?' He snakes out a hand and the glass vanishes under the towel. I can hear him slurping.

'Because whatever you do now you're going to piss somebody off.'

'I'm not scared of any man.'

'You should be scared of Juan. The same goes for Alfredo.'

'What's going to happen, Danny?'

I nudge him with my foot. 'Look over there.'

He stares at me. I'm pointing at the hills but he's angry I touched him. 'Don't do that again.'

'Look at the hills, Charles.'

He twists his head then turns back to me. 'Yes?'

'That's where they'll take you. They'll drive you up there and leave you in a ravine. It's dry up there. You'll be mummified in a week.'

'You know that on this island ...' He sits up and takes another hit on the beer. He looks very relaxed. '... they used to mummify their dead.'

'I didn't know that.'

'The Egyptians are thousands of miles away. It's unlikely they migrated the custom. Parallel development. Interesting, don't you think.'

'Yes. It is.'

'I'm going to work for whoever I want. This is a crusade.'

'You're crazy.'

'They can all pay me if they want.'

'You're dropping me in the shit here too, you know. They want me as some fucking go-between. If you just head home then they'll forget it. The whole idea.'

'I do as I please. There's one thing I wanted to ask you.'

'Yes?'

'Will you help me?'

'I don't understand.'

'Will you actively help me with the crusade, or will you object to it?'

'There is no fucking crusade. They just want to use you to make money.'

'Maybe, but will you be an obstacle?'

'You know my thoughts on it all. I think it's just a brainfuck. No, I won't help you.'

'That's unfortunate but expected.'

'Juan'll be here in a few minutes and he'll give you a wad of notes. Then you're working for him, nobody else. After a day or two Alfredo will send some of his friends in a car and they'll take you up into the hills. The crusade will stop there.'

'You're being dramatic.'

'No, I've seen it happen. Sometimes they fall out, the locals, a few of the foreign workers can get caught up in it. We're only here because no one gives a shit about us back home, Charles. We're drifting. If we mattered we'd be back home making it.'

'I disagree. I'm doing something important here.'

'No. We're here because there's nowhere else. Get going, Charles.'

'Have you considered you own position?'

'Frequently.'

'You haven't spoken with Juan today have you?'

'No.'

Pat is at my side. 'How's it going?'

'It's not. Where's Juan?'

'He's outside.'

'I should speak with him.'

'Yeah, well, he's out there. You coming on-board then, Charles?'

'I told you, I'm flexible.'

'You better go and talk with Juan, Danny.'

'Right now.'

'Maybe we can sort it.'

'I'll be back in a minute.'

It's cool in the lobby. There are some tourists milling around, checking the posters for tonight's entertainment, a drag show or dance act, a lewd comic. Their kids will be out at the clubs, participating, tripping out, diving into the mercury pool that will eat their heads hollow. I wish Charles had gone. Juan's going to be mad and Charles is fucked. My head is screaming with the hangover, I feel sick with it all of a sudden. I'm by the hotel doors out onto the street. I have to sit down on the pavement, feeling faint.

'Danny.' It's Pat, standing over me.

'I'm feeling rough boy. Give me a hand.'

'Get in the car, Danny.' There's a Jeep, a big yellow Jeep pulling into the hotel driveway.

'Pat, man.'

'He says you know the score. You fucked up boy. You're not in on the act no more.'

Juan stops the Jeep and climbs out. They pick me up and I'm on the back seat. I'm shaking. My hands are cold as an ice burn. I'm lying back on the leather, feeling the sweat run past my ears and soaking my hair. 'Where we going?' It takes a few seconds for me to realize how scared I am. This is the mountain run. Juan and Pat mean to kill me. I slump against the seat now, lifting myself. We're out on the circular, I can see it winding up to the hills like a grey river of asphalt.

'Pat this is fucking crazy.'

They're not speaking. They stare straight ahead at the road. The last buildings of the town are flashing by; a lobster-pink apartment block with lime-green awnings, a glass-fronted supermarket and some foreign banks with no windows and heavy wooden doors. The concrete of the town is giving way to the yellow dirt of the island. I try shouting at them but they won't respond. We're moving too fast for me to jump and they'd only stop and pick me up. There's no cover here. The whole island is Juan's domain.

We move up into the strange volcanic core of the island, the road a series of long curves around a sheer rock face, lifting us higher at each turn. The light is intense and I can see strains of minerals and ore buried deep into the rock, gleaming as though illuminated from within. There are bushes and gnarled trees by the dirt borders, some of them decked with odd fruit. Way up above us I can see wooden crosses silhouetted against the sky. The villagers erect them when a loved-one dies.

Juan moves off along a side road, little more than a dirt track and we rattle down into a valley. At the end I can see the ocean. He stops the truck before a huge rock that bars any further progress. We're a long way from the main road now.

'Get out, Danny.'

The ride up here calmed me a little. I know what I have to do. I was trying to remember it all, it's my only way out but I can't face it, I vowed I'd never do it again. But Pat's hopped out of the cab, he's pulling my door open. If I only had the time.

'Pat, I can come around the wall he's put into your head.'

'Shut up, Danny.'

'If we could speak I could work around it. You don't know what you're doing, Pat, listen to me. You have to hear me out. Listen carefully to me, Pat.' I slow my voice, flatten the tone, start with the key words. My hand is in motion behind me to establish the perspective. I'm staring at him, almost reaching him, I catch something in his eyes, a glimmer. Maybe he's not quite sure why he's here, maybe he's beginning the long journey to independent consciousness and then into my control. It's so long since I've tried, I'm flashing back to the last time, the guy I couldn't get out, his face and the dark all around us. I can't afford to think of that. I don't want to die up here.

Juan is next to me, he's made it around the jeep. I feel his hand crash into my back, the fingers pushing, sinking, as though he's trying to rip out an organ. I fall to the ground. I couldn't reach Juan. Charles will have walked right in to Juan and taken over. He's pulling the strings. But Pat I could reach, I could reason through it with him. But I need time to discover the trigger word, to dismantle the obstacles that Charles will have installed to hold me back.

Pat is standing in front of me. He slaps me with the back of his hand. Then Juan has me under the arms and he's shoving me around the rock in front of the Jeep.

'Pat, stop him. Come out of it.'

He shuffles along behind Juan, slipping away from me again. Juan is crushing my chest, I'm finding it hard to breathe. My feet are scraping through the dirt, digging in to delay him but he tears me loose.

As we clear the rock I see the ledge and the rock floor below. The sky is huge above us. The ocean is crashing into the boulders that rim the shore so far beneath me. I flick my head to check Pat a last time.

'He said that this was what you wanted, Danny.'

Juan is lifting me over the edge, my legs are off the ground, flailing in the air. 'No, Pat.'

'He said that this was really all you've wanted for a long time.'

# 'Sangria'

And Juan rips his arms away from me and the ledge is above me now in a mad rush of air. All I can see is the blue stretching off to the line of the horizon, the smudge of land that is the continent. The sky and ocean are joining.

Charlie Hall

'THE BOX'

The light narrows my vision, scorches my eyes. This dry environment is just for waiting and searching; waiting and fretting. I stand with holidaymakers who squeak with excitement of 'the new'. Others, stunned by the effort of flying, gaze around as if they have suddenly been beamed to this place from another time. They shuffle around perplexed.

I should have said goodbye or left a note or something. I don't feel that I've committed a crime against humanity, but ... Well, I should have said 'Goodbye.' But then there would have been a scene, recriminations. I would have been late. The taxi driver, impatient surly fucker, he was bad enough. 'Yes I do mind if you smoke,' that sort of thing, grumbling as he moves all his crap around in the boot to make way for my boxes — like he's doing me a massive favour to come and pick me up.

'It's your bleedin' JOB, for crying out loud!' I think as we arrive at the airport. He opens the boot of his seedy Datsun and we stare at each other. 'I put 'em in, you earn your wedge and lift 'em out,' I think. 'Fuckin' 'ell, next time you'll want me to drive as *well*?' I go and get a trolley and watch him sweat with the record boxes. I ask for a receipt so he has to squeeze himself back into his car and give him the exact amount. Fuck his tip.

I could have said some kind words before I went to sleep, but my travel anxiety was already bubbling and the coke kept me awake, so I smoked a spliff. As I got back into bed, she curved herself into

149

me and it made me feel like I was made of crystal and I was afraid I'd shatter. Jesus, I'd only got back from The Complex buzzing a few hours before. I'd spliffed up with the boys and they'd gone and I was left with her, so I went to bed and lay listening to her wondering if she was awake, the tension throbbing in the air, words on my lips. I could have just said something. Her hot legs on mine, I was so jittery I wanted to punch her but the spliff calmed me down. I managed a halfhearted cuddle which made the words want to come out more. Just as I was drifting off, the alarm went.

We're all gazing up at the screens like obedient school kids. The flight number comes up and we race off with our trolleys. Like I've any confidence my boxes will come bursting joyously first in line on to the carousel! On the other side of the rubber curtains, I can hear the handlers chatting to each other as they sling the bags on to the belt like so many corpses. Here they come: battered suitcases; chirpy rucksacks; sleek executive walk-in wardrobes.

Just about everyone lunges forward at the luggage and then hesitates. 'No, wait a minute. In this light I'm not sure. I thought mine was *bluer*?' They glance around, harassed. The dilemma, 'If anyone grabs it then it's theirs, but if it's mine and I hesitate then it'll go back through the rubber curtains and the handlers will have *carte blanche* to tear it open, squirt toothpaste all over my underwear, nick my ... Oh fuck it, *it's mine, it's mine* ...'

And still I wait, with that niggling feeling that they've taken *my* boxes somewhere else, some *special* place, without telling me. I'll stand here like a spare part until it finally dawns on me and I'll go up to the counter scared and sweating like the first time. There'll be there grins swiped across their faces, 'Bet we had you worried, sir!'

I tough it out, trying to look unconcerned, just wanting a fag. If this was Italy we'd all be puffing away, leaning up on the 'No Smoking' sign, which is always situated by an overflowing ashtray. But this is Sweden where you get nicked for smoking in the *street*.

Fuck, I should have said something. 'Ah, I know what, get her on the old mobie! Good old GSM!' I think. I feel like a better person already as I struggle round behind my back for the phone.

'Hello? Hey it's me. Mmmm. I'm in Sweden. Look are you OK? I'm a twat, I'm sorry. What? No it's me. Yeah. No sorry, I polished it all off at Heathrow. Had to get into *gear*,' I snigger. 'Look I just thought I'd say something ... Well ... sorry ... I'll see you Sunday night ... OK. All right.'

I hardly know her. Usual story — arrived at the club that night whenever it was (last week? last month?) and I saw her again. We'd sort of been on each other's case here and there. You know, a bit of back-room flirting in The Ministry; skinning up together as I waited for David Holmes to finish his set at Final Frontier; plenty of laughs out in the garden at the old Full Circle. We'd had our eye on each other, both thinking maybe we knew each other too well. I used to get home from a night out, lie in bed and she'd come to mind. I'd still be awake with the drugs slowly draining through my system, tweaking the last synapses and I'd want to call her. But I wanted to be good, didn't want to make it all just a wank. I wanted to be *fair*.

I had been on a roll the night we finally got together. High summer and for once London was kicking. You'd come out of a club and there'd be people standing about in the street messing around. The atmosphere was stupendous and *everyone* was there. Good times to be a DJ.

When I was a punk back in the seventies, I was involved, but only as a part of the raw energy. The people who were shaping the movement — the artists, the musicians — were older. I had no desire to be part of the organization. I just wanted to consume, be shaped. We knew that the movers were powerless without us and we were cocky because of that. Now I look out at a throbbing dancefloor and I can feel the energy and this time I'm channelling it. There's the feeling that these are days not to be missed. That something vital and memorable is happening, some sort of axis point and we are there.

I had DJ bookings stretching through till October and I was as high as a fucking kite. That night I was playing for a mate in a sweaty gaff in the basement of a kebab shop on the Edgware Road. The vibe was perfect: underground and mellow. The boys on the gate were super-chilled and you could puff if it was done discreetly. I'd come down with a right posse and it was all laughs and the buzz of being together on a summer night. The pay for the night was crap, but Pete was shifting quality nose-up and I knew my night was going to be one long party, enough for everyone and me too.

When we got in, the place was already pumping. Eren was playing fat beats and mad acappellas and the crowd was right with him. He whipped them along grinning through his thick hair. The ground was just right.

I had a few beers and socialized a bit, trying to stay straight-headed. If I tuck into too much skunk or bugle before I get on the decks all sorts of chaos is likely to follow. It's a question of getting locked into the groove. The ideal night is one where the first mix goes right. There's a surge from the crowd as they sense new energy on the decks and you go with it. After that, you can stuff yourself with what you like — even done it tripping a few times, which is quite a challenge. I've heard a couple of DJs who brag that they play best on a trip. So do I, but it's a *social* one, tense with the anticipation, keeping an eye on my watch.

There're people down here who love my music. They're vibing me up. I want to be good for them, but then on a night like this it doesn't matter too much. It's only a scruffy do. It's worse when the hype's right up. You're expected to 'perform' and you see all the wannabies lurking round the DJ-booth just waiting to hear you fuck up. Not tonight.

It was one of those nights you dream about, when everything falls into place. All the right records were at my fingertips as soon as I dug in the box. Then, halfway through my set, I saw her best mate giving it some shimmy. So *she* was bound to be here! My senses tightened and I concentrated on the set. The records kept on coming, the heat was building, the vinyl grew hazy with condensation as soon as it came out of the sleeve.

The heat was outrageous. I was throwing beers back. We had to cane all the charlie before it sweated up. People were starting to lose it, but they kept right on dancing. We were all locked in together, a rare and utterly fucking wondrous moment: *pure ecstasy*. More coke, more beer, more T-shirts pulled off, more skunk in the air, and when it seemed like there wasn't any further to go, the buzz just kept building, bodies sliding against each other to the music. It was so hot, so scary, everyone was laughing in amazement. They were shrieking, hollering and whistling when it seemed like there just wasn't any more air to even draw breath.

I play house. When I first heard it, I was into reggae and funk and a mate came back from America with a bag of tunes. We had already developed a boys' club — trainspotting Fred Wesley, Maceo, the deep dirty funk from America's East Coast and the crazy Latin boogie from Los Angeles. Washington threw out mad Go-Go beats that had us all sweating our arses off, speeding things up. Then came dark, marijuana nights down in Melon Road, Peckham, with Jah Shaka giving us pumping acid dub. We'd stay out until the break of dawn, dancing all night, fuelled only by ganja and Red Stripe.

We were having a party one night, grooving away, when in comes our mate Jacko with his 'house music'. That shit was *weird*. Like FAST-as-fuck and empty. Machine music. Having been used to the fat bass sounds of funk and reggae this music was ... well it wasn't music, man! 'Take that fucking shit off the deck and put the *funk* back in.'

That was then. And with the help of a few little pills and a bit of understanding, THIS is now.

I play house. I keep it fat and I keep it funky. I want to convey that happy sexy vibe I got through funk, as well as the moody weird shit and the trippy frequencies of dub — like when you realize that you've been dancing for two or three hours just to a rhythm. I want people to feel what I feel. I want them to feel the simple joy of dancing, the release of losing the plot in a little room with a couple of hundred other people who want to do the same. Shit, I *love dancing!*

And tonight I'm jamming! For the first time in what seems like years I've got my shirt off and sweat's popping out of my body. I've got time to slap a track on the deck, listen out for the beat, match it up and then it's in. The new sound heightens the vibe. I tease the dancers by bringing vocals in off the new track, dropping the bass out so there's no kick drum mayhem, then spinning the track back. The twirling scream of the outgoing track encourages more whoops from the crowd.

Then *she* was there and we hugged each other, bursting with a simple feeling of happiness and we held each other tight. I could feel her body pressing against mine in the heat. With sweat streaming down my face, I kissed her mouth and she kissed me back and at that moment I was the fucking king of everything and this was RIGHT.

We stayed up until Tuesday: hanging out in Full Circle, then round someone's house, then off to Strutt, then off to someone else's gaff. We were full of each other, in fucking LOVE mate, buzzing, drugged-up with Es, spliff, charlie and more charlie ...

Got me thinking about that coke. I should get rid of it before I hit customs. They might have a dog, like in Naples. I'm sure that dog isn't a drug dog, it snarls and lunges at *everyone*. You can see the handler making stupid secret noises and twitching the fucker's leash so he goes for me (it's the BOX). I was clean. They gave up when I was down to my Calvin's. So what to do? Go and do it now and risk my boxes getting raped by the handlers when they go back through the rubber curtains unclaimed ... ? Or wait and squeeze into that toilet over there with all my boxes and trolley ... ?

WHAM!!! Ah, that'll be my boxes, last as usual. There're a couple of nice Swedish girls watching me now, a bit of the old DJ mystique. They look furtive and almost interested but I can see they're not ravers, they're just curious in an anthropological

154

way. My first box, a big steel fucker, has ko-ed one of those sad anonymous blue Samsonite copies and scarred the corner and there's a sort of fluid seeping out on to the rubber. My boxes are hardly scratched (I'm always amazed they let these through with regular luggage, it's senseless violence!). The bag's owner, herself a bit of a dented old bag, looks at me with a beaten look on her face like she's used to it and my victory is diminished sizeably.

The toilet's great — typical Scandi hygiene. Loads of shiny, gleaming, sweet-smelling surfaces. Perfect. I'm scooping the gear out and as my eyes sweep the interior of the cubicle I notice a little flash of colour right down behind the toilet bowl. Curiosity drives me and I bend down. I pick up a wrap and it's FULL. The powder twinkles, maybe a little too much, but it's got that right crystalline tweak to it, the overhead lighting glancing off it in wide beams. I take a dab. 'OOH! It's bitter-as-fuck. Yoinks!'

I start off with the rest of my gear, which perks me up and then I cut out a gleaming sexy curve of the new stuff. A quick double-check. It's not ketamin, smack or speed and it's free. Greedy old me. 'If she wasn't sure it was me on the phone, then who did she think it was?' I think. A sharp lancing snap of suspicion in my belly and then gone.

The light outside has improved when I step out of the cubicle. It has a kind of twinkling property that I hadn't noticed before. It's a little bit stuffy but that's bound to be partly down to the drugs. It's weird, the muzak and people's voices blend and then jar slightly.

I look down to check my bags. All present and correct and they look fucking ace: gleaming steel boxes, tools of me trade mate. *I'm the Lone fucking Ranger, blown into your town so strap yourselves down 'cos I'm-a-comin' in! I'm the hired gun with his pistols packin' blazin' HOUSE MUSIK! Come on, let's have you!!* I'm itching to play. I square my shoulders and stride on. Fuck me, this gear's the business.

The old victim's wobbling ahead of me, the liquid still oozing out of her bag. It dribbles on to the (fantastically shiny, sort of like when you look at a deep pond and you can see the surface, but you can see the dark depths as well) brown linoleum floor. It looks like a beautiful glittering cord. Her feet splatter through it. We're going through customs. I'm cool and totally clean and buzzing like a bee. Just then the old woman notices the brook of gunk and starts squawking. I swerve round her, expert in my trolley handling, but the incident has been enough to get some uniformed twit out of his office. First thing he sees are my boxes.

'Pssst!,' goes the official and nods in the direction of the counter. I follow him. His trousers are neat and pressed and halfway up the crack of his arse. His hair is cut neat, halfway up his red neck.

'Passport!' He holds out his hand. I take out my passport and hold it out so he has to reach forward to get it. I'm staring him in the eye. If he wants to play with me, I'll play back. As he grabs it. I let it go so he has to use his other hand and almost goes off balance. I'm clean, without question, so I'll just wind him up a little bit. These straight guys would never go so far as to beat you up or plant some gear so I'll just go with it.

He looks at my passport photo and back at me like I'm a wanted criminal, narrowing his eyes. He's either on a highly sophisticated wind-up or he's so fucking dumb he doesn't think I've seen all this before. Off comes the immaculate cap and he puts it on the steel counter and gently smoothes his pink hand over his blond hair.

'And what is your purpose for coming to Sweden Mr ... S ... m ... ithhh?' He fixes me with another of those killer looks. Well now, with those record boxes, I wonder what I could possibly be doing for fucksake?

'I'm over here to DJ ... Mr ...' I say and peer at his name-tag, but the letters seem to be dancing around. 'Yeh ... Mr.'

'Your bag?'

'Yes, they all are mate,' I reply. I'm not going to pass it straight over to him. He's going all the way so I may as well go with him to see how long it is before he gets fucked off with it. He looks up sharply, now he knows it's 'Game On'.

'Your bags, please. Up here!' He slaps the counter. I move faster than I've ever moved before and in one gorgeous fluid movement

I twist round in a kind of t'ai chi (crane gets angry at monkey picking nuts from tree) move and my heaviest box smashes with a crash on to the counter. A crash that's only partly softened by his cap taking the first hit. He's so gobsmacked at the speed of my move, he hasn't even noticed the cap.

'Open please.' I twist the box round, grinding his cap and smiling 'There! My records! Help yourself!' He's a bit confused. There're almost two hundred tunes there. Is he going to go the whole hog? Go on, I dare you! I think. If he does he has won, because he doesn't actually have to put them back. This is one chance to wind me up.

I got into this business through house music which is all about understanding and togetherness. OK, so we all took drugs too and people have got fucked up, but on any journey there're casualties. The upside of the house movement was amazing, but now commercial interests have elbowed their way in: big-time drug lords, crap clubs, stupid records. More people go to clubs now and with the growing market the quality of drugs is lowered, so more people get sick and the witch-hunt begins. And who is it who gets it in the neck? The most visible members of the movement: those of us marked out by our metal boxes. It's like *we're* the drug dealers.

If I was going to be smuggling drugs I'd scarcely be doing it with a couple of record boxes. I bet that old lady had half a kee of coke in her duffed-up suitcase. It's a battle that I'm used to. It's like the border guards used to be like when you were travelling abroad for the football. One false move and you'd be straight back home, so you had to bite your lip while they treated you like vermin.

He puts his fingers on the records, where to start? I'm just looking at him in a totally unthreatening manner, which will make it worse for him. He's hesitating. I can *feel* his mind clicking away. Shit, I *can* feel it, it's a kind of rapid tremble like a small dog shakes when it wants to do something but is held back. He looks up at me, his eyes have still got some fight in them.

'Come on mate!' So he goes to my holdall, rips it open, throws all my clothes around in a frenzy, thrusts and pokes his thick, clean fingers in corners, but he's moving slowly and missing loads. He goes back to the box and scoops about thirty records out. I notice the beads of sweat on his head. He looks through those records, quite thoroughly, bless him.

He takes my ticket and passport and goes into a back room. 'Oooh,' he's shaken me up a bit. I suck in some air right down into my lungs, charging through bronchial tubes, swelling those little aureole down there, squeezing the oxygen into my bloodstream, powering me up. I let the air hiss back through my teeth. I mustn't grind them. Jesus they're clenched so tight . . .

Then he comes out again. 'Put your bags back on the trolley.' 'I'm free! Then his clean young face crumples up when he sees the ruined cap. He points! In the back of the net!

'Follow me!' The Search Scenario. Here we go, Round Two.

'Can I have your clothes?'

So I strip off in a flash. I feel like my body's in perfect nick, honed down by careful years of drug use and the good life. I flex my muscles gently and stare into his face, still with that nutter's friendly look.

'I see you are used to this,' he sneers.

'It's the Box isn't it? That's why you're doing this,' I say.

'Ah, you know it is my job. You know what I'm looking for.' He's on his trip now, the justification (you're sick with your acid house and children dying in the clubs).

He gives up. I've kept my cool and I'm clean, although a urine test might tell another story. I pick my passport and ticket up and fuck off to the bar on the other side of customs. The ice-cold lager tastes so fucking sweet I feel like eating the glass, so I order four more and tip them down my throat. As the last one goes down I catch a glimpse of myself in the bar mirror. My face is streaked with sweat, there's beer foam round my chops and my eyes are bulging out on bleedin' stalks. What was in that wrap I found? I guess it must have been PCP.

But Sweden made me feel kind of cheap. The punters have to

pay over the odds to get me in their club — wouldn't they be just as happy with one of their homegrown DJs? Isn't this all part of the cheapening of the scene? It makes me yearn for the simple underground. I just want to play house.

Ben Graham

# 'WEEKDAY SERVICE'

I'm watching the Mosque gleaming in the moonlight while Johnny takes a piss around the corner. This is the St John's area of Halifax, built up then abandoned by Victorian industrialists and cotton traders, leaving only their names to these narrow streets, stone terraces and grimy, mattress-strewn alleyways. West of the town centre, stretching up the hill to the army barracks and the rugby ground, it's a warren of long, Gothic avenues converted into crowded flats and tiny, windowless bedsits. The skyline is a mosaic of steep, sloping rooftops, silent chimneys and rusted weather-vanes.

Johnny returns, wiping his hands down the front of his clean, white jeans, and grins at me from beneath his Modish haircut. 'Right then! Are we gonna go and blag some whizz or what?'

We're walking up Gibbet Street, past empty mills and boarded up shops. I occasionally wish I had some kind of religion, but I've never believed in anything. I sometimes envy the chaste, holy life, just meditating on the soul and eternity. But all I believe in is the holy dole, and the order of perpetual apathy. Johnny was brought up a Catholic — he renounces the sins of pride, avarice and ambition, but regularly cultivates new ones, just to avoid self-righteousness.

We're putting our faith in some kind of God just walking through St John's at this time of night anyway. This is a skint and dangerous neighbourhood. Flats are regularly broken into or torched; passing cars are pelted with stones; drunken strays at midnight are waylaid with baseball bats and Stanley knives. The pubs are grim, functional alehouses where giros are cashed in return for a few hours of welcome oblivion. Where a desperate, middle-aged blues band pound away in the corner, and a hollow-eyed housewife screams vainly at her man to come home while he still has money to put food on the table. Sometimes, clichés are all you have left. Another cliché — where there's poverty, fear and desperation, that's where we go to buy our drugs.

We arrive at Den Quigley's place, a through terrace house squeezed on to the end of an already overcrowded street. A yin-yang sticker clings to the grime in the corner of one high window, and next door a thin old woman peers apprehensively at us from behind the net curtains. Inside, the front room is empty, the walls and floor stripped bare — you have to go through to the back before you find any of the familiar comforts of home. Various lank figures slump on the sagging beanbags and ageing armchairs. A long, low sofa, shiny with wear, illustrated with brown fag burns and sudden dips where the springs have sighed their last, fills half the room. The stale air is heavy with incense and cigarettes, and whatever else is being smoked, burnt, scraped or crushed on the overcrowded coffee-table. Echoing, stygian dub and unholy blasts of klonking techno stream from the large, battered speakers that balance precariously at either end of the room. The soundtrack only heightens the sense that we've wandered into some self-contained, alien landscape, entirely detached from the outside world.

Squat, shaven headed and dropped into an orange and blue striped T-shirt, Den Quigley fixes us with lidded eyes.

'Aright lads,' he drawls, his words dragging along his tongue like sandpaper. 'How's it goin'?'

Den Quigley is a redundant electrician who reinvented himself as the goblin prince. DJ, Drug Dealer, Mystic and Pool Hustler, he's the king of the underground, the biggest, ugliest rabbit on Watership Down. Sat at his feet is his girlfriend, Amber, fifteen and pregnant, with the widest, roundest eyes you'll see this side of a Manga cartoon. Together they recline in state, indifferent to the strange court gathered around them. He sucks on a twelve-inch joint, the smoke rising through the leaves of the huge rubber plant that hangs over his glistening head.

We've got five pounds. It's Wednesday night, and we want to get loaded.

'Got any draw, Den?' Johnny flashes his best cheeky, cheesy grin and begins the bartering. Den exhales slowly.

'How much do you want?'

'I'll tell you what the situation is,' Johnny says, reaching into his pocket for a crumpled note. 'I've got a fiver here, and what I'd really like is to buy a wrap of whizz with that, right—' His eyes twinkle as he lets out a little nervous half-laugh, like he knows he's taking the piss, and he knows that Den knows, but on the basis of that understanding he might just be able to get away with it. I'm perched on the edge of the sofa, half hidden in the smoke, trying to avoid Den's gaze.

' — But you know how it is Den, we're gonna get licked on this speed and then we're gonna need a bit of weed aren't we, just to chill out. But if you can do us an eighth on tic, Den, honest to God, I can pay you for it Monday morning, first thing. How about it?'

Den takes a toke, holds it in his lungs for what seems like days, then breathes out noisily. He passes the spliff down to Amber, and a cold smile passes momentarily over his face.

'Yer a cheeky fucker, Johnny. You come up here, I ain't seen you for ages, then when you want some fuckin' draw you turn up on a Wednesday, at fuckin' midnight ...'

I mutter something to the effect that we wouldn't have knocked at the door if we hadn't seen that there was a light on, but Den ignores me.

'I know, I know I'm a cheeky fucker Den, but when have I ever let you down?'

It's all a crazy game. Whatever he says, it's all in the spin of the wheel, the roll of the dice. Whatever is Allah's will. Dope, money, booze, girls, it's only life, some strange dream. What does it matter?

'Go on, then,' he sighs. 'Monday morning. And ay—', he grabs Johnny's wrist as he pushes the money towards him, ' — I mean it Johnny. Monday morning, fifteen quid. You'd better have it.'

I have no idea where we're going to get fifteen quid from on Monday morning, but I don't say anything as Johnny cuts the powder into four lines, one for, me, one for him, one for Den and one for Peppy. Peppy is Den's right-hand man and number-one hanger on, named after Pepe Le Peu because 'He smokes so much skunk he'll turn into one'. Peppy ambles over, long, stringy, straw-coloured hair and a scraggy goatee, mumbling a halfhearted greeting. Normally he just sits on his own in the corner of the room, eyes constantly moving, taking in everything and making mental notes in the vast pyramids of his brain. Occasionally he'll start talking, whether anyone's listening or not, in a soft, steady tone, that once you're tuned in won't let go. He'll talk about different kinds of radiation, and germs that are carried on radio waves, and secret government LSD tests, and alternative energy sources and Nostradamus and *The Tibetan Book of The Dead* ... Sometime's he's fascinating, for a while anyway, but then the candles'll flicker and you'll get a weed rush and suddenly it's like you've fallen off the edge of the world into an abyss where reality, fantasy and paranoia all blur together, and there's no objective yardstick or reference points to tell them apart.

After we've cut up the speed it doesn't look like much, so Peppy produces an E and grinds it up with a pestle and mortar, chopping it out into equal lines. So it's E up one nostril and whizz up the other. East and West, which is best. I snort hard, one after the other.

'Jesus!' I grimace, squeezing the brow of my nose.

'It really burns yer nostrils, dunnit?' grins Johnny.

'You're not kidding,' I reply. 'Fuckin' hell.' I can feel the stuff going to work though. Taste that dry tingling at the back of my throat, feel thousands of brain cells popping and vaporizing behind my eyeballs. As I shake my head and sniff hard, the others hoover up their medicine. Next to me, some guy is talking about how he used to work on the Rowntree Mack's production line, packing up wine gums.

'You can actually get pissed on wine gums,' he says. 'You have to eat a fuck of a lot though, you want to throw up but it's worth it, 'cos you can get really off yer head. We used to knock off early on Fridays and just neck loads of 'em, walk into town fuckin' wazzed.'

I'm beginning to notice how many good-looking girls there are, languorously dipped in the shadows of the room. Long, brown, bare legs snake across the carpet, the painfully exquisite angle of a shoulder here, a pert breast there. Doe eyes gazing blankly out from beneath a shroud of long, dark hair. And I realize how much I ache for sex, a yearning even the drugs can't kill; they just make it abstract, almost detached. But what does it matter? All our emotions and sensations can be reduced down to chemical reactions in the end, and right now I feel in love with the physical world, almost catatonic with desire, but utterly unable — unwilling, even — to act on it.

I was never very good at games at school, and sex is a competition: can you pull, can you keep up the illusion, will you measure up in bed. Drugs are easy. It's only after the chemicals have worn off, when I wake up alone in my big double bed, coming down hard with all the endorphins drained from my body, that I wish I just had someone there to hold. Someone to love me, to give me back my confidence, my ego, my soul. Even when I'm getting high, the hollowness of the next day is already there with me, growing at the back of my mind, like a little reminder of the futility of everything, like Death's home phone number, next to a message saying 'Please call back'.

I wander through into the kitchen. Amber is there, making a round of teas.

'Hi,' she lilts in a soft, high voice. 'Do you want some?' She holds out a packet of muesli towards me. 'You could feed a hundred people with this for weeks. It's really good value.'

'I suppose it is.' I nod, taking a handful. She's a small, skinny girl, barefoot in a long, tassled skirt and a loose, hippyish top.

'We're poisoning ourselves with all the crap we eat and that, and it's ruining the environment,' she says. 'I wrote a poem about the planet the other day. It's the only poem I've ever written, but it's just about how the Earth's our mother and we're killing it.'

Den walks in and passes me a joint. Amber gives me an embarrassed smile and takes the tea through to the other room.

'She's great isn't she?' Den says, coming up close. 'She's changed my life. We've changed each other. She was a virgin when I met her, you know? Hadn't been soiled by no one. Hadn't been opened up to the world of her senses. So I opened the door for her, you know what I mean? I showed her where the light was coming from, and I kicked the doors wide open. But I made sure it was special. I put cocaine all round that sweet little cunt of hers, and I put a dab on the end of me knob, and we just fucked all night. There was blood everywhere, but it was beautiful.'

Den smiles at the memory.

'I won't let her go to school, you know. She wanted to do A-levels and shit, but I told her, fuck that. They just fill your head with junk, man, they tried to do that with me, but it didn't work. I hated school. I already knew what life was about, you know what I mean? I knew in here. You already know when you're two years old, but they try to make you forget. So I said, fucking leave school. I'll teach you everything you need to know. I am the way and the light, you know what I mean? We've been dropping acid together, and I've been trying to enlighten her, 'cos she's having my kid now, and I'm not sending him to school, no way. I'm gonna bring him up right. When the kid's born we're gonna buy a bus and fuck off to Wales or somewhere, middle of nowhere, just the three of us, 'cos the light is within you, innit? The way and the light, you know what I mean?'

Sometimes I think I should stop taking drugs. But it's a hobby, it's something that me and Johnny can do together, and it's the craziness I love, the spirit of adventure. The three a.m. taxi rides round winding, faceless streets and all-night garages, the shady deal in the pub pool room, half a dozen people in one toilet cubicle, waiting in some strange alleyway as the moon plays on the dirty river beside you. Getting high is obviously the main goal: going out, off your face, grinning, or sitting up all night, listening to the Burrito Brothers and confessing to every sick thought and insecurity that's been plaguing us. And I know that Johnny, too, is half in love with the idea that these are the last days, that none of it matters and we can just play out forever.

Across the road from Den's there's an empty church which overlooks a walled up, forgotten graveyard. But I happen to know that there's a gap in the rusted, iron gate where me and Johnny occasionally crawl in on a sunny afternoon, to share a spliff under the angel of death. We climb over the tombstones and explore the ancient, weed-shrouded vaults, then walk up the street like panthers, all of our senses alive with the exhilarating tingle of danger, taking everything in. The buzz of strange languages: the constantly cooking smell of exotic, spicy foods: the second-hand warehouses overflowing with enticing junk. A combat jacketed punk shambles past, hair a shaggy scarlet mop. A Muslim elder with a full, grey beard passes a pale, craggy faced pensioner, hands thrust deep into his anorak pockets, muttering silently to himself. Brightly clothed, laughing brown children chase out of a garden in front of us. Mysterious veiled women with deep, beautiful eyes glance furtively over. We buy sweetmeats from the bright, reclaimed storefronts, and stare at the Nation Of Islam posters on derelict chimneys that once belched poisonous smoke around the world.

The sulphate sets me in motion, and I feel like it's time to leave. I find Johnny, but he's already been cornered by Peppy.

'He's a painter, yeah?' Peppy is saying.

'Who?' asks Johnny.

'Den, man. He's a fucking great painter.'

'Did he paint all these?'

For the first time I notice the paintings that are all around the room, melting, bleeding shapes on canvas, like undercooked Francis Bacon.

'Well, Amber painted them,' Peppy admits. 'But Den paints pictures in people's minds, that's his thing. He's probably painted one in yours tonight, hasn't he? Yeah? So, you know, in a way he did paint those pictures, because he painted them in her mind first. Because, right, she didn't used to paint like that, yeah? It was all like, chocolate-box shit, portraits of her mum and all that. But Den told her, he said, you know, they're crap, burn 'em. So she did, yeah? It's down to him that she's painting all this stuff.'

We leave St John's, retracing our steps out of the labyrinth, chemically insulated against the night. Cutting through People's Park, taking care to avoid the dog shit and condoms, we cross the once ornate bridge over the empty pond. The swan that once swam there was stoned to death years ago. Across the large, neglected lawn, headless statues stand sadly, a cracked fountain is covered with meaningless obscenities. I feel a sudden rush of emotion, loss maybe, or regret, I don't know. It passes. Back at my house we sit in front of the telly, skinning up, strumming guitars, accumulating half full mugs of black tea until the sun starts to peek through the thick, dusty curtains. Pretty soon my housemates will be getting up to go to work. Across town, Gibbet Street keeps dreaming. It's only life.

Jeff Noon

'DJNA'

DJ Helix was *persona non data* at all the legit clubs of Manchester. To get into Shangri's that night he had to fold his body into a dubmix. This wasn't difficult if you had the right mixing gear, which the rogue had in overload. Trouble was, the St Peters were continuously upping their detectors. One false move, buddy, the gates get shut. Goodbye salvation. Nowadays, a superfly judasguy could end up seriously frazzled.

Death by disco.

Fig was with Helix, and Fig was clean, free from sin, so she would go in first. If Helix was caught in the flare at least the girl was inside. At least the girl would get to dance. Helix knew to his loving-cost what happened when Fig didn't get to dance.

Slow death by cold sex. Way too much.

The queue-stream was coiled around the block. Fig and Helix were about a dozen places from the entrance, where the St Peters were clocking the influx. The Official Bouncers of our Lord, dressed in natty black dinner jackets, silver wings stitched to the back, flapping madly through some bulky mechanism. Man, those guys were sure bulky. Angels of the Zion Curtain, checking every skullport. Securibores.

'Yer up for dancing, Helix? All night long?' Fig was straining to be cool, but they'd been waiting an hour to get this close to paradise. Helix could see the fear in her eyes. Every Saturday night the same.

173

'Sure thing, babe. Maybe they'll play your favourite.'

'I doubt it.' She turned to look at the clouds, her eyes shielded.

Fig was once a lone dancer. You've seen her type no doubt, at any provincial disco in the old days; the lonely girl that everybody wanted to go out with, the stunningly *weird* girl that never went out with anybody. She dressed how she pleased, discarding fashion, and her name was always something strange and short; Joolz or Doon or Suze or Kat or, indeed, Fig. Always the first dancer on the floor. Before the petrified English boys and girls got the courage up, there she was, dancing wild and free, making strange patterns. Nobody ever got near her. That was the ruling; Lone Dancer left when the popular tunes came on, slipping away through the crush of sudden bodies.

Fig's real name was Sue Newton; but she was strange as a child and her classmates called her Fig. Her favourite tune was something called 'Forever Breath', a mad scramble of lyrics over a raging beat. Nobody else could dance to it, only the Fig. But that was before the new laws came in, and the Lord descended on to the dancefloor. Dancing alone became an evil act, punishable by fire. But Fig still needed to dance, so she gave in to the laws, much to her chagrin. And then she met Helix, and everything went haywire.

Above the scary pair, as the line crept forward, the logo-beams spelt out CLUB LA SHANGRI, in words written on the clouds. GOOD DANCING FOR THE PURE. GUARANTEED NO DIRTY JUDAS. Now they could see the St Peters processing the entrants. JESUS BOOM, WORKING THE ROOM sang the clouds playfully, turning to rain. DANCE WITH THE LORD. BECOME THE DANCE! There were only four people to go, almost in, thank the download, because they were getting drenched by now, when the flares went off . . .

Sudden, like. Oh shit! The big judgement.

DIRTY SINNER! screamed the clouds, making the testament.

*In the beginning there was only stillness. And the Lord God said let there be dancing. Lo, there was dancing, betwixt Adam and Eve. And the Lord saw it was slammin'. The evening and the morning of every Saturday night.*

Alarms going crazy and for a bad second there Helix thought they'd spotted him early, but then the bouncers were moving in on some poor sinner girl, who started to run, away from heaven, but was too easily caught. Far too easily caught.

Helix didn't recognize her.

There were around five hundred sinners left alive in Manchester. Helix knew about half of them, but mostly they kept themselves to themselves. The attributes of being a Dirty Judas? Loneliness, secrecy, despair. Helix could thank the pagan gods of funk that he had his very own Fig. Most pure souls ran a mile from such association, because most pure souls only wanted to dance with the Lord. And this was Manchester, after all. The city of forever rhythm, where Jesus danced in the rain.

'I'm scared, Lixie,' whispered Fig, using the loving name as they were pushed forward. 'Let's call it off.'

'No way.' The judasgirl was being dragged down to the offices in the club's cellar. From there the dance cops would be called. That night the miscreant would be in the holding cell. Tomorrow morning she would be in court. Twelve hours later she would be in prison for a year and a half. The standard penalty for dirtiness in the soul. A lot of them committed suicide before that. So don't talk to me about standard penalties.

'Let's go home, Helix!' Using the hard name. 'Please!'

'It's OK. This is home.' But he was sweating himself, lying to himself, and he knew that moisture played havoc with his defence mechanisms. It was like a disco war, the club's defences against his latest blocking pattern. 'Stay happy.' This whispered as they entered the club, Fig first, Helix following. Helix pushing his girl forward, like a shield for himself.

Almost like a shield.

Fig made it easy, of course, through to heaven, taking the communion wafer on her tongue, taking the wine, letting the biscuit dissolve through the wine, through to the dancing. Club Jesus Boom. With this my body, shall you dance. With this my blood, shall you love. 'Thank you. I'm grateful,' said Fig, feeling the music enter her system, like a blood-rush. 'No problem,' answered the waitress of love. 'Welcome to Shangri-La's.'

Then the bouncers pushed Helix into the code-breaker, the flarebeams playing over his body, searching, searching ...

DJ Helix, screaming loud.

Because Helix was one of the last natural-born DJs in town. And the DJ now stood for Dirty Judas, those poor children who still suffered from sinful music. Vinyl pirates. Criminals. Having the rapid beat in their soul.

*But the Lord saw that the dancing was turning evil. Eve had succumbed to the snakes, the sexy rhythm, the entwining repetitive beats. She was dancing like a harlot, tempting Adam into the same movements. And the Lord God said let there be no more dancing, unless it celebrate my Love.*

*Let the dancing be pure.*

So the Helix was screaming loud, as he passed through the detectors, but screaming on the inside only, as the search played rigmarole with his soul. While, on the outside, singing the praises in a smile. Sure, just a smile, a well-practised inane smile that told the world he wanted to dance, dance, dance! Dance for the Lord!

A winning lying smile, turning on the dub remix ...

Acceptance.

Through into the antechamber, where a waitress forcefed him the wafer and the wine. 'With this my body, shall you dance,' she chanted. 'With this my blood, shall you forever love.'

'Thank you. I'm grateful.' Easy like, and superfly cool.

'Welcome to heaven, my child.'

Through to the dancefloor, moving like a spectre.

Of course, the wafer and the wine meant nothing to Helix. He was immune to it. The judas worm was snaking through his DNA. It made him one badarse DJ, an enemy of the state. A mere ghost of silence, among the dancing dolls.

*And so a Law was made against the double-serpent beat. Let only those who partake of my flesh and blood enter the dance. Thus spake the Lord, and it was ever so.*

Was it ever so.

For two hours Helix wandered the crowded spaces of the converted warehouse. He had the wafer crumbs still claggy on his tongue, the wine in his stomach, swilling around. His defences had held tight against the doorsaints, thanks to the dubmix, but now he was moving through a wave of hush. All around and pressing tight, the dancers, celebrating the world of beat. Making love to the Jesus Boom, as the Messiah worked the heavenly decks. The night was hot and fruity, but no such music could the Helix hear, as though his body had soundproofing.

DJ was alone.

Because the Lord had sent down this message, no more wild-dancing, and England had responded, *en masse* as always. The Government had quickly keyed into the new religion, using it to force the dancing-gene into submission. 'We cannot allow such wantonness,' the Prime Minister was suddenly fond of saying. 'We must retrieve our children from the devil's grip.'

Over the top and ever so nasty, ever so English, of course, but pretty soon the slogan started to appear on all the TV screens, all the cloud-hoardings. 'RETRIEVE OUR CHILDREN! SAVE OUR CHILDREN!' So the Law of Gentle Pop was passed, the St Peter's Bouncerhood was formed, the clubs were forced to comply. And all over the country, Jesus Boom appeared in the mix, working the decks, working the populace, working the nice 'n' easy dance. Interactive and resurrected, along each groove of pure vinyl. The wafer and the wine were introduced, holy drugs; the only means by which the dancers could actually hear the Shangri-La.

Disco biscuit and Jesus blood.

So the people gladly queued, to have their DNA branded with the new rhythm. The digestive collective. And all those still wanting to dance the serpent? Well then, those bpm sinners were left with the Dirty Judas code, the last natural code. The authorities called it DJNA, the discojockinucleic acid. Easily spotted, unless you had the hiding gear.

Like DJ Helix, for instance, with the gear in overspill. The lone DJ. Through the bouncer's eye, swallowing zero, looking for his drowned love.

Fig was hearing it. She most certainly was! She was drenched in the music, like the wine was falling all over her body, like disco rain. And dragged down by the wafer, a bog of sweet biscuit carrying her under. Into the collective rhythm, so very, very pure and clean and free from wickedness.

Holy communion.

The loving beat. No snakehips, no juiciness. Just the breath of our Lord playing over her body, infiltrating, gentle. Soft clutches.

*So the Lord God sent his only Son to the dancefloor, in order to teach the people the rightful rhythm. The Son gave his blood and body up, in order that the dancers could partake of his blood and body. The wine and the biscuit. And the people did the good dance, succumbing. Becoming one with the Lord.*

Pass me some biscuit, pass me more wine ...

Helix was pushing himself through the dancers, pretending to dance, working his false rhythms. Thinking that Jesus Boom was just a myth, not real at all. Something created by the Government. Until he saw Fig, somewhere over there, somewhere and somewhere, dancing with some clean and normal Jesus-fuck. Jesus-fuck! So he cut in, gave the dancer a vicious stare, enough to make a back-off. And then, suddenly, Helix was doing it, he was dancing with the Fig. Alone and together in the whirl. With Helix copying the Fig's movements, arm to arm, beat to beat, soul to soul. Not to be caught out.

*So the Lord made a remix of Earth, dubbing out the devil.*

A spirit of the outlaw beats-per-minute, dancing to his lover's slow move. Making her happy, even as the monitors played over his shielded body. Angels of bulk, hoping for a weakness. But Helix never gave them that opening. He just danced like the cold music was loud in his mind, making some ice, clutching his girl to his body. But the Fig-girl was protesting about Helix's lack of pure rhythm. 'How can you be so fevered?' she asked.

'It's the way I'm built. Should I apologise?'

'I think you should.'

'And to think you were once so wild,' Helix said; 'a real lone dancer. What happened to you, Fig? Did you give in?'

'Yeah, I gave in to you.'

Helix was mad at this. What did he have to do, to get this woman on his side, once and forever? 'Excuse me a minute. I've gotta piss.'

'Sure thing,' answered Fig. 'Don't hurry back.'

'You betcha.'

Helix never touched the toilet. Instead he was heading up the stairs, towards the control-booth. A gang of St Peters were standing guard on the door. 'What you after, mate?' one of them asked.

'I've got a request for Jesus Boom.'

'Jesus doesn't do requests.'

'It's for my girlfriend. Her favourite tune. 'Forever Breath'. We're having an argument, you see, and I just thought—'

'Jesus doesn't do requests.' The automated response. 'Especially that kind of tune.'

'But I thought he was all-loving?'

'Well you're wrong, buddy. Now get the fuck outa here.'

'I'm gone.'

So Helix retreated, back to the balcony. He looked over and down to spot Fig in the crowd. Nowhere to be seen, until . . .

There she was, dancing slow and close with yet another Jesus-fucker.

Helix left the club, went home, getting drenched on the journey. Who the fuck was she dancing with, anyway? Who the fuck?

No answer. Night over, sleep alone. Fig never came home.

And Sunday was the same. No Fig to suck.

Bye-bye and no love, with so many hours to travel.

On the next Saturday along, Helix played a gig at the Mirage, an illegal club in North Manchester, way beyond the horizon. Pirate beats. Helix wasn't much good at love, but he was excellent at spinning the world with dirty music. The latest twelve-inchers, scratching them to hell and back and mixing like a maniac on the twindecks. The dancing crowd were loving his movements, outlaw-stylee. Because some believers still couldn't quite believe, despite the Lord, and thank the Lord. 'Repeat the beat!' he chanted over the mix, 'Don't beat the retreat!'

All the time he was looking out of the booth, hoping to spot Fig down there on the floor, dancing her heart out. He played his personal dub of 'Forever Breath' seven times over. Almost cut the groove to nowhere. Favourite song of the Fig, surely ...

Oh well, no such luck.

Fig would never come to one of his gigs anyway, saying it was far too dangerous. Like visiting the Jesus Boom was easy, and all for love?

Oh well and double shit.

Then he spotted something. Could it really be? Helix gave the decks over to his business partner, DJ Plasma, and then descended. Into the wicked dance, so beautiful. OK, there she was. No, not Fig; the other girl, the judasgirl he had seen being taken out by the doorsaints.

'Hi, how yer doing?' He introduced himself. 'I'm DJ Helix.'

An empty stare, coming back at him.

'I saw you last Saturday,' he continued. 'At the Shangri-La. You were discovered. You're a judas, right? What's your moniker?'

Again, the stare. Eyes of vacuum. And then, after an age, 'Simone.'

'I thought you'd be in prison by now?'

No answer.

'You want to visit the booth, DJ girl? Simone? Maybe play some tunes?'

The girl nodded sleepily, so Helix led her up the stairs, let her take over from Plasma. Plasma protested, but then relented. But the girl's hands were slippy on the decks, and the music went haywire. The dancers were arguing already, and Plasma was shouting to Helix, over the noise. 'What's going on? This some groupie of yours?'

'No. She's a DJ, really she is.'

'Make her act like one. Before we lose the crowd.'

But the noise just got worse, and the crowd started to wander, so that Plasma had to jump in, to steal the decks from the girl's clumsy fingers. 'Will you please get that trash out of here!'

So Helix led the Simone girl out of the booth. She looked at him once, her eyes so dark, he could see the loss seeping out of them. This girl was dead. The standing-up dead.

'Jesus! What's happened to you?' he asked. 'What did they do in heaven?'

But the girl could only run away, always on the run, down the stairs to the dancefloor. Helix couldn't dare follow her. He leaned over the balcony, watching the revellers who still dared to revel. Oh hum. Plasma was doing his best to retrieve the beat, and more power to his mixing. Because DJ Helix was deep in sorrow, and no way could he work the dance that night.

No living way.

Just then someone tapped him on the shoulder. 'Will you get the fuck off me!' he shouted, turning around. 'No requests, OK?'

'It's me, Lixie. I heard you playing the tune.'

'Oh.' Helix turned fully around, real cool. 'I thought you'd left me?'

'I had. But now I'm back. I made a mistake.'

'What?'

'Jesus ain't enough for me.'

'Oh. Here she comes, the Lone Dancer.'

'I want to love you.'

'Hi ho, Silver! Really?'

'Really.'

'I'm not so sure.'

'Neither am I.'

'You ran away, Fig.'

181

'No, I just went dancing.'

'With whom?'

'With the Lord, of course.'

'Nobody real?'

'Nobody real.'

'Shit.'

So the Helix took the Fig back into his arms, and they kissed, and they kissed, and they kissed. And the kissing made the music go crazy, because the next second DJ Plasma was rushing up to Helix, dragging him away from the loving. 'What's happening?' cried Helix.

'The Godcops are here. It's a bust!'

'Jesus!'

'You said it.'

The next second, Plasma was gone. As the Jesus Boom worked its way into the house-system. THIS IS THE LORD TALKING! PLEASE STOP DANCING. DJs, HANG UP YOUR DECKS. NOBODY GETS OUT OF HERE ALIVE.

Helix pushed Fig towards a no-exit door. 'Let's boogie!' But all the time he was looking out for the judasgirl, Simone, Simone ... hoping to save her soul.

No such luck, as the Lord descended ...

*In the beginning there was only stillness. And the Lord God said let there be forever stillness. The evening and the morning of every Saturday night.*

And later that night, DJ Helix was lying in his bed, and clutching at his Fig, as though she were the only fruit of happiness. And afterwards, three hours afterwards: 'How far will you go, Lixie?' she asked.

'All the way, my love.'

'Fine. Take me there. Take me dancing.'

Take me anywhere.

Morning came calling, and Helix learned from the papers that a certain DJ Simone had been found in a cheap bathtub, white and pale and dead, bleeding from both wrists. They called it suicide.

*So the Lord made a remix of Earth, dubbing out the devil.*

Two days later DJ Plasma was found dead in his flat, an overload of drugs in his system. Helix spent the week just moping around, thinking about what had been lost, what had been found. Plasma gone, Simone gone, with the Fig found again. But for how long? How long for anything? And all down to the Jesus Boom.

So then, the next Saturday . . .

Fig was with Helix, and Fig was clean, fully tested, so she would go in first. If Helix was caught in the flare at least the girl was inside. At least the girl could get to dance. Helix knew to his loving-cost what happened . . .

Loneliness. Burning loneliness.

'Hope yer up for dancing, Lixie? All night long?' Fig was trying to be cool, every Saturday night the same. But this time Helix had supercharged his dubhead. Spent most of his savings on some new equipment. No way would those angels catch him now. Anything to get his lover back. Anything at all . . .

'OK, let's stay happy.'

Helix followed Fig through the monitors.

This time they both took the wine and the wafer together, and danced together, and stayed together, all through the long night. Helix made sure of that. Until he had to go to the gents. 'Excuse me a minute,' he shouted into Fig's earhole, working the silence. 'I've gotta piss.'

'Sure thing,' answered Fig. 'Hurry back.'

'You bet.'

No such love, actually. Or else too much. Because Helix was heading up the stairs, towards the control-booth. The same gang of St Peters were still standing guard on the door. 'What you after, mate?' one of them asked. And, from another: 'Don't we know you?'

'I've got a request for Jesus,' Helix answered, cooling it down.

'Jesus don't do requests. Now get the fuck out.'

'"Forever Breath". This one's for DJ Plasma and DJ Simone.'

'What the fuck—'

'And all the other DJs you've crashed!' With this scream Helix made a sudden lurch for the booth-door. The two angels were in shock from his words. Helix banged through the swinging door, falling, falling . . .

Oh shit!

The booth was empty. Just the twindecks spinning around, even though the vinyl was being scratched. Invisible hands were working the beats.

'OK, bud.'

Helix turned to face the two bouncers. 'What is this? Where's Jesus Boom?'

'Come easy now.'

'He's a fucking robot?'

'Nice and easy does it.'

'Jesus!'

'We like to think so.'

Needle spinning the groove, as DJ Helix heard the call from the beat, dragging him downwards, screaming, really screaming this time.

No defences.

At two o'clock in the morning, after waiting so long for Helix to come back, Fig called it a night. Angry with herself, she slipped out of the club, made her lonely way home, walking through cold rain, lit by logo-beams.

Helix was waiting for her there, sitting in the dark at the kitchen table.

'Where did you get to?' Fig asked, getting the first shot. 'Must you always keep leaving me like this?'

Helix just murmured something. Something wet and thick.

'Well, I've had a good time, anyway.' Her carefully sexy claims could only retrieve the same murmured response.

'Mmmm . . .'

'Lixie, love, is there something wrong?'

'Mmmm . . .'

'Are you ill?'

'Mmmm . . .'

Fig turned on the light. Helix didn't bother to shield his eyes. This wasn't a normal drunken spree, Fig could see that now. She went up close, looked deep. Saw nothing. Nothing at all from his damaged eyes. 'Helix?' Fig was now distraught. 'What have they done to you?'

Helix got up slowly from the table, made a murmuring way to the back door.

'Helix? Please!'

So far gone. Bye-bye and no love. Needle spinning the groove, almost cut to zero. The police found his body the following Monday. The illegal DJ had booked into the Organza Hotel early Sunday morning. He had asked for a double room, even though he was alone. The maid had come round, seen the Do Not Disturb notice hanging on the knob, left him alone. At three o'clock, needing the room for new guests, security staff had opened the door with a pass-key. There they found him, DJ Helix lying on the still-made-up bed, a smile on his clean and tidy dead face.

Autopsy report. The guest had taken thirty-seven disco wafers, washed down with six bottles of dance wine. The authorities were at a loss to explain how he had gotten hold of such restricted substances.

There was no note, only a twelve-inch vinyl record resting on his chest. It was a song called 'Forever Breath', broken into thirty-seven pieces.

They called it suicide. Death by disco.

Oh well. There you go.

It took Fig three months to get over it, the savage betrayal. And by the time she returned to the dancefloor, racked with guilt, the music had changed fashions at least five times, so she was feeling rather left out. Rather lonely out there on the floor, under the lights and inside her head. Rather too old. Sure the biscuit and the wine were doing their stuff, as promised, but something good was missing. She fended off six Jesus-fuck proposals, drank a few beers, chatted to a few youngster girls, all so eager to dance with the Lord. She gave in to not connecting anymore.

*Boom!* Music is a whirling shape that flies all around the dancefloor, something unseen but all mighty. *Shackalacka!* If you have the right equipment, the wine and the biscuit. *Boom!* Music can be heard. *Shackalacka!* The big bass goes boom and the treble goes shackalacka. *Boom shackalacka! Boom shackalacka!* Music is a force, a riot of information, a collective explosion, fed by all the DJs who ever lived and died. *Boom!* DJ Plasma was in the mix, DJ Simone also. All the captured DJs. Their bodies had died to give up the ghost. *Shackalacka!* Their knowledge of scratching and mixing and bpm seguing, all stolen and floating through the system, adding to the *Boom shackalacka!* DJ Helix was in the mix. Helix was music, a part of the whole, disembodied.

*Jesus Boom shackalacka!* He had a little secret song.

Fig was all set to leave when the first chords of 'Forever Breath' came over the communion. What was this? Never before had the Jesus Boom played that song, it was too harsh, far too repetitive. Far too loving.

> *Some kinds of love cut a deeper groove.*
> *Deep down along the vinyl, a feather.*
> *Floating the music like a dream unfurled.*
> *Making my love a breath forever.*

Fig moved back on to the dancefloor. Already most of the other dancers had left the floor, judging the beats too sinful. But Fig danced. How she danced. She danced in love. Like the world was ending tomorrow, or else just beginning. On a forever breath, she danced for three hours straight, while all around her the system went crazy, trying to still the raging beat. The bouncers in their wings tried to stop her, only to be repelled by the music. Jesus Boom tried to close her soul. No such power. Like the music was a force, until the system crashed and lights went out. The bad music reached into the booth controls, screaming feedback, causing a spark to ignite. An alarm went off, sending the crowd wild for the doors.

*In the beginning there was only stillness. And the Lord God said let there be dancing. Lo, there was dancing, betwixt Adam and Eve. And the Lord could do fuck all about it.*

Dancers fled the fire. Bouncers fled. Jesus Boom melted into plastic, mere plastic. Only a single wisp of music slithered from the dancehall inferno.

Floating.

Douglas Rushkoff

# 'THE SNOW THAT KILLED
MANUEL JARROW'

'So it's, like, cool, this doesn't hurt,' he said. 'It's a free ride from now on.'

'Is it really?'

'Fer sure. I'm just waiting for the clear light. Sorry about the piss, though. It must stink. I couldn't help it.'

'Quit it, OK?'

'Is that the sirens?' he asked, staring up at the flashing strobes. 'The lights?' The boy lay on his back at the far edge of the dancefloor. Most everyone else had gone back to their partying — he was just another tripped out kid. Couldn't handle the scene. Or did they ignore him for fear of caring too much? The empathy of E can work in reverse: you simply avoid what you don't want to meld with. 'Fuckers,' he said, half laughing. 'Can't wait till they see the stretcher.'

'Don't,' she said.

'I'm just talking, Bess,' he said. 'Makes it easier to stay awake. I'll stop.'

'No. It's better to stay awake. That's true. I've heard that. Say what you have to. Even if it's mean.'

'It's not a concussion, you know. It's not like I'm going to keep myself out of a coma. It's not that at all. I'm dying here.'

'Don't talk that way. Someone's coming with water. You'll be fine. If you don't give up. Feel yourself free. Just think "life".'

'Did you read that on some rave flyer? Something in LA?

191

Or was it some TV ad against abortion? You can be so dumb sometimes.'

'And you can be cruel, Manuel.'

He watched the other kids dancing, oblivious to his plight. It was a madhouse, he thought. Some essentially good vibe had been there at the outset. Back in the early nineties. Maybe. But now the energy and karma of all these kids was just being siphoned out as cash by some businessmen. They had been sucked dry. Pure energy converted to pure marketing.

And, to Manuel Jarrow, this place seemed to symbolize it all. A much-too-shiny New York nightclub pretending to be a rave venue. No matter how late it was — two? three? — or how many of the Day-Glo kids pressed together in the room, the whole place reeked of business, grime and scam-artists. New York really was a terrible place to try to throw a party. It was a nightmare to get anywhere. In the UK, a rave meant a road trip. In SF it meant a hike to the beach. But in NYC, it meant a subway ride (with two transfers) through rat-, bum- and cop-infested tunnels that smelled like human piss — just to get to stand in line in the cold and wait for a fat guy with a walkie-talkie to decide whether you were cool or rich enough to be let inside.

Bess went off to try again for some water and to see if the ambulance was coming. Manuel couldn't tell if it was the lights or his head making everything spin so. He wished he had his camcorder. To document the fall of the scene. There were so many scenes he wouldn't ever have the chance to tape. So many he should have, too, but didn't. Now he never would.

The dehydration wasn't bothering him any more. He had been so thirsty before. Back when he went to the bathroom only to find all the sinks shut off. But now he wasn't thirsty at all. Just tired. Ready.

'The girl at the Smart Bar gave me this,' Bess said, returning with a small plastic cup of orange liquid. 'She said it would help.'

Manuel waved it off, but Bess knelt beside him and held his head on her knee as she moved the cup to his lips. 'You have to try.'

He swallowed a gulp or two and smiled. Then he wretched it out all over her leg. 'I'm sorry, Bess,' he said, 'but I told you ...'

'I wish we never came here tonight,' she said. 'The raves were never like this in San Francisco. We never should have come to New York at all.'

'It was your fucking idea.'

'That's not fair,' she said. 'You wanted to come, too. You thought you'd get a job doing guerrilla TV, remember?'

'You were the one who loved it here. The big city. The real people. So close to Europe and history.'

'I liked it until now,' she said. 'What did we do to deserve this?'

'It was the coke,' Manuel said. 'I shouldn't have spent that last tenner on the blow. We were so thirsty, too. I should have seen what was happening. But the water cost three-fifty a pop and we hadn't done any coke in so long. The E was so pure, too. Nothing speedy in it and I was starting to fade. I guess I learned my lesson.'

'But you didn't deserve this.'

'Deserve to die?'

'That's not what I meant. You're going to be OK,' she told him. 'Everything is going to be OK.'

'Yeah. You just keep telling yourself that.'

'You do it,' she said. 'I'm too beat.'

*Now in his mind he saw the hillsides of Santa Cruz, just behind the university. The place they called Elf Land. He was sitting on a rock with a bunch of college students — a few years older than he was. They were all drumming together into the night.*

*Mushrooms were such a special drug. So natural. So real. They made you dissolve into the woods and then get born all over again as part of the Earth's green network of creation. Like Swamp Thing. The beats of the boys' drums — the rhythms mixed with the many rhythms of the forest. The crickets sang along, their high-pitched chrips in tentative syncopation with the human tribal celebration.*

*This was one of the things he had saved to shoot. Close-ups on the hands as they pounded the skins, intercut with high-magnifications of cricket legs scratching together. He meant to go back there and find those kids again, but with his camcorder and maybe some battery-powered lights. Blues and greens to match the woods.*

*The idea came shortly after dosing in a dorm room. They knew nothing about drumming but felt called upon to add to the pool of resonance in which they found their heads already swimming. Someone just grabbed a drum and headed outside and it felt so right to follow. They had wandered for hours before finding the spot. The special spot where, as the 'shrooms came on, all five boys realized at once they had meant to be united forever in time.*

*The music began in clumsy fits and starts. Military beats with strict male conformity, eventually giving way to affected tribal rhythms and Zepplinesque flourishes. Questions and answers. Day-o, Day-o, Manuel thought, like tourists on a cruise ship. The harder they tried, the more pretentious it got.*

*But once they gave up trying, something happened. They were no longer playing with one another, listening consciously and trying to fit in or assert a new counterpoint. The form and meter just disintegrated into dots of beat. Waves of sound, disconnected from each other yet completely articulate as a whole. They just danced around one another's rhythms — no one leading, no one relegated to the click track. Spiralling hands against animal skin, generating waveforms that reverberated against the trees. Perfect and unstoppable. Infinite yet contained. A total sound so complete it may as well have been squeezed out of a toothpaste tube. Another image he would never record.*

*He got an e-mail maybe six months later that one of the boys had died in a wreck. On the way back up the hill from a Full Moon rave on the Santa Cruz beach. The van just toppled over the cliff. It took the cops hours to extract him from the car. They were trying to keep his neck from moving, but he died of internal injuries in the meantime.*

'We never went to that guy's funeral, did we?' he asked the girl who was kneeling beside him on the floor of the club, now, on Manhattan's lower West Side.

'We couldn't get a ride, remember?'

'Why should I remember that?'

194

'We could never get rides out of San Francisco. That's part of why we came here.'

'Right. To suffer together and then die.'

'Why are you being like this?' she asked. 'You're not going to die, OK? And even if you are, why kill everything else, too?'

'Am I killing something? Really? You should know.'

'Stop it, OK? You're being such an asshole.'

'Look, I'm a little freaked-out, OK?' he said, retreating into the convenience of his own demise. 'Don't listen to me. I always loved you, ok?' He didn't know whether he wanted to go with the tables cleared off or not. 'I won't bring up all the nasty stuff again, ok?' he said.

'You can be so sweet when you want to.'

'And it's all fake. It always was.'

'You fucker. Why are you doing this?'

'I don't want to ignore anything. I want to look. I don't want to chicken out.'

He dozed off for a few seconds that seemed like minutes. There was still no sign of an ambulance, and the kids on dancefloor were all pressed up against one another on the other side of the room. Pete-E, the kid who had sold them the doses was bending down over Manuel, trying to get him to drink some water from his canteen.

'Bess went to call for the ambulance again,' Pete-E said. 'You should really try to drink. You're dehydrated, that's all. Just drink some water.'

'Those fucking club promoters want to squeeze every last dime out of us,' Manuel said. 'It's not enough to charge fifteen to get in. We won't buy their fucking alcohol so they plug up the sinks to make us pay for their mineral crap.'

'It sucks, I know,' Pete-E said. 'We've got a petition started. But right now you have to drink something. If you don't they'll stick an IV in you when they come. You don't want that, do you?' Pete shuffled uncomfortably as he stood over his wan, corpse-like customer. 'We don't need that kind of mess, Manuel, do we?'

So that was it. Compassion always turns out to have that 'ass' in it. 'I better leave you with this water and go. You won't say anything about me when they come, will you?'

'You're clear,' he said. 'Go.'

Manuel was thinking about Bess. He knew she had faults from the time he met her. But the fact that she was so rich seemed to make her immune to the grabby-grabbies that now infected everyone else in the scene. All anyone cared about anymore was how to make money off newbies. Sell the vibe. Make better flyers than the competition. Have a better-stocked smart bar. Hell, there were already ten brands of 'herbal ecstasy' on the market, all practically identical except for the packaging. And every one of those smart drink powders came from the same damn company in Southern California. Club promoters just printed out their own labels on the Mac, slapped them on and then marketed the same old stuff as something unique.

Bess didn't care about making any money. She had her trust fund, and if she was looking for anything it was some traction. Friction. Some meaning in the from of conflict. That's why she took to Manuel, even though he was just a squatter in the Mission district. He was doing something real, and she could appreciate it.

Meanwhile, Manuel could appreciate her indifference to the demands of the social marketplace. Plus, she could cut the line at any club in town. The fact that she paid for his Sony Hi-8 camcorder, didn't hurt either.

Did he love her? Who knew? As long as he didn't think about it too much, everything was pretty cool. She had a great figure and a really pretty face. At twenty-six she was a few years older than him, but that was cool, too. It meant she didn't fall for all the posers and their wide-eyed schemes. Well, none of the posers except for Manuel, which was fine by him.

He never should have left for that camcorder conference in

Berlin. The video he shot of the homeless in the Panhandle clashing with city police put his work on the map, and an all-expenses-paid trip to Europe — his first time abroad — was too tempting to pass up. That's what gave it all away. It broke the sham. He was in it for the promise of stardom, and nothing he told her about the opportunity to network and exchange ideas with other camcorder artists sounded real. He could have gone — that wasn't the point. It was how much he panted over the whole thing.

Plus, she was seven weeks pregnant. At twenty-one the last thing he needed was a baby, but he wasn't going to be the one to make a life-or-death decision about a foetus. That was the girl's job.

So he left Bess and the whole dilemma behind to go gallivanting in Berlin with the coolest of the cool, squatting in buildings bombed-out since the Second World War. So what if he was being a bit irresponsible? He was the younger one, after all. The artist with no allegiance other than his work.

The fifteen-year-old girl he met at the pub in what used to be East Berlin and just had to sleep with didn't help matters, either. It wasn't for love, he insisted later, but for the pure aesthetic adventure. She was five feet eleven, blonde, blue-eyed, and just through puberty: the perfect Aryan princess. The kind of girl they put a bunch of make-up on and photograph for the cover of *Vogue*. It was a mythic experience no artist should pass up.

But he shouldn't have taken the E and then called Bess at four in the morning to confess the whole thing. By the time he got back to San Francisco two weeks later, Bess had aborted their baby and made plans to move to New York.

The two eventually made up leaving their respective indiscretions unchallenged. The only term of their reconciliation was that she would be more in charge of things than him from now on. She'd pay the rent in New York, and he'd stay out of trouble — not legal or artistic trouble, mind you — only the kind of trouble she didn't approve of.

*He flashed on that big house in Oakland where everyone would go for the whole* weekend and do LSD. These parties weren't raves. They were more like what he imagined went on at Timothy Leary's Millbrook estate back in the sixties. Each room of the four-storey Victorian was dedicated to a different theme. Some were just 'ambients', like a room with corduroy-upholstered walls, floor and pillows with some Brian Eno music playing in the background. You just went into a room and chose your trip.

Up in the attic, three pretty girls drew pictures with crayons. The whole space was converted into a mock playpen. As he looked about the room his perceptual apparatus transformed its subjects into three year olds at a nursery school. He wished he had his camera. He had always planned to go back and shoot one of those parties.

He remembered being higher in that house than he had ever been, and standing at the foot of the long staircase, holding on to a banister while everything spun around him. Then a huge dog, some kind of hound, began lumbering down the staircase towards him. The animal stepped on a pile of VHS cassettes that slid out from beneath his paw. Manuel watched as, seemingly in slow motion, the dog bounced down from step to step, flipping over himself several times, his paws flailing for a level surface, step after step, until he landed smack on his chin on to the hardwood floor at Manuel's feet. He and the dog regarded one another for a while. The dog was not embarrassed by his clumsiness. The dog was a Buddha, the boy decided. He was revealing to Manuel his own inner state. The pile of videotapes. It all made sense. If he had only brought his camera. He had been there. The right place and right time. But now he'd never be able to go back.

And that guy with the funny last name. Sekula, maybe. He had taken a whole page of blotter and then locked himself in the downstairs bathroom. Every once in a while someone would knock and ask if he was all right, but he just told them not to distract him. He was keeping the world in motion and the smallest miscalculation would throw the Earth out of orbit and the time-wave continuum. Irreparably. But by four in the morning one of the guys who lived at the house finally pried the door open with a crowbar, and everyone peered into the bathroom to find Sekula sitting on the toilet, naked, trying to jerk off. His eyes frozen wide with fright.

'Are you feeling any better?' she asked him. 'Did you drink some of the water?'

He saw her but could no longer remember her name. She was the one who cared about him. She really did; he could feel it. It wasn't just the E. Beneath the vicarious thrills she got out of living with a squat-loser, she felt for him in real life, too. He had underestimated what they shared. 'I don't feel anything at all,' he said. 'I don't want to feel anymore. I don't want any water.'

'You should drink, honey, really.'

'I'm going to die, babe. There's no more "shoulds".'

'You're going to be just fine,' she tried to sound like she knew this to be true.

'You're a great girl, whoever you are. Just don't listen to me any more.'

As she looked down at him he contemplated her breasts. The videos she let him make of her dancing around the apartment naked. The ones he wanted to get on public access. Then he felt it. A weird cold cloud down by his feet. It was death — competing with the rays of warmth from the E. It was harshing his mellow in a big way.

'Do you know how to use my camera?' he asked.

'No. You never let me touch it.'

'I should have.'

*There were all those real movies he had wanted to make, too. Feature films with commercial prospects. He could produce them low-budget with his friends. Why hadn't he ever gotten around to it? He finished the whole script for that one film, a horror movie called* Spike, *named after the weapon that the retarded hardware store box-boy, Mike, used to kill his victims.*

*In one scene, the hardware store boss's daughter goes on a date with a popular boy from school. Mike follows secretly and sits behind them at the movie theatre. Just as the audience screams in terror at an image on the screen, Mike plunges his spike through the back of his rival's seat, piercing him through.*

*Then later, when the girl has hidden away at grandma's house, Mike tracks her down and rings the bell. The tiny old woman uses a stool to climb up to the peephole in her door, when Mike plunges the spike through the glass lens, puncturing her eyeball and boring a hole through the back of her skull. Dying, the woman*

*kicks the chair out from beneath herself, and dangles against the door, suspended
by nothing but the spike through her head.*

*Bess called the script 'disgusting', and told him it had no social merit
whatsoever. He thought it was cool in its grossness. But he saw her point.
How would it have helped the vibe at all?*

*But now it was just another movie he would never make.*

For a moment Manuel thought that maybe she was right. He was
going to be fine after all. This was just some kind of bad E trip.
He had fooled himself into a panic. He hadn't felt that cold grip
in his abdomen for a long while now. Maybe death had passed
him by. Not likely. She wouldn't let go. She was just resting for
a minute. Or maybe he had gotten used to her. He could feel his
heart speeding up yet diminishing in strength at the same time. A
tiny, rapid flutter in his chest.

'Try to drink again,' Bess said. 'They're on their way.'

'Let me just rest a minute.'

*Back in high school he and his friend Henry had bought a sea-monkeys kit from
an ad in a comic book. They were both smart enough to know it was a scam,
but they wanted to see what sort of monkeys might come in the mail, anyway.
When they put the little sugar packets of freeze-dried monkeys into the water,
they hadn't expected anything at all to come to life. But sure enough, a few
days later there were these tiny translucent creatures swimming around in the
clear plastic box that was shipped along with them. The sides of the box had
little bumps that served as magnifying glasses, and through them you could see
the almost-microscopic brine shrimp a little better.*

*That next weekend the boys got proofed and rejected by the doorman at a big
rave club South of Market, so they decided to go home and throw their own party
with the sea monkeys. Henry put a speaker on either side of the sea monkeys'
plastic home and turned up the music. The water vibrated from the bass — all
they had back then was techno and maybe a little garage. These were the vintage
rave days when everything still felt virtuous and European. When it was just
kids throwing parties for other kids. By the time Manuel was old enough to go
clubbing for real, the whole scene was dying anyway.*

*The sea monkeys really got off on the music. Or maybe it was just the waves in their water that made them swim around that way. And what really was the difference? Waves are waves. Were the monkeys merely swaying passively in the currents, or were they flapping their little arms intentionally? Did it matter? Even if they expressed no conscious will, weren't the sea monkeys moving in a way prescribed by the aerodynamics of their little bodies, in a manner dictated by centuries of sea monkey evolution? Didn't that count as active participation?*

*After they took a couple of bong hits, Manuel and Henry felt certain that the monkeys were fully engaged in a total trance dance, and that the tiny ravers were ready for some drugs. The boys took a whole hit of E from their meagre stash and dedicated it to the monkey communion. Henry opened the capsule and let the powder fall into the water. They shook the whole tank to help it dissolve, then placed it back between the speakers. The monkeys contorted in renewed frenzy — motions that could have easily been captured with a macro-focus lens, but Manuel didn't own his camera yet, and now it would be too late to capture the image ever again.*

*Or the time about a month later when Henry fashioned a bong out of Lego and rubber tubing. They would fill the air chamber with pot smoke, then turn a tiny spigot releasing a balloonful of nitrous oxide that would push the smoke and then itself into the user's lungs. The look on Henry's face as he realized why Manuel wanted him to try it first. Because Manuel was chicken to play the guinea pig. Henry would always have to go first. And at that precise moment, as the nitrous filled Henry's lungs and Manuel waited watching with baited breath, they both knew who was the true adventurer among them.*

'Manuel?' she asked him. 'Can you hear me?'

'Hmm,' he mustered. The cold weight was bearing down on his chest now and he could barely speak. He thought he could see the lights from the ambulance near the entrance to the club.

'You fell asleep. I got scared.'

He just wanted some air, but he was trapped in a stone cold vacuum. Had they stopped the music? He couldn't hear anything at all. They kept turning the lights lower and lower. And the music. Where was the music? He wanted to tell her to pull the cement off his body, but he couldn't make the words come out. He squinted from the pain. Then the pressure just went away all by itself.

When he opened his eyes he saw the other kids in the club gathering around him. They were smiling, unafraid of his body on the ground. Some boys in fractal T-shirts knelt around him and slowly lifted him above their heads. The room was bathed in soft blue light as they carried him across the club.

'Sorry we didn't see what was happening to you, Manuel,' one of them said as they gently guided him to a table they had prepared a table with a pitcher of water and some glasses. The club promoters were all gone. It was just the kids from the scene, and they had all the water they wanted.

They sat him down. He wasn't dizzy anymore. He felt like he could finally take a drink. The snow had been the whole problem, he realized. That's what freaked him out. Why do coke when you've got E? Coke is the total ego drug. It covers everything up in bullshit, personal pride. Coke is so ... New York City.

'You had us worried there a minute,' Pete-E said to him, handing him the glass. 'But it looks like you're going to be all right now.'

He drank the water all down.

'Don't drink it too fast,' Pete-E advised, lovingly taking the glass from him and filling it up again.

The DJ put on some gentle ambient music and a few of the kids peeled off to dance a little. They weren't moving away from Manuel as they did before, though. They just let their bodies respond to the smooth sounds coming from the speakers. It was completely natural.

The scene hadn't really disappeared, it had just gone away for a while. He could feel the E taking hold again, letting him become one with the gently throbbing mass of people, yet somehow conscious, unique, and an observer at the same time. He thought of a documentary he had seen once, a long time ago, of Tibetan monks on a snowy mountaintop in China, chanting and swaying to the sounds of gongs and the little clicky-clacky things they swung back and forth in their hands. And then Manuel knew where he was going.

Bess had been looking down at Manuel's prone form for some time. He was just a child, she thought. She had gotten lost in his face — the way he habitually curled his bottom lip up in an angry pucker like a bulldog puppy, just to prove he disapproved, but now it looked like a snarl, frozen.

The ambulance drivers cleared a path through the oblivious club kids to find Manuel lying on the ground with Bess kneeling beside him. They lifted him on to a stretcher. One of the men checked for a pulse and then shook his head. Bess didn't let herself understand.

'Sir,' she asked one of the men in white. 'Excuse me, sir, is he going to be OK?' Both men just looked down and attended to their business, strapping the lifeless body to the clean linen.

She shouted after his corpse as they wheeled him out. 'Manuel! Please.'

The DJ had enough presence of mind to turn the music off while they wheeled the fallen raver out of the building. It only made the beating of Bess's own heart sound that much louder.

Dean Cavanagh

# 'MILE HIGH MELTDOWN'

It turns out Clement's American Express Gold Card was a snide. He'd had it mocked up in James Spader's name to impress his clients. He confessed that he couldn't believe that the off-licencee had really fallen for it. I could easily believe it as I'd done many a credit card fraud on shopkeepers in the past. Piece of piss!

I payed for mine and Clement's one-way ticket to Alicante and told him that he owed me one. He thanked me but added that it was only fair as the Scratch Card had been his originally. I had wondered how long it would be before he brought that up again. Affirmative action was needed. I took a hold of Clement's arm and led him into the airport bogs.

He looked a little dazed when I walled up against a crapper door. I gave him it straight. No fucking beating about the bush. I made it clear that if he had any designs on my dosh he'd better scrap them because there was no way I was splitting it. I reminded him that he had given me the Scratch Card. It was fair and square. He could come with me to Benidorm and I'd see he didn't starve, or he could stay at home and get banged up for torching that cabbie ... The choice was his. I was itching to CS gas him just to let him know who was running the show, but my conscience got the worse of me and I let him off ... He knew I wasn't fucking about so I didn't expect any more mithering from him.

We had a couple of hours to kill before take-off so we hit the bar. It was full of birds supping their brandies and Babychams

207

before they set off on their annual shagathon fortnights in the sun. We piled straight into a couple of lasses from Staines. I introduced Clement as James Spader and myself as his manager. I was beginning to wish that Clement was Tom fucking Cruise's double because neither one of the slappers had ever heard of James Spader. I bought us all a drink and came clean with them that we weren't really James Spader and his manager — but two male models on our way to Spain for a photo shoot. The cunts pissed themselves laughing. The gobbiest one of the two asked me if I was modelling socks, then started laying into Clement; she asked him if he was modelling chemotherapy machines, the saucy twat. Clement took it a bit too light-heartedly for my liking, so I pulled him up and told him that I'd have striped her with my cut-throat if she'd have implied that I was a Bengali-lancer victim. The daft cunt obviously hadn't caught my drift because he just kept on laughing with the slappers.

I'd had enough of their rib-tickling wit so I went and propped up the bar, and proceeded to get gloriously wasted on the finest gin they had to offer. There was a lad at the bar with a Man United shirt on so I had no choice but to take the piss out of him. He took it on the chin and once I'd run out of material we got chatting.

The gin was weaving it's maudlin effect on my noggin. The Man U fan had to fuck off and catch his flight to Ibiza. Clement looked like he'd clicked with one of the slappers from Staines so I took my cue to break up the party. I mean, I was funding the jolly, and there was no fucking way he was getting his end away before me.

I staggered over and started abusing the gobby bint. Clement told me to cool it. The gobby bint started up again with the slaver. I'd had enough so I offered her outside. I was deadly serious but the fucker just laughed at me. She started getting really saucy. It was probably a combination of too much gin, sleep depravation, low calorie intake and the fact that I hadn't had a decent brew for ages that caused me to pull out the CS gas and squirt it in her peepers; either that or the fact that I hadn't checked it out and I knew from experience that chemical weapons weren't always what they were cracked up to be.

She was squealing like a nervous pig. I was chuffed that I hadn't bought a dud. Clement was flapping again so I yanked him out of the bar and ran like fuck with him to our terminal. Luckily, he hadn't let on to them where we were bound, so the airport cops wouldn't have had a cat in hell's chance of collaring us. Good old Clement. He'd kept his fucking trap shut for once.

We got through the security check without any hassle, but I must admit that they were eyeballing Clement something rotten. He did look a right sight though; his bald bonce was bleeding again, it wasn't gushing but it was enough to cause concern among the blinding air hostess's, who asked if they could possibly dress his cuts as it might frighten the other passengers. They led Clement off to the front of the plane, lucky bastard!, and fixed his head up.

We buckled up and settled down in our seats. My mind was already on the duty-free drinks trolley. I noticed that some black geezers were fucking about with wires and shit down the front of the cabin. I hoped that we weren't going to be delayed. It would give those slappers from Staines the opportunity to finger us and I wasn't relishing the prospect of getting banged up for a CS gas attack.

The Captain's velvet tones came over the tannoy and everything was cool. 'I'd like to welcome you aboard the British Airways 10.20 flight to Alicante ... On behalf of myself and my co-pilot, and the cabin crew, I'd like to wish you a pleasant flight. We will be landing, weather allowing, at Alicante airport at approximately 1.30 a.m. Spanish time. I believe the temperature in Alicante is in the 80s ... We'll be cruising at around 30,000 feet. We'll fly across the Channel, down through France and over the Pyrenees ... We'll then be heading straight down through Spain and over to the Costa Blanca ... There will be a chance for you to purchase refreshments and duty-free gifts from our charming hostesses: Nicky, Jade, Belinda and Claire. If you require their assistance, feel free to signal them as they are here to see that you are well looked after ... May I remind you that there is No Smoking during take-off and landing ... Nicky will now take you through the evacuation drill ... Oh yes ... You may have noticed that we are fortunate to have on board with us the respected junglists Kenny Ken, Fabio and Mickey Finn, who are on course for Spain's first Jungle Festival ... As a special treat I've asked them if they wouldn't mind dropping a bit of science for us ... We've managed to rig up their equipment, but we're not too sure how the cabin's rather basic PA system will handle it ... So don't be too critical of the sound quality if it's your first taste of jungle ... For those of you who'd rather not open your mind to the wicked drum 'n' bass excursions of Kenny, Fabio and Mickey, may I suggest that you slip on the headphones that are provided ... Take it from me, though, you'll be missing out on some real ill shit if you do choose to tune into the muzak channel ... Once again, may I wish you a very pleasant trip and hope you all have a wonderful time in España. Toodle pip, over and out.'

There was much head scratching and conferring among the passengers. The air hostesses were in great demand, having to explain to the grave-dodgers just what the fuck the Captain was on about. The younger passengers were well chuffed that the in-flight entertainment would be provided by the junglist DJs. Jungle and hardcore has never really been my musical cup of tea, but I had to applaud the Captain for his initiative.

As soon as we'd hit cruise altitude the DJs kicked up. Kenny Ken took to the decks and started mashing up the beats. He was letting off some serious sub-bass breakbeat. Clement wasn't familiar with junglism so I gave him a brief explanation. He didn't seem any the wiser when I'd done my best to fill him in; I just told him to sit back and enjoy it.

The faces on the older passengers were a fucking picture. Most of them sat there with their gobs nearly down to their hairy tits. I knew it wouldn't be long before the moaning old fuckhooks got on their high horses. The lads and lasses down the front where really getting into it. This young black scally got up and started MCing along to Kenny Ken's Technics wizardry: 'Kenny Ken On The Ones An' Twos ... Ruff Junglist Massive Make Sum Noize ... Droppin' Dat Drum 'n' Bass Ting Kenny Ken! ... Big Hup! ... Rewind, Ye Wanta Rewind? ... Rewind Kenny Ken ...'

The air hostesses were getting pulled up left, right and centre. There were a hell of a lot of pissed-off punters aboard that plane. The hostesses did their best. They were very diplomatic with the gripers but told them that it was the Captain's idea to have them DJing and there was very little they could do about it. A couple of old lasses were carrying on like fuck. One of them fainted and her mate started bawling. A middle-aged geezer was demanding to see the Captain, a couple of young lasses told him to get the fuck off the plane if he didn't like it ... It was getting mighty leery, I was fucking loving it.

We hit a spot of turbulence and Kenny Ken was thrown off a little. The middle-aged geezer was going fucking bonkers: 'Now can we please have a little sanity ... This irresponsible tomfoolery is upsetting people. I'll see that your all fired do you hear? Fired! ... We demand to see the Captain!'

Kenny Ken got back into the groove and dropped a crucial slab of reggae-fused breakbeat. I wasn't too sure whether he was mixing Desmond Dekker's seminal 'Israelites' into the track but it definitely sounded like it, I recognized the: 'So Thata Every Mouth Can Be Fed' refrain.

A gang of disgruntled passengers pushed past the junglists and made their way towards the cockpit. The hostesses tried to stop them but it was totally futile ... A couple of minutes later they were legging it back to their seats with terrified looks on their ugly mugs. The fucking Captain only follows them out brandishing a piece in one hand and a crack-pipe in the other. He was obviously wired on blow and intent on letting the DJs do their thing. He looked like shit and double-scary to boot. There was no doubt in everyone's mind that he would let off a couple of caps in the next fucker who got up to complain about the in-flight entertainment.

Even Fabio and Mickey Finn looked a little worried. Kenny Ken was too busy cutting up the dubplates to notice. The Captain grabbed the mike off of the scally MC: 'Now listen to me you ungrateful bastards. I've gone to great trouble to lay this show on. The DJs agreed to do this out of the kindness of their hearts. I think the least you can do is give their music a chance. OK, I understand that many of you weren't expecting to hear some authentic jungle on this flight, but may I suggest that you take this opportunity to sample the delights of this electrifying new music ... Open your fucking minds for God sake!'

With that rather eloquent piece of advice, he handed the mike back over to the MC, got his lighter out and had a toot on his pipe ... Suffice to say that there were no more complaints. Kenny Ken went on to finish his set with a storming junglist version of Eek-A-Mouse's 'Ganja Smuggling', before throwing down the gauntlet to Fabio to keep it rocking 'Inna Ruff Tuff Drum'n'Bass Stylee'.

I earwigged in on one of the hostesses telling the mortified couple sat behind me that the Captain had been under a lot of pressure lately, and had recently been talking about handing in his pilot's licence and opening a junglist club in Stoke Newington.

Good luck to him I thought. I admire people who know exactly what they want to do with their lives. The only people worth bothering with in this life are those who simply do not give a flying fuck about convention. Risk-taking, creating and destroying, fucking people's minds up a little — that's where it's at. I felt secure in the knowledge that our Captain was a crack-tooting, piece-wielding junglist. You know where you stand with these kind of people.

Me and Clement got shit-faced and soaked up the vibes. I made a few attempts at trying to charm the hostesses into initiating us into their legendary 'Mile High Club' but they weren't wearing it. Shagging was probably low on their list of priorities with most of the punters spewing up, shaking like shite-ing dogs and scaring the fuck out of each other by administering the Last Rites to themselves.

The Captain made another appearance. I knew he wouldn't let me down. This time he had his shirt off, his cap on back to front and he was sweating like a Vietnamese pot-bellied pig. Fabio was spinning and the Captain was shocking out big-time to the grooves. He swung his piece above his head; whooping and hee-awing, and screaming every now and then like a deranged cowboy after a heavy session on the moonshine. You could smell the fear in the air. It's a pity that planes aren't fitted with equipment in case of fucking bowel evacuations — we could have done with it on that flight.

Mickey Finn was the last up on 'The Wheels Of Steel' (as some DJs have been known to call their Technics decks). The Captain was so far out of it by now that he was forcing the passengers who'd dared to complain, to toot on his crack at gunpoint. I'd never partaken of the much hyped crack but I thought better of cadging a go off of him in his state.

The junglists were looking extremely edgy by then. I think they felt a little embarrassed for supplying the soundtrack to the Captain's one-man cabaret, but they were in the same boat as everyone else; one false move and the mutinous Captain could have plunged us all into everlasting oblivion.

After he'd turned a couple of blue-rinsed old bints on to the joys of Chinese Rocks he grabbed a hold of the mike off of the seriously shitting-it scally MC again: 'Right Ladies and Gentlemen, we should be making our descent into Alicante in approximately (it took about fifteen minutes of squinting to work out the time on his watch) . . . Oh! is that the . . . Well we should be landing soon. Um . . . I trust you've enjoyed your flight with us . . . We hope to see you again on your return flight . . . I'd like you to give it up big style for um . . . Kenny Ken, Fabio and Mickey Finn. Come on, make some fucking noise Alicante posse!' The passengers didn't have much choice but to give the DJs a good ovation with the Captain waving his piece about: 'Oh yes! One last thing . . . Please extinguish your cigarettes during the landing.' With that polite request he fucked off back to his equally stressed-out co-pilot in the cockpit.

When we touched down we were greeted by the heavily

tooled-up Spanish militia. I was hoping that the Captain would put up a bit of a struggle, and maybe take out a couple of spics before turning the piece on himself and doing the honourable thing. It was not to be though. He let me down. He gave himself up like a nipper on their first shoplifting collar ... The fucker deserved the chair for shattering my illusion of him as man of greatness.

Two Fingers

'PUFF'

It has been hot in London — as hot as the northern tip of Africa — a capital city reduced to a quivering wreck by the heat. The working masses head into the city in their short-sleeved shirts and shorts, revelling in the sun, mercury rising to 36, then 37, then 38 degrees. St John Ambulance are put on special alert for dehydrated commuters. The London Underground put on extra tubes to stop overcrowding in rush hour and rent out air-conditioning units to blast freezer-cold air along the platform. People are dropping left, right and centre. Dehydration. Sun stroke.

Then the sun slips over the horizon. Night comes slowly, its darkness no longer menacing, but a respite from the sun's penetrating glare. There is a calmness about the night. Heat is trapped in the sharp confines of the city, but the night air is soft and gentle, warm breezes caressing the skin, promising sexual rewards.

Joe has been puffing all night long. In actual fact, he has been puffing all his life. Well, not all his life, but long enough. He stops for a moment to let Rush catch up. Rush is weaving along the road, yelling at the empty office blocks above them.

'Fuck all a'y'all. Yeah you heard me, fuck all a'y'all . . .' He spins in a tight circle, arms out, head back, moving faster and faster — inner ear deceived his legs miss his next step and he stumbles into the wall, which curves and stretches away.

He breathes the night air — so easy to breathe! He can feel his chest lightening with every intake, now that he is out of the thick muggy room. The hard smell of weed had engulfed the air as the five of them sat smoking joint after joint, their eyes red and unfocused as they tried to argue over something, before they collapsed into a gale of giggles. Over what he can't now remember. They'd been sent out for munchies, maybe. He wasn't quite sure now. He had money in his pocket and was walking like he knew where he was going, but? He pulls himself up off the floor, his spiderleg-thin frame unfolding. He stands wobbly, looking unsure and whispers conspiratorially, 'What we doing?' It comes out in a rush. His mouth is dry.

'Getting food,' says Joe.

'What we getting food for?'

'Got the munchies.'

'Have you?'

'Yeah.'

'So have I.'

They walk further. Joe has a cigarette in his mouth before he's thought about it, forefinger snapping across the flint wheel, flame illuminating his face. He bends slowly like a slow motion replay. 'Let's look at that one again Jimmy.' He bends even slower, the flame shaping the contours of his face as if, until that light had illuminated it, he hadn't had one, just a smooth mask, uncluttered with features or expression. He bends slowly, a Polaroid capturing the slightly cleft chin and sultry eyes: deep set and hooded, lids lowered. A pulse throbs across his forehead, as his lips gently hold on to the filter. His eyes close as the smoke slides into his chest. There are two ways to inhale the smoke: long and deep or shallow and short.

On average it takes seven and a half minutes to smoke a cigarette. 'Seven and a half minutes,' he thinks. Long enough, just long enough. He inhales again and follows Rush, the scarecrow from the *Wizard of Oz*. As he walks, he leans back and blows out smoke rings, his mouth an 'O' as they float into the dark sky. He watches them dispersing in front of the stars. The Big Dipper, Ursa Major, Ursa Minor, Sirius. That's about as many constellations as he knows, but he always feels a rush of excitement when he finds them in the night sky. The cigarette's a stub so he tosses it and walks faster to catch up Rush who is standing at the edge of the road watching the lights change.

'You know they put subliminal messages in traffic lights?' says Rush.

'Since when?'

'Since forever. They've been putting them in and making us walk when they want us to and stop when they want us to. It's Big Brother taking over. They know where you were born, where you live, what you like to eat, how much you make. They can find you anywhere.'

'Who can?'

'*They* can. They can do anything . . .'

'It's just a fucking traffic light. Come on.' Rush is limp as Joe pulls him across the street. The tar is slightly sticky as it cools after the sun's assault. Joe pulls his head back and howls, remembering the times he thought that he was actually a werewolf. Rush doesn't even shift focus.

Through the long avenues of buildings can be heard a dull throb. It's like a pixie at the edge of your vision. Moving your head to one side or the other just makes it disappear. Makes you wonder whether you had seen it at all. But when you forget to look, it slips back. An angel on your shoulder, whispering directions. Rush cocks his head to one side, standing stock still.

'You hear that?' he says.

'Yeah.'

'Jungle! Must be a club somewhere.' He looks at Joe, that sly smile slipping across his lips, curving his cheeks, bringing out his dimples. His mind is racing down fantasy lane. 'Let's go!' he says.

'Getting munchies.'

'There's munchies inside.'

'You got any weed on you?'

'Fuck!'

'Then you know I ain't going inside.'

'Come on.' Rush hates to beg. 'Be spontane, spontane . . .' His head tries to wrap itself around the word. 'Spontaneous. Munchies can wait.'

'I ain't going in there without no weed. Fuck, I hate standing around when everyone's burning and I ain't got none,' says Joe.

'We can score inside.'

'With what?'

Rush pulls out a wad of bills from his shorts.

'I said no.'

'Look either you come with me, or I'm'a fuck you up right now.'

'You gonna fuck me up? You gonna fuck me up?'

'Yeah I'm'a fuck you up, who da fuck do you think you are? I'll fuck you up, right fucking now. You pussy,' rants Rush.

'Who you calling pussy, you Goodfella's quoting cunt?'

'Fuck you, hoe.'

'Don't call me that.'

'What? Hoe!'

'Listen I ain't going into no club, with no weed.'

Rush's hand tightens on Joe's wrist and he pulls him along. Joe tries to haul against him, but Rush is stronger. He has always been stronger. They race down the street, breath loud in their ears, amazingly athletic for men who spend most of their time inhaling smoke. Air-Max clad feet slap the concrete as they race. They slide over the bonnet of a parked car, *Starsky and Hutch* style, the theme-tune in their ears. Time warps and they're striding the streets in kipper ties and bell bottoms with tight leather jackets and sparkling white teeth. They stop and do the Hustle Bump, the Mash Potato, the Fly. Then Soul Train is within them and they wiggle and grind, people all around them urging them on.

'You go girl!'

'Lay it out there daddy o!'

'That nigga be crazy!'

'Oooooooohhhhhhhhhhhwweeeeeeeeeee!'

Time unbends and they are still running through London, only slower. The smoke catching them up. The music is louder, like galloping horses, through a canyon. Rush stops and kneels on the floor, placing his head to the concrete. 'I always wanted to do this,' he laughs. He points. 'It's thataway.'

'You're fucking crazy.' It's all Joe can say through gritted teeth as he tries to breathe and stand at the same time. They walk now, catching their breath. The sweat cools their flesh and dampens their thin T-shirts. The music is closer now. He can distinguish between the treble and the bassline. Maybe even catch an echo of the words.

While Rush walks on, Joe pulls out a cigarette, lights it, and inhales. 'Inhale,' he thinks. 'Probably the most beautiful word in the world next to "moist".' To inhale. To be moist. The worlds wrap themselves around his head in a rain dance. Chanting rhythmically, he closes his eyes and pictures them. He mouths them as he walks, bringing the cigarette up to his lips to inhale again. He stretches them, until the words become pure sound. He invokes them as a magician would a secret incantation. He exhales the smoke one last time and opens his eyes.

It's called Incarnation. Well, that was what the bouncer said. But who believes bouncers? They'd just as soon kick shit out of you than let you in. Oversized bodies in undersized clothes. Joe hates bouncers — not as much as he hates being in a club with no weed, but almost. He hates them for the way that they look at you and check the girl you're with, because for that moment they have the power of life or death. They can let you in or not. When your life is built around the weekend, when going out is all, then the bouncer is God. But that doesn't mean you have to like them. Joe has never liked them.

Inside it's as hot as sin, even in the chill-out room. The coolness of the night replaced by a steaming, condensation-filled arena, writhing bodies packed into too little space. The lights alternately dazzle you then slip you back into darkness. Joe checks the money in his pocket as he weaves to the bar. A nudge of a shoulder here. A touch of the waist there. A little caress of a spine. Somehow, he squeezes through the small gaps between bodies. He doesn't bother to look back to see where Rush is. He knows that he will find him.

The air is heavy with the scent of sweat and too much perfume splashed on to try and cover the stink. But cutting through all of it is the smell of weed. Joe closes his eyes and lets the different aromas assail him. His nose can make out at least three different types of weed. It's agony to stand there and not know where to get some. He rests his head in his hands on the bar-top and feels the sticky alcohol, coating the hairs on his arms.

Looking up, he seeks the red glow, the sharp intake of breath. His eyes dart from group to group, noting which ones are burning or just smoking cigarettes. *There.* The light-skinned honey in the white Lycra, laughing in her friend's ear. Her friend is in the shadows, but her scarlet dress picks her out. She puffs deep, holding it tight. His eyes slip away from the puckering lips and hollowed cheeks as she inhales again, and scan the room.

A group of niggers lean against the wall, their heads bobbing, covered in hoods attached to puffer jackets. The glow from the spliff lights the lower portions of their faces as they pass two around at once, while another skins up in his palm. Meanwhile, a white boy and his girlfriend lean on the bar, way down the end, puffing slow, deep in conversation. Their pupils are dilated-like-fuck as the rush sets in from some tablet they've dropped and they're cutting the edge off it with the weed.

A beer sits in Joe's hand, the bottle cool on his palm. He drinks it quickly. He knows he can't stay here. Too much weed. His eyes search for Rush and see him leaning over a short girl: wide through the chest, hips and butt and encased in hot pants and a halter top. He grabs at a cigarette like a drowning man, pops it into his mouth, lights it, inhales and pushes his way out from the bar.

He walks through the long room, hearing the snatches of conversation, smelling the weed-laden air, tasting it on his tongue. He watches people mill and reel, groups within groups. Women standing together waiting for the approach. Males, eyes hungry, their tongues darting across suddenly dry lips and smiling. Hair flicked out of eyes. Knuckles rubbing softly along the curve of an arm. A palm gripping tight on a buttock. He sees all of this with feverish eyes, his pupils circled with red.

A side-room beckons with strobing lasers, burning flesh, loud techno beats and hands raised in genuflection. He slips in, drifting, trying to make out expressions through the dazzling light show. Pupils wide and dilated stare back, smiles splitting pink and straining faces, bodies drenched in waterfalls of liquid. He doesn't want to stay, but is somehow entranced. He stands and lets it all wash over him, but it's all artificial, false, chemically-induced. The sounds are hollow. He's unable to connect with it. The heavy THUD THUD THUD THUD THUD THUD THUD THUD makes him feel unclean. He turns to leave.

'Are you up yet?'

Joe looks at the bright face with eager swelling eyes. He moves away from the touch, as if burnt.

'It's great isn't it?' The face moves away, hands driving off into the crowd. Joe stands there for a fraction before moving slowly away.

Joe walks unsteadily into the dark interior of the main room. His eyes adjust to the lower illumination level as the volume overwhelms his ears. The MC is chatting hard on the mike, his patois balancing precariously over the beat. An aural acrobat slipping out of time then back. His voice, his ego, connects the DJ with the crowd, while the crowd communicate their enjoyment through him. He's the vital link between those that dance and listen and those that make and play the music.

Joe's eyes scan the people — the black people. He feels his

heart swell as the music does. The horns in the tune ring in his head. His head nods. He shifts deeper into the mass, feeling their energy and excitement envelop him. He's aware of the weed around him, but the music takes the edge off his longing.

High spiralling patterns of sound dance over a subliminal bassline. He finds himself in front of a gargantuan speaker (at least six feet high) and feels the bass thumping into his back like a fist. His own heartbeat becomes inseparable from the computer-created one behind him. He closes his eyes and lets the lights flash across his lowered lids, sparkles of orange, amber, red, yellow dance on his pupils like rain storms, tornadoes, cloud formations. He dips his shoulder, slides his feet, repeats to the other side. Got his groove on. The bassline holds everything together.

The MC sounds as if he's about to explode. *'Rewind my selector! rewind. Hey! hey! hey! Oh my good golly gosh!! Oh Gosh! Man know we run tings, set speed.'*

An intro rolls followed hard by that driving bassline. Hands go up, palms flat, whistles crack the air, then it's in with the foghorns.

*'Where's the Lighter Massive!'*

A split-second later the floors is a weaving mass of flames, which flicker out, then snap back into life, as thumbs spin the wheel. Joe watches as he moves with the beat and feels a collective bonding, 'togetherness', even though people bounce against him, nudge him in the back, lean on him as they fight their way past.

In front of the DJ, malevolence pours off a circle of rude bwoys. They're wanting to do some damage, daring someone they don't know to step to them. The bass is taking them back to tribal times, savage times. Race memory kick-started and slipped into overdrive.

He sees the girls: tall, thin, short, fat. They're dancing, butts out, hips moving in circular motion, unchained and free in here as they can never be outside. You can look, but don't touch. The fierceness of their glares, matched by the fierceness of their joy. White teeth bared.

He sees a man, naked, body shiny, beckoning him over. The speaker underneath his feet is solid, fixed, but it trembles under the power of his pounding dancing. Joe blinks, looks back and the man is still there. Still naked, still beckoning. He looks away and lowers his head, closes his eyes and listens to the music.

He listens to the way the bass rolls — regular, rhythmic. He feels the force of it, and sinks deeper in. Above it, the hard staccato percussion constantly changes tack, weaving structures in the mind. The whole becomes more than the sum of the parts. The intro is a taster to get you excited. Hard on its heels comes the drum blueprint, wickedly intense and forceful. Bringing it all together is that bassline — whether long and flowing, or chopped and brutal.

Throbbing drums hammer out the rhythm. Bare feet, hard and callused, stamp. The bodies reel and spiral, dark of complexion, skin leathery, toughened from aeons of exposure to the sun. Throats are raw from screaming exultation. All knowledge is forgotten, leaving only sensation. An awareness of the heaving mass surrounding you. The soul is adrift in race memory.

There ahead of Joe *he* stands. His body, shiny with sweat. Chest bobbing with the influx of oxygen. His hand out-stretched towards Joe. Fingers long and flexible, joints able to move in both directions. The man is smiling. His hand unclenches and within the palm is something long and white. Joe's mouth is already dry at the prospect. Is he dreaming? Is it a mirage? He snatches it from the hand and in a shimmer the man and his smile vanishes, leaving a spliff left in Joe's hand. He checks to see if it's real. Sniffs. Powerful scent, intoxicating. He feels his lids lowering, just from the scent. *Just from the scent.* There's an expansion at the top of his skull and a rapid coldness descending through his head, neck and shoulders. The strength of it takes him off his feet. He's overwhelmed by a closeness in his throat and a desire to get out into the cool air.

Joe stands outside the room, blinking the sweat from his eyes, looking for Rush. Moving away from the wall, he has to force his feet to step one in front of the other. The music is no longer taking him to other planes of existence. His expanded mind slowly shrinking. He's frustrated that he can't remember what happened. The long spliff in his hand is the only relic.

Suddenly, Rush is there, up in his face like a stiff one.

'Where you been?' he asks.

'Where *you* been?' says Joe.

'Talking to Maxine. You remember her, went to school with Michael?'

'She's grown since then.'

'You telling me.'

'We got to go'

'It's just starting. It's only . . .'

He looks at his wrist and finding there's no watch there he shrugs. Oh well.

'They'll be waiting for us.'

'Fuck 'em, enjoy yourself.'

'You score yet?'

'Haven't been looking, I been getting high on the music.'

Joe's hand unclenches and he holds the mystery spliff up for Rush's inspection.

'Since when you learn to roll your own?' Rush laughs.

The thought crosses Joe's mind: to tell or not to tell? It would be so much easier not to tell and already what he could have told has slipped away, a foggy memory like childhood.

'So you gonna spark it or what?'

Joe's hand closes on it. He reaches into his pocket for a cigarette, flips it on to his lip and lights that instead.

'Naw, I'm'a wait a while.'

Alex Garland

# 'BLINK AND YOU MISS IT'

About twenty seconds ago, I blinked, saw a window and outside it, my next-door neighbour's kid, Sammy. Sammy recently turned five. He was standing on the far side of the road and wanted to cross over. I knew there were no cars around without having to look, because even through the glass I'd have heard them. I grew up on this street so I'm finely tuned in to that sort of thing. But Sammy, who's only been living here for the five years, was less sure. He solemnly checked in both directions, twice each way, and only then set off for the other side. He used measured strides because he's so little and liable to lose balance, but to me, he looked like a miniature explosives expert, walking from the lit fuse instead of running.

Five years old. Packed with common sense. Say, eight or nine years left to go before the common sense starts to desert him. Twelve years to go until he's in an abject free-fall, if he's anything like me. And he could well be. At five, I was certainly the kind of kid who looked both ways before crossing the road.

This is what happened.

It was a bright sunny day. No surprise. It was a beach, so if there hadn't been sun we wouldn't have been there. So, sunny day, on a beach, and I was sitting in a circle of people. In the centre sat the beach guru.

The beach guru.

Pushing forty, possibly past it, though all you could do was guess because being stuck in a young person's world, he was pretty coy about divulging his age. Encyclopaedic knowledge of substances. Receding hairline, number-one all over to hide it, nineties version of the comb-over. A keen eye for any of us he suspected he could get into bed. Or, being a beach guru, sheet, laid out on the sand.

Being seventeen and in a free-fall, I didn't see this guy for what he was. So I listened to his stupid travel stories. I didn't cringe when he said, 'Yeah, respect,' or, 'Chill.' I didn't ever kick his head in when he instructed me to not say a word and just check out the sunset man. Let it wash over you. Feel its ancient touch.

Bright and sunny though the day was, we were mainly concentrating on the night. A full moon was coming in forty-eight hours, which spelt big party, and party-goers coming from miles around to partake. Miles as in thousands. Point of departure, Goa or Koh Phangan.

Lots of organizing to do, because you didn't want to let these people down. Centre of the organization centre of the circle, the beach guru. He liked to get involved. He needed these young faces looking up at him, or down to where he reclined on the sand, and asking — Where we going to get this? How are we going to do that? The sound system is fuzzy. What are we going to do?

Nine times out of ten, all we had to do was chill. *Chill guys.* The generator will be working. I've got Phuoy on the case. The weather will hold. I burnt an offering this morning to the monsoon God. One time out of ten, a gleam would come into his opiate eyes, he'd click his fingers like Tony Bennett, and he'd say, 'OK, lets sort this sucker out.'

Substances, a shortage of. The bust had come a week ago, a horde of green uniformed men, ripping through the beach huts and upending backpacks. No one had been nabbed, because we'd known it had been coming. The owner of the Zoom-Zoom café had tipped us off half an hour before. Half an hour, half of which was spent spreading the news. In the remaining fifteen minutes a collective panic set in, oddly euphoric, in which people ran around, throwing their various stashes into the sea or into the bushes, or digging holes.

In the aftermath, the scale of our problem became clear. Stash in the bushes had been found. Stash in the sea had been ruined. Stash in holes was safe and sound, except most people couldn't remember where they'd dug the holes. Sand is sand, soaked by dew, dried by sun, blown around, patterned with changing foot prints. Doesn't offer much in the way of reliable orientation.

For the next few days, the beach looked like it had been hit by a plague of moles. And all the hippy sharing ideals went straight out the window. Those that had, hoarded, and those that had not, hung around like jackals hoping for scraps of the lion's kill. Worse, we couldn't just head off and score. As the green uniforms hadn't found anyone in possession and had made no arrests, they were pissed off. That meant the local dealers were keeping a low profile and magic-mushroom omelettes were off the café menus. Even the island's chemist was jumpy and turning us away. You had to hack up blood before he'd give you any cough medicine, or be comatose before he'd give you any speed. The only thing he'd give us was rohypmol. Not such a bad thing, unless rohypmol was all there was.

This, then, was the *sucker to be sorted*, and we were all extremely worried about it. Our full-moon party was going to be BYOE.

'I,' the beach guru said, 'have a contact.'

He let that hang in the air a little while before picking up the thread.

'Don't use him often. Uh-uh. Only use him when I have to. Uh-huh.'

He bent forward in his squatting position and rubbed a hand over his face and the sizeable bald part of his scalp.

'Gonna use him now. This contact, gonna use him now ... with ... someone here. Gotta take someone with me ... Don't know who it's gonna be ... Eeny meeny ...'

231

We all looked at each other. He did this pretty often. A sort of power thing, which we lapped up. Which of us was going to be the lucky boy or girl to help the guru achieve his aim.

'Who's it gonna be? Gonna be ... Gonna take ...'

Eney meeny miny mo, catch a fella by his toe, if he hollers let him go, eeny meeny miny ...

I was mo.

'Yeah,' the beach guru murmured. 'It'll be you. You'll be mo.'

'OK,' I said readily. 'What do I have to do?'

He didn't answer my question. His expression had suddenly changed, twisted into something like distaste or anger.

Shit, I thought. What did I do wrong?

'Eugh,' said the beach guru. 'I just swallowed a bug.'

The contact was in town, an hour or so truck ride from our beach. I had to pay our hitch-hiking fare, naturally, as the guru didn't believe in cash unless it was someone else's. As we bumped down the road, getting thrown about in the pickup, I was told a bit more about what was in store.

'Every time there's a major bust, I use our contact. You want to know why?'

I nodded.

'Because after a bust, he's the only guy who's guaranteed to be holding the goods.'

I considered this for a few moments.

'He's police?'

'Chief of.'

I raised my eyebrows. 'We're scoring off the chief of police?'

'Uh-huh.'

I didn't know what to say. Of course, I know what I should have said now. I should have tapped on the driver's window and told him to pull over. Got off the truck and walked home. And the idea did cross my mind, but at the same time I was imagining the reactions of everyone when I got back. So I kept my mouth shut. Just looked at the road-side scenery flash past us, palm trees and nipa huts.

At town, we jumped out and started making our way through the side-streets. This, at least, was good. I'd had an idea we'd be marching straight into the police station, which, regardless of the guru's sage credentials, would have been beyond the limit of my trust

I was being led, I quickly realized, to the docks area. Not where the ferry came in, but where the fishing boats dropped their catch. And that struck me as another good thing, because, naïve and innocent as I was, it seemed to me that the docks was the sort of place where this kind of unusual deal happened. Lots of dirt and confusion, people shouting rushing around with crates, easier to pass unnoticed.

So all in all, by the time we reached the waterfront, I was relatively relaxed. Guard down, only swearing from the sun, no alarm bells ringing.

'Money,' said the guru.

'Got it here.'

'Let's have it.'

I handed the banknotes over, thinking: the last good sign. Even if we get busted, he'll be the one that gets screwed worst.

The guru folded the money into a wad and tucked it into the waist-band of his shorts.

'OK. Now, see that guy over there?' He pointed to a man reading a newspaper, sitting on the far side of the road on which we stood.

'Yep. See him.'

'He's the guy you want to talk to.'

'Oh ...' I frowned. 'Aren't you going to be doing the talking? I mean, seeing as you already know him.'

'No. You'll be doing the talking.'

'Really?'

'Uh-huh.'

'Well ... what do I say?'

I got a pat on the back. 'That's a good question. You walk up to him and say, "I want to buy some drugs". That's all.'

'Drugs?'

'Yeah. Don't be specific.'

I hesitated. I couldn't imagine why it was wrong to be specific, but took the instruction on good faith.

'Drugs. OK. What then?'

'Nothing. Just like the rising and falling of the tides, the turning of the world, everything will take care of itself.'

'. . . Right.'

We set off across the road.

I didn't look left and right.

If I had looked left and right, I'd probably have spotted the green uniforms. Flickering between the bare-backed dockers and their crates of shining mackerel. I would have *had* to have spotted them. There were so many. They arrived so fast.

'I want to buy some drugs,' I said, and the next thing I knew I was in a half-nelson, lying face down in a seafront puddle of salt water and fish blood.

A memory as bad as the taste it left in my mouth. Salt water and fish blood, you have to experience it to know how bad it really is. And incredibly, the next memory is even worse.

Dragged away, trying to scream and struggle, held in a choke-hold that was close to stopping me from breathing. The police chief and the guru, in amiable conversation. The wad of banknotes in the guru's hand. Saw it in the whirling figures, pulled this way and that, spinning round. The image freezing as I saw the police chief slip the banknotes into his back pocket.

Everyone happy, you'd have to say, apart from me.

Police happy because they got their arrest.

Dealers happy because the police were off their case.

Travellers happy because they got their full moon party.

Beach guru happy because he's a conscienceless cunt.

Sammy, Sammy. He was two when I left England. And now he's five, and on the other side of the world.

But still, I keep a close eye on him. I watch his every move. I see him rise in the morning and go to bed at night. I see his limbs lengthen, and his reading and writing improve. He'll be starting at primary school pretty soon, where I'm sure he'll do very well.

Last Christmas, I sent him a card.

Friendly enough, normal old Christmas card. Tree on it and snow.

Hi, how you doing, hope you got good presents. Cars, space-ships, whatever. And listen, do you look both ways before you cross the road? How's your common sense? Watch out for that, Sam! It'll start to go when you hit thirteen! By seventeen you'll be in a free-fall!

Love, etc.

You wouldn't believe the hassle it was getting a Christmas card in a Buddhist country, let alone doing it from behind bars. And all the hassle for nothing. Frankly, I don't think the card ever reached him. Though it reached his parents, I can be sure of that. The card was returned to me with a note attached from his father. Polite enough, but pretty firm.

Please don't write anymore. We can bring him up fine on our own.

(Which means I guess they got the other letters too.)

Matthew De Abaitua

'INBETWEEN'

'Don't stop,' says Si.

I am slumped against flakes of leather and foam, kissing the dry sponge innards of the seat. We all fall from left to right with the swinging motion of Job's driving, the centrifuge of the turn splays my limbs, it plants a foot beneath my belly and rolls me over — sometimes to fall where I can see the revolution of a neon sign or the wind pushing a trolley across a car park, sometimes to press my face down into the seat where I inhale its hide.

And Job says, 'There is another junction down here somewhere, another road — takes us out the city, I think — you know it's like what I said to El with all her blah blah blah, I said to her I don't need anymore choices. I just want sex but you keep givin' me options, knowarramean?' Job laughs.

The car accelerates towards the point where the road bisects. Next to me, Si finally manages to open his softpack of Marlboro Lights. I ask for one, and he decides to light two simultaneously. Staring at the point between the two cigarettes splayed in Si's mouth — while still deranged from my uncontrollable consumption of El's cunt in the club car park — I see my mouth squat upon and between her thin, deeply white legs. A zippo flame wavers. The car turns suddenly and I find myself gagging against the closed window.

'You know I think they've fucked up all the signs,' says Job. A sudden jolt to the left and the car bounces over a mini-roundabout.

I pull another impassive face out of my bag and slap it over my fear. When Job is driving, I always like to have some impassive faces to hand. He has never been one for patience, for taking his time. Job began the drive at a hundred miles an hour, and although I tried to feed him spliffs to slow him down — each joint normally shaves ten mph off his pace — this time he wouldn't let up. Wouldn't stop.

'I mean how many different ways can there be — another fuckin' turn off — Si, grab Nelson, we're going round, if he's sick he's out — another road, what do all these signs say? Si can you read them, tell me what they say. Si? Si? Nelson?'

We wheel around a superstore car park, and let the security cameras get a good view of us. Like, cover all our angles. A second trolley is released from the pack, then a third with its chain rattling after it like a tail, then a fourth. 'Strong wind,' I say, against the glass. Si points to the escaping trolleys — I see some kids helping them on their way with malignant concentration — and whispers, 'Slowly all the cages are released.' He leans away from me, smug in his observation. I can't open the window.

The gearstick yields to Job's advances. We slosh aimlessly around in the back of the car. Job drives and narrates, narrates when he stops, drives when he stops narrating, drives as if he is narrating. Push-start-go. His narrative is structured along a series of risks. He seems to have been accelerating for the last twenty minutes, only squeezing the brake when he wants to swerve ostentatiously around parked cars, or these shopping trolleys clunking out into the road. The car leaps down an alleyway and inbetween a pair of bollards. We bounce out into another street and get a cuff on the wing mirror for our impudence. Job changes gear like a singer changes an octave.

I take a cigarette from Si's mouth, and it is like we are dividing El between us. A leg each, as it were. There is a fault in his vision, a lack of focus to him. The way his eyes fail to settle remind me of a baby lolling stupidly in its pram, unable to see beyond its own hands. Of course, since I was born my eyesight has never stopped improving. If I could just get the window open, I could see for miles.

Job continues an observation, one I missed the beginning (and probably the middle) of: 'Of course it's the lights. When I lived in the countryside it took me a while to get used to . . . the streetlights come on about four and then that's it, you get this kinda, well sort of amber, sick amber, sick decaying amber light over everything, like some pallor of the skin. Seewarramean? Pallor as in disease, I think I'm making a point here lads, as in interesting, as in definitely not your average blah blah blah. See, in the countryside it gets dark slowly, and you get to see every gradient of the light but here you get the same quality of light from about four o'clock on. Which fucks with your mind.'

I manage to claw my way up the back of Job's seat. Si is sitting to my left. On his face is an expression of agonized surpise. I wrap my hand about his, and steady the flame beneath the tip of his cigarette. You have her next, pass the light from one to another, it doesn't matter to me anymore.

With one inhalation, Si switches moods, pulls his agony and all his twists back inside. Deliberately, with one methodical bifurcating stroke of thumb and forefinger, Si sharpens his eyebrows. 'I know what Job means about the light. I was thinking about the birds. They have these floodlights down the docks which are so bright the birds sing day and night before they lose it in some fucked-up bird neuroses. It's the lack of twilight, see? Confuses day and night for them.'

The crucifix dances beneath Job's earlobe to the rhythm of the potholes and gutters and tarmac flaws. Hours are lost as the route repeats itself. It is one long sentence of roads, and I am hard pressed to remember where we are going, or even where we began.

Job says, 'Where are we going? Anyone tell me? Like if neither of you can read the signs maybe you expect me to navigate by the stars. We could be three not so wise men, if you seewarramean Nelson?'

'Yeh, but you try skinning up with a block of frankincense,'

241

I say, trying to catch the hook of Job's carelessly cast allusion. Once he gets on one of his meaning trips, he has to be placated. Nothing annoys him more than people listening to the how and the why of his conversation rather than the what. When he was sectioned, they ignored his prophecies, and such indifference only drove him to further distraction. They couldn't stop his ranting, only turn the volume down.

'Don't stop.' Si unfurls his fist, lets his hand open into a half-claw, and he doesn't even notice it when the cigarette falls from his fingers.

'What did he say?'

'He said don't stop. I think stopping gives him the heeb.' I retrieve the fag, and Si snatches it from me, as if offended.

'The what?'

'The heeb, the vibe. The heeb and the vibe. The fear, you know.'

'Say to Si that I can understand how he feels and say I can understand why he thinks that but he has to understand what I am thinking.'

'Don't stop.'

'He says don't stop.'

'Do you remember El's directions? I said, I said write them down and I said to you Nelson write them down, so where are they or am I to have nothing as a guide for this entire trip. I should lay a down-payment on some nothing, maybe I'll finish the hire-purchase payments and they'll let me own it outright, a stack of nothing, a pile of state-of-the-art, digitized bollocks with wanking black matt finish nothings in a red carrying case, do you think that's what I should use to find my way with, or do you think we should fall back on that old cliché, the map?'

'I drew the map. I put it in my coat pocket.' I suggested to El that we go out into the car park, where the light was better, so she could sketch out our destination for us. She said 'Have you got anything to lean on?' I knelt down and offered my shaven head.

'Nelson, always the gentleman,' she said, before pressing the paper down against my pate.

'And, fucking AND?'

'And I left my coat ... behind. We should go and look for my coat. I left it in the club. I didn't want it to get messed up. Cost me fucking hundreds that leather. Maybe I should go back and get it.' El grabbed the collar of the coat to haul my head further into her, tightening the seams around my throat. She was heavy on my shoulders, and it was difficult to get any purchase with her sliding over the leather like that. I slipped the coat off, and redoubled my efforts.

'Oh yeah that's smart Nelson. Let's go back to the fucking club, let's just walk back in and say, sorry, we forgot our coats, we'll just pick them up and be on our way. Don't mind us. Besides do you know the way to the club? I mean do you have a fucking map to the club?'

'No, I don't.' Job is prone to blackouts. I realize that while he is gripped by the emotion of flight, he cannot recall the beginning of that emotion. He has woken up in the middle of it. I guess even if he had been standing over me while I gave his girlfriend head, holding my coat, he wouldn't remember it. Just wake up in the middle of his jealousy. These days, he forgets reasons.

'Don't stop.'

'Will you tell him we're not fucking stopping. Like I have a whole head full of intentions, and stopping is not one of them.'

I lean close to Si, amazed by the length of his face. A face built to mourn. A face only capable of the long emotions.

'How are you doing, Si?'

'Is he stopping?'

'No, he's going on.'

'Good. I'm fine. You?'

'Dizzy,' I say and hook a horseshoe of arms around my knees. 'His driving freaks me out a little.'

'It means a lot to him, to drive like this.'

'What are you two saying?'

'You see, Job likes arguing with the road.'

'I think I have had my fill of arguments.'

'You want to stop?'

'Just to piss, just to get some fresh air.' To escape before Job's forgetting ceases.

'Come here.'

Job turns on the indicators, turns the headlights off, turns them back on again — all before he eventually finds the switch for the windscreen wipers. Raindrops are methodically swept from the windscreen, the car mops the sweat from its brow. As Job withdraws his hand from the switch, I see it shaking. The car turns again and my head judders over the cattle-grid of Si's thighs. I gnaw the inside of my cheek for protection, using the incisiors to prick a length of skin, and then the molars to chew it.

Once, when in much the same state of mind as this, I needed to be convinced of my invunerability, so I took a knitting needle and ran it across my palate. Si stopped me before it reached my throat. In the club, mortality was barely a concern, especially as it impeded pleasure. But come-downs always leave you susceptible to regret. To pause here, on Si's lap, is some comfort. For me, at least.

Job says, 'Actually I think we've been here before.'

'When?' I say, lifting my head to ride the carousel of kebab shops, Turkish drinking dens, curry houses and all-night garages. It all looks the same. Any attempts to navigate are frustrated and confused by the Escher procession of brands up and down the streets.

'We should just go left, always left. It's the way of the criminal.'

'Are those like official directions, Si? Because although I may look like the man with the plan, I am getting little messages off the ether that tell me we're not actually getting anywhere. Certainly not to El's anyway.'

I panic slightly, again: 'We're not going to El's. We're going to Danny's to clean up.'

'Since when are we going to Danny's?' asks Job, indifferent to the blood in his hair and the come on his T-shirt.

'I thought we were going out to the moors.' Wistful, Si hankers over pastoral idylls, he has a passion for grass and open spaces that he never manages to fulfil. 'I thought we were getting away from this. Straight out of the city like an arrow.'

Already Job's forehead is scabbing over, the wound entwines his hair in its repairs, matting it over the scratches.

'I mean, don't stop.'

'But we're not going anywhere, I mean do you want — like are you asking that I drive around all night until eventually the car falls apart, or we run out of petrol or Nelson throws up, with the same old techno going around and around, and the same roads . . . Christ will one of you read the fucking signs out to me, you know how they get all blurred when I'm driving. Was that a one-way? I missed it. Anyway are we going round the roundabout until one of you decides to help me out, or are you going to sit there and do your usual fuck all. S'like I was saying to El, your conversation is like techno, one repetition after another with speed the only variation and I can never figure out the point of it. I mean are you two listening? 'Cos I tell you this is none of your usual tittle-tattle, your normal blah blah blah. This is no small talk.'

'It's small talk every fucking day of your life.'

I see the roundabout approach and wait for Job to ease into lane. He races straight through, skidding hard into the turn-off. He accelerates again on the cusp of the bend. Just when I thought the car couldn't go any faster.

Job is half my size, his arms remind me of the bones lacing a bird's wing. He ducks down to mess with the stereo, he uses his knees to steer. Once the tape is clicked off, we listen to the whine of the suspension, the ache of the engine. He seems to forget about his hand, he leaves it hanging between the stereo and the wheel. He is suffering from severe shakes. I haven't seen shakes like that since Stanley The Accountant and his notorious DT's. When I worked behind the bar, Stanley used to make a great play of putting the exact money for his large Scotch into my hand. This precison was a leftover from his financial career. But he had the DT's so bad that he used to drill the money into my palm. I want to tell this story to them, but I can't get it together.

Another wedge of headlights scan the interior of the car, our privacy peels away. In the flush of light, I see that Job is not sweating, he is leaking. I want to wipe him clean, give something back for all I am about to take.

'Job?' His name is all I can muster.

'If you say a fucking word about stopping, Nelson, I swear I'll put us through a shop window.' The come is dry on his T-shirt. He takes his eye off the road to pick at it, initially bemused. I can feel the memory of what he did swimming towards full recollection, both in his mind and in my own. I don't want that memory to hit him as we are driving a hundred miles an hour across the city.

'Couldn't we at least swap over. You could take a rest.'

'No. None of you are in a state to drive, if we are going to get anywhere then we are going to do it my way, with my system. Like Blake, you know Blake, "I must create a system or be enslaved by another man's" and like the highway code and the traffic lights and all these rules painted out on the road is their fucking system, so I have my own system of driving and believe me I'd take a serious fall before I'd bow down to — I mean it's all pernicious, this highway code is subliminal conformity. The only path for us is to develop an anti-system. Read the laws of chaos, Nelson, and then you can come back to me and tell me you don't like the way I drive.'

I fall back into the seat and gnaw at my cuticles as nightclub crowds are divulged, smears of crowd scenes — an after-image of a taxi driver's waving fist and the doppling echo of outraged horns. Si has wound down the window, his head is out of the car.

'You getting some air?' I ask, realizing that it is my turn to show some concern.

I don't catch his reply. It is spoken out into the wind. Then I realize that it wasn t a reply, but a scrap of dia-logue. Si is talking to someone out of the window. Dozens of worst-case scenarios occur to me. I must have blacked out and missed us being pulled over. Si leans further out of the window, nods in agreement to some remark. They seem to be questioning him.

'When did we stop?' I ask, bemused.

This remark causes panic in the front seat, Job starts banging around like a bird in a bag. He puts his fist into the speedometer. The glass doesn't make a sound, it caves in without complaint. Si is nodding at his interlocuter. He slides his hand out of the window to aid his explanation.

'Did I black out? When did we stop?'

With exaggerated caution, Si lowers himself back into the car, turns the drag of his face to me and says 'Don't stop, not yet'. Then, after apologizing to whatever is outside the window, he resumes his conversation. Still I can't hear a word he is saying.

Job becomes this great mud-slide of vitriol and unanswerable questions.

'Where are your minds? The fucking road is moving and what kind of game is this? Telling me I've stopped when ... Jesus, I'm doubting my own eyes, I mean look at the street. Isn't it moving? Are we getting anywhere? Does this look like some fucking stationary position to you two? I mean who here can tell me what speed we're going, the speedometer is like just numbers. I cut my hand, I cut my head. I got to drive with one hand because these numbers don't match the street, and then you go telling me we were stopped an' all and, fuck, I nearly got out the car. Christ, you fucked with my mind. If you want to fucking stay alive here then we'll avoid anymore little trips like that one. Come here, Nelson.'

It is cold, the gale raging around Si's end of the seat chills my thick nauseous sweats. Leaning forward places an unbearable pressure on my stomach. I hang over Job's shoulder, the good angel that I am.

'Does it look like we've stopped?' says Job, his question is uncertain.

'No, the houses are definitely moving. Where are we? It looks residential.'

'Well fuck off then,' screams Si at the wind. He winds up the window and sits very quietly in the corner. There is this pall of self-consciousness to him, like he has just conducted a very public lover's quarrel. Restraint has been in short supply all evening, consciousness has been dashed on the rocks leaving, in its place, a set of incomprehensible impulses and hallucinations. Si is stricken, clearly bemused by whatever happened to him when he stuck his head out of the window. There is no reason behind any of our actions, and tonight we only become aware of them once they have begun.

I have not forgotten watching one of the wasted dance against the wall of the club, each gesticulation against the beat drew blood on his kunckles, his forehead, and not comprehending the pain, the wasted began smashing himself systematically against the brick. I paused long enough to conceive an image of the wasted's self-destruction 'Oh yeah, that's like when a dog bites its own wound, as if the pain was an enemy it could kill,' and then I left him to his mania. I have not forgotten my head lolling against the white tiles above the urinal, when their bitter cold lay across my brow. I have not forgotten realizing — as my forehead drifted back from the tiles — that the wasted dancer smashing himself up against the wall was Job.

At first I thought one of them had punched me; it was only when I was hit a second time that I realized the blows were coming from beneath us. There was something under the car, obviously very large and keen to break in. There was a general loss of self in the car — plenty of screaming and questions that rode in on a great wave of panic. I remember the car riding up on to the pavement. I remember hitting a dog and laughing at the sheer incongruity of it spinning off over a lawn.

I look back down the street — dreading to see if we had shook off whatever was clinging to the underside of the car.

'Speedbumps, it was only speedbumps.' I am pleased to throw this particular solution out to the group.

'What the fuck else did you think it was? Course it was fucking speedbumps. God help us if we didn't have you around to point out the fucking blatant every three and a half minutes.'

'We hit a dog too,' I say, somewhat sullen at Job's rebuke.

'Really? I thought it was just flying by.'

'We hit a dog?'

Si isn't very phlegmatic about the dog. I talk him down by getting him to look into my eyes. It isn't very difficult to focus on his pupils, they are a wide target.

'We should stop,' says Si. 'We should stop and see if its still alive.'

Neither Job nor I bother to answer. I hand out some fags, they reward me by staying silent while they inhale. The road signs are getting bigger, and bluer.

'We must be near a motorway. We should get on to a motorway.' The further we can get from El, the better. I don't want her and Job to fight and then have to face up to her needing my sympathy, my consolation.

'How far are we from the ring road?'

'Nelson?'

I am back in my seat, biting back my body's latest attempt to purge itself. I tell them to give me a minute.

'We're not going near the motorway — we got to get off the road somewhere. As she said to me, El said to me, Job you got to realize that you're getting filmed on all the fast roads, and you got to stay away from the shopping centres because that's we're they'll be too and you got to avoid your classic honey traps so don't go downwind of a pub, and your motorways — see your motorways are your zenith of observation. Mind you, El's all fucked up over discretion. I think discretion is easy, you just got to be overt about it. Like if you are hiding, you'll always be seen.'

Si laughs, forgets about the last five minutes. 'Yeah it attracts them. If you look away, they look right at you.' Si looks right at me, I look away. He laughs as if this proves his point.

'What do you mean?' Job is steering with his knees again, as if dancing, his free hands weave in and out of one another, the fag expires and he spits it out the window. We descend into the thrumming claustrophobia of tunnel walls. I repeat my question; 'What do you mean?'

'What do you mean what do I mean?'

'Are you saying that we go very fast so as not to attract attention?' Our eyes meet in the rearview mirror. I watch the grimace of his explanation, the way he hardens the muscles of his cheeks to spit out his contempt towards my ignorance of his anti-system.

'We go very fast so that we can't get caught, but — dear Nelson, dear fucking Nelson — we go very fast in places where we don't get seen. Do you understand this, or do you want me to pull over and draw out some diagrams for you?'

I hang in silence for a while; desperate because I want to be on foot, in control, inconspicuous. I want to say this is a disaster, that we are driving right into disaster, as well as away from it. Yet I am hooked upon Job's reflected stare.

'Do you ever feed the birds?' says Si. Neither Job nor I answer him, presuming that this is a scrap from another one of his imaginary dialogues.

'I said do you ever feed the birds?'

'Yes,' I say. Job's eyes flick out of the mirror. The tunnel gives way to a great roaring ascent, the river behind us is visible only in its absence of streetlights and houses, the dock is a hole in the city.

'When you feed the birds, do you ever notice that if you are sitting on a bench, with no birds around you, say you're just eating a sandwich or something, if you break some of that sandwich off and throw it out in front of you, then the birds immediately come down and pick it up. Do you see? Do you see what I mean? So it means that the birds are watching you the whole time you are eating. It's raw surveillance.'

Si has to wipe the saliva from his lips, such is his relish at this observation. I let my head loll again over the back of the seat, left hand pulling Si's sleeve. He leans over my face, his breath is at once rotting and metallic, perhaps rusty.

'What are you saying?' Every time he mentioned watching, he gave me a conspiratorial leer, and in my present state of mind, my suspicions are particularly susceptible to being aroused.

'I am saying you don't always know when the birds are watching you. When they might be catching you in the act.' I need to separate Si and Job, I have to make sure Si — with his knowledge and his stupor — doesn't tell Job about El. I whisper to him, 'Do you want to walk from here?'

This suggestion sinks slowly into his face, dragging his expression after it, a weight dropped into a pallid cloth.

'He's not finished. Don't stop, remember. Wasn't that what she said to you: don't stop?'

'We could ... we could hide out in a park.'

'Why do you want to hide, Nelson? It's like Job said, you try to hide something and everyone can see it. We're having fun.'

The central locking clunks around us, the nodule retreats into the door, out of reach.

'What are you saying?' Job guns the engine, raising its pitch, he interrogates us with revs.

'Talking about the birds,' I say, unable to move my head in case the shift in perspective sends my stomach into a tail-spin.

'You gonna fly away, is that what you're fucking saying? Have you got what you need out of Job now, is that it, you think you're not in this up to your fucking eyeballs, is that it, you think you were somehow invisible, that no one saw you, you think if you close your eyes then the world will disappear and you'll be able to hide behind your lids, is that it? Is that it?'

'We were just talking about the birds.'

'And exactly what were you saying about the birds?'

'I remembered reading something about them being spies.'

'Nelson wants to walk,' says Si. 'He wants to stop.'

A housing estate is laid out beneath the flyover, lit here and there by halogen security lamps. Job swerves into the slow lane without decelerating. The car drifts over on to the hard shoulder and begins vibrating. The flash bulb of the automatic camera bursts

251

right in our face, recording us. The light clings to Si as he squints against it. Job unlocks the car.

'Get out if you want. Get out now, and we'll say no more. But if you stay, you have got to tell me about this,' he pulls the hair back from his bloodied brow, 'and you better explain this,' he stretches his T-shirt out, magnifying the stains, 'and maybe if I like what you say then I won't drive into the nearest fucking wall.'

Job wants to break everything, though he himself is far too easily broken; he believed his pamphlets could destroy the world, if only he had enough money to photocopy them; he believed in direct action, and beating up anyone who flaunted their subscription to capitalism is about as direct an action you can get; now he just believes in something he used to be. 'You attacked someone again. It was funny, almost. This bloke kept coming in the chill-out room with his cock out wanking, writhing around on his back wanking, he couldn't stop. Do you remember?'

In the mirror, Job blinks once in assent. Gradually, I confess. 'And you tried to throw him out, and he came all over you.'

Job blinks again. I twist the importance of this essentially meaningless detail of the evening. He was right; if you want to hide something, put it out in the open — and hope that all the background information will conceal it. Job said it himself, though I take no pleasure in making him a victim of his own insight.

'And you put the boot in, like I haven't seen you put the boot in for a while. Not since Kev tore the heads off those pigeons outside Burger King and you lost it. Not that he didn't deserve it, that's not what I am saying. But El kept telling you to stop, it was freaking her out, so I took her out to the car park and put her in a cab. That's it, nothing really. I mean, yeah we should just make ourselves scarce in case you hurt him. It did look bad. I think you finally crossed the line between petty and serious crime. But that's it, it'll be business as usual in a couple of day's time. Just lie low for a while.'

I wear my smile well, it fits snugly inbetween Job and myself. You can always rely on the easily broken to swallow a reassuring smile. You can always rely on them to stop halfway down the road to revelation.


We pull into the Happy Eater just as dawn is giving way to the brittle light of a sore-headed morning. In the car the idea of a slap-up breakfast had been taken up with the fervour of a new messiah, though as soon as we saw the banal, bright meat we realized we had been in love with the platonic idea of an English breakfast rather than its actuality. Inevitably, breakfast was limited to coffee and cigarettes. Another meal of appetite supprests, we buy as much starvation as we can afford before tromping back to the car. I call El while Job and Si recline on the bonnet. All four doors are open, the boot is up, the whole car sits there gasping.

'Today, El, let's leave today.'

'Where are we going?'

'Leave that to me. I've got it all set up. I know just the place.'

My explanation is limited to a single ten-pence piece. Besides, I have had my fill of conversation.

I wander back to the car. Si and Job are just finishing their after-dinner course of fags and banter.

'So where we going now?'

'Around and around, until we find somewhere decent.'

'And when will we know this place, this somewhere decent?'

'I'll know it. The first rule of the anti-system is you don't find what you look for. Haven't you been listening to a word — a fucking word — I have been saying?'

Three not so wise men.

'THE SPARROW'

In the land of the blind the one eyed man is King.
In London town the sparrow sings in the wind
and good news it brings.
News from the South, from the East, from the West.

'The river of PEACE is coming. The sun of JOY is shining.'

But, why does the little girl on the streets of Brixton cry?
Why is sadness swimming in her eye?

It's because a white man has killed a black man
and a black man has killed a white man.

They fight for equal rights
and bullets fly like silver arrows in the night

Knives cut flesh

And one gang shouts —
'WE ARE THE BEST — FUCK THE REST'

So this is why the little girl cries and sadness swims in her eyes

The sparrow lands at her feet and from her hand golden bread it
eats.

It sings a sweet lullaby and on the concrete the little girl sleeps

The sparrow faces East, West and North
and in the girl's mind a purple dream comes forth

Martin Luther King had a dream
but not one full of jelly and cream

In her sleep. The world turns and no more houses burn.
In her sleep. A metallic gun is turned to chewing gum
In her sleep. London is free and everyone is allowed to and say
'I'm black
I'm white
I'm yellow
I'm red
but that still allows me
to be me.'
The sparrow kisses the little girl's hair
as the polished shoes of society stand there and stare.

Do they care?

The sparrow flies high in the sky, it spins in the air.
It sings in the wind and good news it brings
news from the South, from the East, from the West
In the land of the blind the one eyed man is BLESSED.

As darkness falls, in a leafy tree the sparrow sits
and watches creepy creatures crawl

The ravers are wide awake
they make their way to the date
It has got to be late or to them it's just fake
It has got to be fresh 'n' funky
so their bodies can shake 'n' bake

# 'The Sparrow'

It needs to be sexy to give them a chance to dance, romance
and mate
In the shadows, stand shady fellows.
The drug dealers wait to communicate, the price, the weight
E, crack, tweed, shit, it's give 'n' take, they don't hesitate
it's about the dollars you make
They got to bite to eat even if takes all night
fuck the heat, no time to sleep

They've got no chance, all they got is the cocaine dance
A little shuffle to the left, a shuffle to the right, hop, hop,
step, step.
A little shuffle to the left, a shuffle to the right, hop, hop,
step, step.

The sparrow flutters it wings as it pontificates

A black jeep with windows down pumps a jungle beat
that rolls down the street and moves the crowd.
In the leather seat is a youth posing like he's wearing a crown
Brand names are the game his claim to fame
His pockets are full of dollars 'n' pounds
The name is Kane, hell, there ain't no one better.
He parleys like an undercover lover
but the brother's a cop
but he ain't there to stop the bop
or to shop the dealers for selling rocks
Kane's got his mind on bigger things fit for a king.

They've got no chance, all they got is the cocaine dance
A little shuffle to the left, a shuffle to the right, hop, hop,
step, step.
A little shuffle to the left, a shuffle to the right, hop, hop, step, step.

The sparrow circles the multicoloured rave

Bouncers wait for the ravers to misbehave
the line is thick 'n' long
The bouncers are big 'n' strong
All the ravers want is to get into the musical arena
to taste the flavour
to feel the fever
get deeper
to hear the songs
drop like bombs


Through a hole in the warehouse, the sparrow PUSHES its head,
then its body, on a beam it surveys the scene.


A DJ spins vinyl on the wheels of steel
A pretty sweaty youth shouts — 'I feel so real'
the crowd are shoulder to shoulder
back to back
soul to soul
head to head the tighter the rinse, the sweeter, the fever.
The steaming young bods shower their hair with bottled water
The DJ has them in her hands they are lambs being led to
slaughter
Each record is carefully selected, some are rejected,
the grooves are either scratched or infected
Only the best is good enough, it's got to be ruff 'n' tuff
the idea is to make them cream when they scream
The needle hits the wax the drum 'n' bass shakes the place
the crowd roar to the track


They chant — 'Music! Music! Music! Music!'


Kane the cop, squeezes through the heaving mass,
he cusses under his breath, there is very little air left
he is shaken and stirred from side to side

on a cosmic roller-coaster ride

Mr Big the Don of Stonebride estate is in the corner.
Kane frowns, he shakes himself down
this is no time to break, make a mistake, if he does he'll
be a goner.
Mr Big is not smoking cigs only Havana cigars are fit to
touch his lips
Champagne eases, releases the pain, helps to delete, keep sane, the
brain in frame
he is to blame for his wooden leg and his silver cane.

Mr Big, catches Kane's gleaming eyes through the people
this is the showdown, the sequel, he has finally met his equal
Violent thoughts gun, run through his mind like a raging river
Kane is the only man standing in his way
He's got to make him pay for killing the night 'n' spoiling the
day
Stopping him from getting bigger 'n' bigger.
In his mind he would like to call him a nigger
but he stops and shakes Kane's hand with a cruel snigger.

'Ah don't ave di dollars,' says Mr Big, pulling confidently on
the cigar.
'I can't hear you,' says Kane. 'Let's talk by the bar.'
Mr Big grins. 'Yu ave di jugs?'
'Jugs?'
'Yes jugs.'
'Oh you mean drugs.'
'Dat's wha' ah fuckin' said, jugs.'
Kane nods. 'In the jeep, the drugs are in the jeep. It's a new line
called golden dove.'

The sparrow flew over to the bar
it swerved around the hologram of a silver star

Kane got in first. 'Where are your boys?'

'Ah lef dem ah 'ome playin' wid dem guns an toys.'

'I've kept my part of the deal.'

'Dat 'ow yu feel?'

'OK. I'll keep the goods until my pockets get their fill.'

'Ah did want tu heat but now yu kill mi hunger. Kill.'

'Eat?'

'Yes heat? Yu fuckin def or wha?'

'So you expect me to give you the drugs just like that?'

'Wha'ever 'appen tu trus'? Bredda don't treat me like dat.'

'Like what? You've wasted my time, that is a crime, you're no brother of mine.'

'Careful, don't raise yu voice or yu'll leave mi no choice.'

'If that is a threat, I ain't got it yet.'

'If ah ever mek ah move rudebwoy, yu'll be dead before yu 'it di ground. Yu get me?'

'Make it. I can take it.'

'Yu fakin' it.'

'Do you wanna feel my steel?'

'Ow much yu got?'

'Nine millimetres and let me tell you this shit is real.'


Kane opened his jacket.

Mr Big coughed.

The revolver glistened.

Kane smiled.

Mr Big threw his cigar on the floor.

The jungle beat shook his feet, he had to admit defeat.


'Ow di fuck yu get dat in 'ere?'

'You can do a lot if you've got money to spare?'

'An inside job.'

'The intelligence of a street God. Now move towards the exit.'

'Quit, while yu ahead, or before sunrise yu'll be dead.'

'Move.'

# 'The Sparrow'

'A! A! A! A! Relax, rudebwoy. Don't poke di gun so 'ard in mi
back, is dat henywey tu treat ah man wid ah wooden leg?'
'I know your reputation. There are a lot of men pushing up daisies
just because you decided to go crazy, I'm staying sharp my mind
ain't lazy.'

So back through the metal hole the sparrow went,
to see how the night would be spent.
Would Mr Big win? Would Kane remain King?
Would one brother kill another?

They've got no chance, all they got is the cocaine dance
A little shuffle to the left, a shuffle to the right, hop, hop,
step, step.
A little shuffle to the left, a shuffle to the right, hop, hop,
step, step.

Six shots rang out

Booyaka! Booyaka! Booyaka! Booyaka! Booyaka! Booyaka!

For a second the sparrow was in doubt.
A body was on the ground
blood was gushing, rushing
It did not make a sound
Sprawled out like a rag doll
it's skull cracked by the fall

The Kane was dead.
Mr Big's hench men were waiting in a car in the parking lot
and what Kane got was hot.
Mr Big's wooden leg moved with grace, pace
he had a grimace on his face
'Tu di fuckin' jeep! Tu di jeep,' was his battle cry. 'Ah tol' di
fucker dat 'E wuz goin' tu die. Ah got di keys. Ah got di keys.'

The sparrow flew in front of his face. Mr Big punched the air.

Black jeep.
Key in lock.
Turn.
Click.
Bag under the seat.
Drugs.
Golden dove.
Open bag
Mr Big's fat finger dabs the white powder.

He tasted it and shouted. 'Dis is Rebbish, not rubbish, rebbish, rebbish, rebbish, rebbish. Di fucker 'as jus' lef us wid sugar. Mek haste we mus' escape, ah 'ear di soun' ah sirens comin' from di East.'

They've got no chance, all they got is the cocaine dance
A little shuffle to the left, a shuffle to the right, hop, hop, step, step.
A little shuffle to the left, a shuffle to the right, hop, hop, step, step.

The police arrive before Mr Big can make a dive.
Their guns are cocked the road is blocked.
Mr Big looked at his hench men. 'Do we live or die.'
One of them shivered, he was tall with a boney figure. 'Mi noh ready fi dat pie in di sky, star. Yu get mi? Ah got mi ah daughter who is six ah wanna see har get big 'n' rich.'
'Let's rush 'n' crush dem pussys,' said Mr Big. 'Me nah go out like ah bitch.'

So more bullets rang out and Mr Big's bones snapped like sticks.

## 'The Sparrow'

Booyaka! Booyaka! Booyaka! Booyaka! Booyaka! Booyaka!
Booyaka! Booyaka! Booyaka! Booyaka! Booyaka! Booyaka!
Booyaka! Booyaka! Booyaka! Booyaka! Booyaka! Booyaka!
Booyaka! Booyaka! Booyaka! Booyaka! Booyaka! Booyaka!

The sparrow circled and then back to its nest it went,
it had seen how the night had been spent.

The sun will rise and the new day will bring a fresh surprise,
But now it understood why there were tears in the little girl's
eyes
Why on the street of Brixton she crys.
It is because a white man has killed a black man
and a black man has killed a white man.

They fight for equal rights and bullets fly like silver arrows in
the night.

Booyaka! Booyaka! Booyaka!

And one gang shouts —
'WE ARE THE BEST — FUCK THE REST.'

So this is why the little girl cries and sadness swims in her eyes.

They've got no chance, all they got is the cocaine dance
A little shuffle to the left, a shuffle to the right, hop, hop,
step, step.
A little shuffle to the left, a shuffle to the right hop, hop,
step, step.
They've got no chance, all they got is the cocaine dance

Alan Warner

'BITTER SALVAGE'

Two guys, Choker and The Lad Who *Was* Choked come stumbling down the late-night city street fourteen-pints-drunk when they see the suitcase leaning against a litter bin. Rain has saturated the upper sections of the suitcase and wetness stains have seeped down the clay-coloured flanks.

Choker reaches the suitcase first, lifts it by its handle and carries it, walking onwards without loss of pace. 'Twenty kilos contraband,' announces Choker, pretending to expertly weigh-up the case; but The Lad Who *Was* Choked can hear no weight straining his comrade's voice.

'Open it on up then,' demands The Lad Who *Was* Choked.

'Let's show a little restraint till we get back to our ark,' Choker insists.

'Something to live for?' asks The Lad Who *Was* Choked who is wearing a soaked satin jacket with SATIN LIVES painted unsteadily on its back.

'Precisely,' says Choker.

They walk on till another unemptied District Council litter bin emerges from the collective muck of drizzles.

'Why not try for a little salvage of your own?' dares Choker.

The Lad Who *Was* Choked rolls up a wet satin sleeve then fishes deep into the full litter bin, searching for the lesser of many evils. 'One man's dustbin is always anothers heaven,' he reminds, cheek horizontal against the fresh garbage. Choker nods gravely in agreement without putting down his suitcase.

The Lad Who *Was* Choked, calls out, 'Seize the day!' heaving backwards, bearing aloft a child-sized accordian box. He lowers it and begins to jig and furiously squeeze the keys but dry clicks are the only sound until the singular miracle of:

Dooooooooooo

Lonesome: *one*, key on the accordian still works.

Doooooooooooooooooo

They walk ahead, The Lad Who *Was* Choked skipping and unflaggingly pumping the squeeze box. He goes in for a bit syncopation:

Doo

Doo

Doo

'Ah, if music be the food of love, *play on!*' cries Choker.

The sodium streetlights turn the little tics of drizzle stuck to each strand of their hair orange.

Approaching a busier thoroughfare The Lad Who *Was* Choked halts, aghast. 'Listen,' he whispers.

Do Do Do Do

Do Do Do Do

Holding down the key The Lad Who *Was* Choked is simply jerking the box rhythmically to engender the repetitive note.

Do Do Do Do

Do Do Do Do

'What?' asks Choker.

'Well, surely you recognize the tune?'

'That!?'

'It was Number One for weeks man!' The Lad Who *Was* Choked performs the work.

Do Do Do Do

'O Superman'

Do Do Do Do

'O Superman'

'Laurie Anderson ... her with the fiddle that lit up. Amazing, an accordian that plays O Superman.'

\*     \*     \*

Choker is holding his suitcase off the wet pavement and The Lad Who *Was* Choked stands on the concrete. He has removed one boot and placed it before him to collect any coins of appreciation from the infrequent passers-by.

Two young women, wearing black Levis and sharing a brolly, approach down the middle of the road. By way of greeting, Choker shouts, 'Why do you stray to the centre of this broad road when such fine pavements are provided?'

'Cause the pavements are thick in dog shite,' chirps the one in high-heeled boots.

'... And the crappiest buskers,' says the other by way of an epitaph, who wears a T-shirt which reads:

BABE

The Lad Who *Was* Choked presses on.

## Do Do Do Do

### 'O Superman'

The two young women go into the hysterics of laughter and walk on. The Lad Who *Was* Choked steps into his boot and with Choker they make instant pursuit. They catch up with the girls where they are waiting for the green man at a traffic light.

## Do Do Do Do

### 'O Superman'

'Oh no.'

'Face it girls. He's going to go on singing that unless you accompany us for a drink.'

'Can't,' says High-heeled Boots, 'we're going to the Work's Night Out.'

Babe says, 'It's not just the Work's Night Out, it's the Work's Night Out of *The Three Branches*.'

'Gosh. All three of them!' Choker looks at The Lad Who *Was* Choked then both men turn their attention to the girls.

'Are yous from a circus or something?' High-heeled Boots asks.

'No ma'am, we're new in town and looking for a place to stay,' says Choker jiggling the suitcase.

'Could we perhaps accompany you to the Work's Night Out?' smiles The Lad Who *Was* Choked.

'... of The Three Branches,' Choker quickly adds.

'Suppose you're kinda cute,' says High-heeled Boots.

'That's only cause their hair is wet,' warns Babe. 'And his jacket is absolutely bloody frightening ...'

'I know what labels are on *all* your clothes.' The girls look at him and Choker, underlining it in the wet air with a finger reads out, 'Made. In. Heaven.'

'Ha! Charmer eh,' she suddenly stands on one leg. 'The heel fell off my boot last night and I glued it back on so if it falls off yous had better not laugh at me.'

'Promise.'

'Cross my heart.'

'Right, well, we'll get yous in then.'

The Lad Who *Was* Choked throws away the child's accordian which lands, with not even a squeak, beside the traffic lights.

The two girls lead the way. The guys follow, The Lad Who *Was* Choked's wet laces are clicking. Without turning round High-heeled Boots says, ''Nother time I was asked out. Guy arrived on a big motorbike with a helmet; I had to ride on the back. When we got to the dance my foot'd been resting on the exhaust and my boot heel was all melted away. He had to carry me in and I had to take off my boots to dance . . .'

Another filled District Council litter bin appears. The Lad Who *Was* Choked thrusts his hand in, removes what looks like a scarf but as he pulls, more and more fabric emerges, metres and metres of it that he shoves up his jacket.

The four of them reach a hotel. A porter asks if he may carry Choker's luggage. The girls giggle. 'Certainly *not*,' says Choker.

They make their way to the darkened Function Room. A disco is in progress. The DJ is only playing the 45s of Funkadelic, A sides and B sides in chronological order (implying the lucky bastard has two copies of each single): 'Better By The Pound', 'Stuffs & Things', 'Let's Take It To The Stage', 'Undisco Kid' etc.

Choker puts down his suitcase and in the darkness, among the flashing lights, he strides up to the buffet, eating everything remaining he can find, eventually holding a plate of sausage rolls under his mouth, he watches the crowded dancefloor where The Lad Who *Was* Choked is dancing with High-heeled Boots and Babe.

A jet of dry ice curls up into a bank, collapses then slides across the wooden dancefloor. Soon no one can see far ... the flashing lights — mainly blue and yellow, red on the bass drum — push through the white vapour. The Lad Who *Was* Choked has removed the long, long coils of fabric from under his jacket; he clutches one end then tosses the other, high and curling into the bank of smoke. A fresh, thick supply of dry ice pushes through the thinning gaps and the line of fabric immediately taughtens as a tug-of-war begins between The Lad Who *Was* Choked, High-heeled Boots, Babe, several other dancers and unseen opponents on the other end of the taught line away through the banks of dry ice. The beat increases (it's 'How Do Yeaw View You?'). At one point it seems as if this side of the dry ice is going to win and Choker can see the sliding shoes of the first member in the opposing team appear, the legs angled back, vanishing in the blue-then yellow-stained smoke. But the fabric snaps and the team of about ten people camel-step backwards to the buffet table then crash down in great mirth, a bump so big the record jumps and they're back up dancing — High-heeled Boots seems especially energetic in her exertions — arms spinning; then Choker notices the heel of her boot has gone for a burton.

It's still raining — Choker and The Lad Who *Was* Choked are carrying High-heeled Boots on an old wooden door they found in a skip. Babe is carrying Choker's suitcase and the brolly; she's smoking a cigarette without touching it, blowing the ash off the end with these little snorts.

'This is it here.'

'Very posh,' says Choker, tossing the door aside and wiping his hands on each other as High-heeled Boots hops up the path and puts a key in.

'God's honest truth, ladies: we were hoping for a little bit of shelter through the night ... a cut of the cake.'

'A piece of the action,' says The Lad Who *Was* Choked.

'Huh, even the old goat must lick the salt I guess; well that's not our idea of fun with yous, we just like putting on bizarre clothes then taking polaroids of each other ... thats all the photos in they boxes. Look at them if you want.'

'All with your clothes *on*?'

'Want to see what we wear under our clothes?'

'Yes.'

'Yes.'

Babe and High-heeled Boots (though she's taken the remaining one and a half off) jump up and lift their tops. All under is wrapped in layers of silver kitchen foil.

'It's warm as toast.'

'No short skirts for us.'

'No man is worth pneumonia.'

The girls start reaching in under their clothes, tearing chunks of the silver foil out from beneath, reaching down the back of their necks and heaving out the layers. 'This is the best bit,' says Babe, leaning over and pulling out a semi pipe-shape from the bottom of her Levis.

'Ohhh ...' Choker groans ... 'Sure there's nothing left in there I could fetch out?; wouldn't want you to get hit by lightning.'

'C'mon beefy, get with it,' High-heeled Boots has produced a game called *Butthead* and tosses the packet at Choker. There are words on the side of the *Butthead* packet written in a foreign language:

## DEUX CHAPEAUX RIDICULES

The girls sit on piles of clothes, in chronic laughter watching Choker and The Lad Who *Was* Choked play *Butthead*: two velcro multicoloured hats are strapped to their heads. The object of the game is to throw the big pink sticky balls at the opponent's head, the areas above the temples scoring the highest points. Both players breenge around madly, several balls stuck to their heads, trying to turn away from their opponent, shooting at him and picking up spent balls simultaneously along with the blindness when the girls take a flash photo with the Polaroid and let out minutes of deep laughter as they peel the pictures.

Choker and The Lad Who *Was* Choked crack their heads together and crash to the ground.

'Usually with guys we let them play strip Twister with us.'

'Using lots of body oil.'

'That was much funnier though.'

After a long pause staring at the girls The Lad Who *Was* Choked says, 'I'm hungry.'

'Are you a veggie?' asks Babe.

'No,' answers The Lad *Who* Was Choked

'Are you?'

''Course not,' says Choker.

'We're not veggies either are we?'

'Nut.'

'But we only kiss veggies don't we?'

'Aye.'

'Do you want some salt and vinegar crisps warmed up in the microwave? That's about all we've got; some juice in a box or something for a warm sandwich?'

There's a table with a bunch of grapes lying in the centre, no bowl, nothing on the table, just a bunch of grapes sat in the middle.

'I'll have these.'

'Look at that. He doesn't even wash them.' High-heeled Boots yawns. Choker notes the liquidity of the left eye after yawning. He longs for the unforgettable dark rose of a girl's first touch.

Babe says, 'Well I'm gonna crash. You guys can fight over the vibro-couch next door, I'll show you.'

She opens the door. It's a room with a small fish-tank, a couch, and it is decorated with lots of bright-coloured condoms that have been inflated and fixed in the corners of the ceiling.

'You'll find the couch vibrates — it's the pump from the fish-tank. Don't dare switch it off. If you hear noises in the night it's the fat fish sliding the stones around on the bottom in the dark.'

'Where's that go?' Choker points to the door.

'Down to the drying green and out, nite nite.' She shuts the door.

'Oh my *God*,' agonizes Choker.

The Lad Who *Was* Choked nods, 'It's like John Brotherhood used to say, she could shove my toothbrush up her arse as far as it would go and I'd still use it without Macleans.' Then they hear the breathing, the blowing:

Inhalation Inhalation Inhalation

Phoooo Phoooo Phoooo

'Shh, it's *both* of them.'

'Thought so. Lesbos. Must be, knocking us back, all that crap about other guys.'

'Only we could see them at it.'

'C'mon let's just walk in on them together.'

Choker and The Lad Who *Was* Choked step into the room. High-heeled Boots is lying on a beach Li-lo with a thin sheet over her. She's wearing a motorcycle helmet. Babe kneels, leaning over another Li-lo she is blowing up; she pauses, pinching the nipple she has been blowing into.

From within the helmet, High-heeled Boots says, 'No beds. We sleep on Li-los. You should try buying them in winter! It's near impossible. We had to go out to the airport.'

'Why do you wear a helmet?'

'Comfy. Dont need pillows.'

Babe says, 'We usually blow them up with the foot pump but we didn't want to wake yous.'

''Sides, it sounds to the people downstairs like we're getting

277

shagged. They sometimes bang the ceiling with a broom.'
High-heeled Boots slips down the visor.

Choker spins on his heels and strides back into their room.
The Lad Who *Was* Choked says, 'Mmm I was wondering if you
had a cigarette.'

Babe says, 'I don't kiss people who smoke.'

'But you're not going to kiss me and *you* smoke!'

'That's right, I'm not going to snog you and I *do* smoke but
I don't kiss guys that smoke.'

'Yous are just crazy,' says The Lad Who *Was* Choked and
he walks back into the condom/fish-tank room and slams the
door. 'Let's get out of here,' he says and nods at the door to
the back green.

Choker nods to the corner of the room, 'Aye but there might
be some bitter salvage from the night's ruins yet.' They both look
at the suitcase.

The dual click as Choker fires off both catches then lifts the
lid.

There are clothes inside. Women's clothes: old-style bloomers.
Choker rummages about but there are just all these pairs of red
and lace bloomers.

'Fuck's *sake*,' announces Choker. Then the two guys notice
something odd about the bloomers: it's not loads of pairs; it's
one pair ... one *massive* pair of bloomers, big enough to go on
a baby elephant ... they are as big as a car.

'They must be from a circus or a theatre or something.'

The two men begin to laugh, they unlock the door and laugh
all the way down the stairs to where they shush each other and
hang the massive bloomers on the highest line of the back green
imagining the neighbours, staring down on those bloomers outside
the girls' flat in the morning.

Choker is still laughing when they walk through the streets
and he gets The Lad Who *Was* Choked up against a shop wall
and squeezes the life out of him — stopping *just* when he knows to

stop, then lifting his mate and helping him cough back to laughter as they stumble into the dawn, the persistence of the first bird's singing and their Mickey Mouse heads: the velcro helmets with the pink balls stuck on them, still strapped to their skulls.

Steve Aylett

'REPEATER'

After an hour recording park birds I strolled back through town, the mike in my shoulder-bag laying down the traffic. Streets like the deeps of a full ashtray. A plain-garb cop trundled up offering drugs. I declined and was arrested. At the kennel the cops were embarrassed and angry when I replayed the proof of my lamblike innocence. As they handed me my jaw on a plate I had an idea. Saw it all red and gold and full of justice. Put it at the front of a piece of Debussy and let the music carry it forward, filling it out. A notion and a half. Have to ask the old soldier.

The beating was over and I hadn't noticed. Cops regarding me with stall-cod eyes. Time to get up — but don't do it again.

Back on the street feeling four snapped ribs — I've had worse and laughed with the correct medication. It was partly my fault for taking that route. The area was famous for the cops' planting of drugs and users had begun flocking there in the hope of being able to keep some in exchange for violence. But I wondered what Dogger would say.

The old soldier lived in a shed apparently made of biscuit and was never without his dog, Fire, the calling of whose name caused alarm and mayhem. Dogger had dodged so many bad laws his spine had corkscrewed. In classic style he had swallowed media promises of a better life and then overstepped the boundary of etiquette by actually trying to secure one. He was like Fagin without the charm and carried lemons in his coat as a teargas precaution. He

283

was so real his toaster ran on diesel. As I descended the railway embankment I heard him yelling in the hut. 'The chains of your repression are as familiar to you as the teeth in your head. Born to it you were.'

'Hello Dogger,' I said cautiously, entering — he was alone. I told him about the cops' theft of my equipment.

'There's no limit to what a dying system will demand of you, Hypnojerry,' he laughed, showing braces like a knuckleduster. 'Only a narrow land could end at one stroke the right to sound and the right to silence.' He was referring to a brace of new laws which curtailed the activities of those with an aptitude for reflection and enjoyment. 'For fear of copycat outbreaks of happiness and laughter. Not that the deeper implications matter to a public soundproofed by indifference. Sad as a galleon in a bottle.'

His hands flew over the eight-track sound desk. He was messing with the sound of a prefab saying 'nothing you need fear' — it was reversed, accelerated, cracked like a whip. 'They did the same to me — tried to send me to clench for heseltine possession.' This was a laugh as cocaine will have slowed Dogger's thoughts to a constabulary crawl. He had an eight-track mind. 'It's genius envy, Jell, pure and sour. I felt pity for the bastards so as not to get too angry. Injustice rings down through history to a deserted callbox. Let stress get into your tripes you'll end up in surgery under a blithe knife. Watch this.' And he played the word 'fear' while pointing to a screen where the sound was rendered as a geometrical netshape which bulbed like a soapbubble. He tapped at a keyboard which froze the shape, then flipped it inside-out like a mitten. 'Now let's play this shape as a noise,' he said, and pressed return. The system emitted the worst fart I'd ever heard.

Dogger explained that he had found a way to disclose the inner nature of a recorded verbal statement. Some remarks produced the zenlike sound of a gong. Others — particularly those of the young — the howl of a desert wind. Politicians from both dum and dee almost always created flatulence.

It was the latest in a long course of experimentation. Dogger had discovered birdsong slowed down was whalenoise and whalenoise speeded up was birdsong. He found that Nixon's resignation speech reversed was an invocation to the devil in exquisitely pronounced Lithuanian. When he heard about the rave laws outlawing repetitive beats he examined the issue in fly-leg detail. Rhythm requires an alternation between sound and silence, or one sound and another. Dogger had considered whether the legislation could apply to repetitive injustice and bullshit but these activities were so constant as to be a seamless, mundane hum. Only regular interruptions of this mundanity could set up a beat. That was why raves were against the law — so that the unjust and dishonest would not be seen to be part of an illegal process. 'It's all in the game, Hypnojerry. Mischief distinguishes man from the other animals — that and the opposable thumb.'

A train shrieked past and Fire woke up, raising his ears and eyebrows.

The next evening we retrieved my gear with the help of Antifrog. We figured since two wrongs don't make a right our act would not stand out against the general corruption. Antifrog was a gay black youth with a strong Irish accent and herbal trousers. When this montage of minorities swanned into the kennel the cops couldn't believe their luck and set about his punishment. Truncheons leapt like salmon as he tried to report a theft. Dogger and I slipped past before the party was dampened by blood and boredom.

Since the passing of the new laws so much sound equipment had been seized we had learned that the safest thing to do was break into the cop confiscation store and dump our stuff there without a tag. Other than drugs they never touched a thing. But with the party approaching we'd need the gear and for once we had a legitimate reason for entry — my recording rig. Dogger kept up a running commentary as he worked the bolt cutters — he'd speak till the bitter, amp-smashing end. 'Almost gave up on your generation, Jell. Tunnel vision without a flashlight.

A passionless blank. Then by god the colour started seeping out of the walls. Back from the dead — and me too. Should have seen me in the eighties, boy — so out of it I had sideburns on someone else's face. Then one day I strode towards the horizon and was damn near garrotted by a rainbow.'

We were into the storeroom — I found my gear and knew this was the only way I could have retrieved it. The truth is easiest to disprove. Its defences are down.

Dogger meanwhile was flashing a Mysteron beam over amplifier stacks — the stuff of villainy. 'Jell, disorder's an offence with no mappable contours and the ideal fog for all occasions. Laws have gone by like motes on the film of my eye and with as much effect — but disorder? By god it's a beauty.'

'We're in a hurry-up,' I reminded him.

But Dogger had a philosophy you could stand a spoon in — he took a book from a shelf, blowing at the dust and frowning. '*After London.* Damn fine book — you can keep your triffids. Jefferies got there first, with a flood. Well written too.'

'Most books are so well written they barely have any effect on the reader's senses,' I told him urgently. 'Let's conclude this procedure and get out.'

'With a bang or a whimper though, Jell, how'd you picture it ending? The world, I mean?'

We lifted the stack amp between us and started off. 'Here's how I see it,' Dogger grunted through his exertions. 'Denial. Vacuum competes with vacuum. Laws outlaw the harmless to make the effective inconceivable. Scholarly incomprehension. No questions asked. Banality given the terms and prestige of science. Ignorance worn like a heraldic crest. Mediocrity loudly rewarded. Misery by instalments. Hypocrisy too extreme to process. Maintenance of a feeble public imagination. Lavish access to useless data. Fashion as misdirection. Social meltdown in a cascade pattern, consumed by a drought of significance. Drabness as ordered as the grey cells of a deserted waspnest.'

'It's a thought.'

On the way out we were approached by someone as featureless as a figure in a crash procedure diagram. It asked who we were and we pretended to be cops by saying we didn't know.

A few days later we visited Antifrog in hospital. The beating had been worse than we expected but he wished us well through a broken mouth. We taped the irregular bleep of his coronary monitor and set off for the country. A convoy of cars processioned through darkness towards a repeated thumping which could have been the heartbeat of the land itself. By degrees it became audible as Ravel's 'Bolero', played across a fallow field stretching so far it seemed not to end. Acres of grass were blown to italics. Fire leapt from the van and started across the field, eager for fun.

By midnight the field was a sea of ethnic trousers and Evian bottles. I remember weird strobe images of Dogger looking as spooky as a pickled alien. Lasers of jade and red gold were fanning and dipping as Antifrog's heartrate formed the grid for a soundscape sampled from the net and forced through a 50,000 watt sound system. In the crowd it was hard to tell where one smile ended and another began. Without lying there was nothing bad to be said about it. The press would have a field day.

Dogger and I had wired ourselves and some others with cop-style bodymikes which relayed crowdnoise through an oscillating sampler. Dogger disappeared but I heard him talking again, taking full advantage of the mike — rantbites were firing off and jarring with the ambience. 'Cancering anxiety. Sneering at tradition. A government openly at war with its people. Why be covert in the last ditch?' I waded through the scene to strangle him — no polemics, Dogger, not now.

I saw blurlights playing over a marquee wall and wondered how a set of old pub strobes had got in here. A repetitive siren effect was cranked up in the mix — this sound is illegal, I thought vaguely, and passing outside found it was caused by countless police cars surrounding the area. Blue lights strobed in the night.

The cops stood expecting our amusement to be paralysed in

deference. Many had confused their profession with full human identity. I thought a few had guns, and asked someone why.

'To assure us that nice people carry guns too.'

One cop was yelling inaudibly through a loudhailer. I learned later that this official warning to leave was a mere formality, but as the cop put the hailer aside and signalled the others to move in, a loop of his statement volleyed from the speakerstacks. Most of the ravers took it as a joke but a thousand wandered out and the cops, finding they had lost the element of surprise, panicked.

Looking back I can see all the components of hell were assembled. The cops terrified the crowd in an ironic and postmodern attempt to provoke order. A few less educated ravers didn't get the reference and became angry. These signals were elaborately ignored and the order to move on repeated. Again, someone's mike picked up the message and rendered it audible, increasing the crowd outside the main tent. The cops said that failure to comply would be considered an act of aggression. Dizzy with the notion that a thing could be considered something it wasn't, the crowd yelled back that cop helmets would be considered anchovies and that the cops themselves were chimps in cashmere. There was a cold explosion.

Add velocity to ignorance and you get a police car. One sped into the crowd and screeched to a halt as a girl twisted through the air and landed in a heap. A new sound spat out of the speakers — a crack and then a squelch, like someone treading on a snail. Near the cop ranks someone's head had been rolled over — grey brain tangled with grey hair. It was Dogger.

Amid the sequencers and scenes of riot several wired subjects were beaten repeatedly, each blow being re-broadcast from the rave stacks. A mile away, plaster ducks fell from cottage walls as the sound of a skull being struck repeatedly echoed through the early hours. The regular succession of blows made looping redundant. The rhythm of three different beatings merged and intersected like a multitracking beatbox, the occasional bone-snap an added punctuation. Rather than look vigilantly the other way, senior officers drove the mayhem. Blood dark as spilled petrol flared pillar-box red in the streak of torchbeams. Shots were followed by screams. Windscreens spiderwebbed, smoke drifted and the volume increased as shadowy figures became meaningless smudges of chaotic movement.

A cold sun rose over the ghost of a good time. A few survivors wandered dazed. Picking through a dawn of Chaplin grey I wished Dogger were alive or wrong. But he was neither and his passing was a deadbolt on any objective reflection. As far as I was concerned there had once been giants in the earth and now there was only plastic. Truth withered on the vine as the raid was declared a victory for common sense. Four deaths not including Dogger, who didn't count because he was old, and twelve others who didn't count because they weren't cops either. It was clarified that repetitive beating of a live skull in the course of police duty was legal but that acoustic amplification of the sound was not. The rave organizers, who had hired the land, decided to save money by trespassing for the next event.

I had Fire to look after. This charge looked to me in expectation of something I couldn't guess. Finally he decided I wasn't Dogger and wandered off. My generation lacked some essential element — I only hoped this made us unpredictable.

The authorities had taken action hoping some miracle would prevent an equal and opposite reaction, but no miracle materialized. Youth retaliation was swift and violent though sad beyond its years. Dogger had called us a dull bruise pounded over and over. A sleepy generation with the rave scene acting as a giant alarm. And he never would listen when I told him the weariness was understandable, for a brood overseen by those who make the same mistake and act surprised at the same result again and again and again and again and again and again and again and again.

## SARAH CHAMPION

Childhood ambitions were to become a stunt-woman, magician or to play for Manchester United. She became a freelance music journalist instead, joining *New Musical Express* at sixteen. As well as being the pop columnist for the *Manchester Evening News*, she is author of *And God Created Manchester*, documenting the city's music scene. She has also worked as a publicist, private detective, mystery customer and hot-air baloonist. Still only twenty-six, she is now a global party correspondent and the compiler of techno and drum'n'bass CDs 'Trance Europe Express' and 'Breakbeat Science'.

## NICHOLAS BLINCOE

Nicholas Blincoe is an Aquarian, born in Rochdale, but he usually claims it was Manchester. He has never held down a proper job and hardly ever even got an interview. But he's doing OK now, married to a beautiful Russian spy and author of *Acid Casuals*, the best selling pulp club thriller which is still screaming for attention down your local bookshop. His forthcoming novel, *Jello Salad*, is an oblique tribute to 24-hour service stations and the only kind of food they seem to sell.

## MIKE BENSON

Writer and film-maker living and working in London. Previous writing credits include theatre and film works made in the UK, Europe and Canada. His book of one-page stories was recently published in collaboration with the album 'Music For Babies' by Howie B. At present he is working on an animated music film and his first novel entitled *another day on planet fuck*.

## IRVINE WELSH

Irvine Welsh lives in Amsterdam. His first book, *Trainspotting* (1993), has been dramatized and filmed to enormous acclaim. His collection of stories 'The Acid House' (1994) and his second and third novels *Marabou Stork Nightmares* (1995) and *Ecstasy* (1996) will also be translated to stage and screen.

## GAVIN HILLS

Gavin Hills stumbled into journalism working for the London listings magazine *City Limits*. It closed very shortly after. Subsequently, he made a living alternating between covering major foreign news events and writing about clubs, drugs and football. He is noted for his work on the trendy magazine, *The Face*.

He has won a variety of awards for sports and music journalism as well as winning an Amnesty International press award for his work on the Angolan war. He is the author of two books on skateboarding, one a children's bestseller, the other a complete flop.

Gavin Hills would like it on record that he has never, or knows of no one who has ever, taken ecstasy. He spends his spare time as a Volunteer Rifleman in the Royal Green Jackets.

## MARTIN MILLAR

Comes from Glasgow but has lived in South London for a long

time. He has written five novels: *Milk Sulphate and Alby Starvation*, *Lux The Poet*, *Ruby And The Stone Age Diet*, *The Good Fairies of New York* and *Dreams of Sex and Stage Diving*. He also wrote the novelization of the film *Tank Girl*. His new book *Love and Peace with Melody Paradise* will be out sometime soon.

## MICHAEL RIVER

Michael River was born in London. He lives in various places and curates a junk-art shrine in a lock-up. Two of his stories have previously appeared in the Pulp Faction collections *Skin* and *Fission* and he has recently completed a novel, *hurtle/below*. Thanks to μ-Ziq and the Sabres for soundtracking the writing of this story. Michael River remains open to lucrative sponsorship deals.

## KEVIN WILLIAMSON

Born in the sixties. Lives and works in Edinburgh. Occupations have included: trainee nuclear scientist, cocktail barman, door-to-door salesman, journalist, library gopher, pool shark, adult education tutor, and now editor of the Rebel Inc imprint of Canongate Books. Founded, edited and published *Rebel Inc* magazine from 1992–6. Co-wrote *A Visitors Guide To Edinburgh* with Irvine Welsh in 1993. Launched 'Scotland Against Drugs Hypocrisy' campaign in 1996. His first book, *Drugs And The Party Line*, was published in October 1996. Top clubs are Manga and Luvly.

## JONATHAN BROOK

Jonathan Brook was born in Los Angeles in 1967, but has spent most of his life in the UK. For eight years he toured and recorded as a guitarist for Desmond Dekker and various ska and acid jazz bands

— until despondency set in after a nightmare tour of Japan in the company of earthquakes and alcoholics. He has published three novels for teenagers *Slackness*, *Big Up!* and *Herbsman* (Backstreets) and written another novel that he is trying to place. He lives in London.

## CHARLIE HALL

Born in Kent. Educated in the fuck-up system they call private education. Expelled for marijuana-smoking and not-fitting-in. Came to London on Silver Jubilee Day 1977. Embraced punk rock with gusto. Memorable drug scenario in the toilet of the infamous Speakeasy club with Johnny Thunders, Sid Vicious and Paula Yates, led to a career as a heroin addict until 1981. Cleaned up and wrote his first (unpublished) novel and got a degree from Sunderland Polytechnic. Memorable dancing scenario in Sunderland's Drum Club led to a career as a DJ. Became host of London's Drum Club and half of the techno-death-stomp merchants of the same name. Runs a twisted house label: MC Projects.

## BEN GRAHAM

Ben Graham was born in Halifax in 1971. He took a degree in American Studies and Philosophy in London and New York, but ended up back in Halifax, playing in bands, reading stand-up poetry and editing *News From Nowhere* fanzine. 'Weekday Service' is his first published story.

## JEFF NOON

Jeff Noon is living and dreaming in Manchester. Is dreaming about escape. Is writing these dreams down. Is calling the first dream *Vurt*, the second *Pollen*, the third *Automated Alice*. Is liking to make things up. Is writing to music: blues or dub or jazz or country or drum'n'bass. Is wanting to let words escape. Is wanting to give a voice to Manchester. Is not wanting to die in Manchester.

## DOUGLAS RUSHKOFF

Douglas Rushkoff's forthcoming novel *The Ecstasy Club*, is about a San Francisco rave collective that takes paranoia to a whole new level. His previous books, *Cyberia*, *Media Virus* and most recently *Children of Chaos* (*Playing The Future* in the US edition) all look at technology and the cultures they spawn as expressions of nature and the benevolent force of chaos. Rushkoff writes about cyberculture, rave, technology, and media for magazines including *Esquire*, *Details*, *Men's Journal* and the *Guardian*, and gets in trouble for being an American who tells his audiences that everything is going to be just fine.

## DEAN CAVANAGH

Dean Cavanagh lives on the outskirts of Bradford in a prefab caboose. He adheres to the maxim: 'Avoid Falling Into The Pit Of Because And Perishing With The Dogs Of Reason'. 'Mile High Meltdown' is an extract from his forthcoming novel *Rubber Ring Halos*.

## TWO FINGERS

A devoted fan of *The Simpsons* and *Star Trek*, young Mr Fingers spends most of his time watching Cable and eating chocolate biscuits. Inbetween, he writes a little, including two books about young black people in London, *Junglist* and *Bass Instinct*.

# ALEX GARLAND

Alex Garland was born in London in 1970. His first novel, *The Beach*, was published in 1996.

# MATTHEW DE ABAITUA

Matthew De Abaitua was born in 1971, raised in Liverpool and lowered by London. Inbetween he was nurtured in York, twisted by Manchester and isolated in Suffolk. He co-edited *The Idler's Companion* published by Fourth Estate and has written for the *Guardian*, the *Observer* and *Esquire*.

# Q

Q is a Londoner. His first novel *Deadmeat* will be published by Sceptre in May 1997.

# ALAN WARNER

Alan Warner, who wrote *Morvern Callar* (Jonathan Cape), recently fell sideways out of a door before eight p.m. His next novel, *These Demented Lands*, will be published in 1997. From Oban, Argyll, Scotland, he lives in Spain. He writes this on the boat to Ibiza.

# STEVE AYLETT

Steve Aylett was born in 1967. Twenty years later a replica of his brain was found in a shipment of tropical fruit. When analyzed, the brain was discovered to be made of cast iron and was hollow. It contained traces of lard.

# Contributors

In 1993 Aylett smoked a common bulrush and disappeared for twelve days, returning with the manuscript of *The Crime Studio* and a ritually lacerated chest. Published by Serif in 1994, the book was widely regarded as a cry for help. His second, *Bigot Hall*, appeared in 1995. Aylett has successfully toured a one-man show in which he impersonates the Shroud of Turin. He has produced a third book with one squeeze of an ink-filled bellows.

Aylett's ego is linked to a large and uninteresting orbital satellite.

# Acknowledgements

'The State Of The Party' copyright Irvine Welsh, 1995 (first appeared in *The Face*)

'Room Full Of Angels' copyright Mike Benson, 1996

'Ardwick Green' copyright Nicholas Blincoe, 1996

'White Burger Danny' copyright Gavin Hills, 1996

'How Sunshine Star-Traveller Lost His Girlfriend' copyright Martin Millar, 1996

'Electrovoodooo' copyright Michael River, 1996

'Heart Of The Bass' copyright Kevin Williamson, 1996

'Sangria' copyright Jonathan Brook, 1996

'The Box' copyright Charlie Hall, 1996

'Weekday Service' copyright Ben Graham, 1996

'DJNA' copyright Jeff Noon, 1996

'The Snow That Killed Manuel Jarrow' copyright Douglas Rushkoff, 1996

'Mile High Meltdown' copyright Dean Cavanagh, 1996 (extract from the forthcoming novel *Rubber Ring Halos*)

'Puff' copyright Andrew Green, 1996

'Blink And You Miss It' copyright Alex Garland, 1996

'Inbetween' copyright Matthew De Abaitua, 1996

'The Sparrow' copyright Q, 1996

# Acknowledgements

'Bitter Salvage' copyright Alan Warner, 1996

'Repeater' copyright Steve Aylett 1995 (first published by Pulp Faction in *Techno Pagan*, 1995)

The words of 'Mr Pharmacist' by Jeff Nowlen appear with permission of Habana M.P. Ltd (UK & Eire) Copyright 1967, 1995 Neil Music Inc, USA.

The words of 'O Superman' by Laurie Anderson appear courtesy of Difficult Music/BMG Music Publishing Ltd.

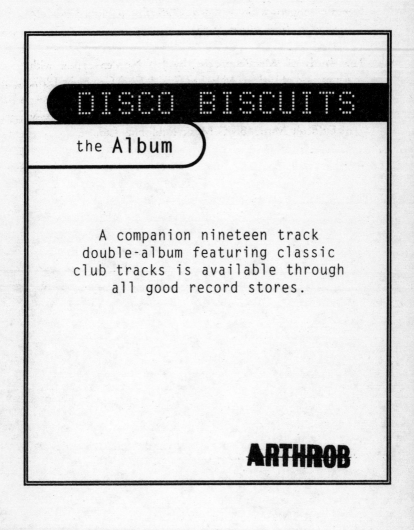

DISCO BISCUITS
the Album

A companion nineteen track
double-album featuring classic
club tracks is available through
all good record stores.

ARTHROB